FREEDOM CODE

SLEEPER SEALS, BOOK 11

ELAINE LEVINE

This book is a work of fiction. Names, characters, businesses, places, events, and incidents are either the products of the author's imagination or used in a fictitious manner. Any resemblance to actual persons, living or dead, or actual events is purely coincidental.

All rights reserved. Except as permitted under the U.S. Copyright Act of 1976, no part of this publication may be reproduced, distributed or transmitted in any form or by any means, or stored in a database or retrieval system, without the prior written permission of the publisher. To obtain permission to excerpt portions of the text, please contact the author at elevine@elainelevine.com

Published by Elaine Levine
Copyright © 2018 Elaine Levine
Last Updated: February 7, 1018
Editing by Arran McNicol @ editing720
Proofing by Carol Agnew @ Attention to Detail Proofreading

All rights reserved.

Print ISBNs:
ISBN-13: 978-1985068872
ISBN-10: 1985068877

FREEDOM CODE BLURB
SLEEPER SEALS #11

The Sleeper SEALs are former U.S. Navy SEALs recruited by a new counterterror division to handle solo dark ops missions to combat terrorism on U.S. soil.

∼

When a CIA agent is found beheaded in a Boulder, Colorado alley just hours after speaking to an informant about a potential terrorist cell, retired Navy SEAL Levi Jones is activated to find his killer. The informant herself is a suspected co-conspirator, but Levi has to rely on her to get him inside the close-knit community.

Zaida Hassan is used to going against the grain in her family. Not only does she write sexy romance stories, but she hasn't married and settled down as expected, and has no plans to in the near future. She has a personal mission to carry out first. When someone finds out about her covert activities, though, and leverages that information against her, she asks a friend to send help.

The handsome, hard-hearted man who shows up seems to have stepped right out of one of her novels, but Zaida quickly figures out that Levi Jones hasn't come to bring her fantasies to life, or even to help her. He's there to avenge the death of her friend, whom he thinks she sold out.

∾

Each book in this multi-author branded series is a standalone novel, and the series does not have to be read in order.

DEDICATION

Between researching payload capacities for small drones, components of claymore bombs, Tahrir al-Sham cells, floor plans of some public buildings, and a huge variety of guns and ammo, my Google search history looks like something from one of my terrorist characters.

I swear my sweet husband must sneak up to my office each night after I'm asleep and erase my web history, since the big black SUVs haven't shown up yet...

ACKNOWLEDGMENTS

Almost a year ago, my friend Becky McGraw invited me to join a group of amazing authors writing a military romance series with the edgy and super fun premise of former U.S. Navy SEALs called up for dark ops missions against terrorists in the U.S.

How could I pass up the opportunity to work with some of the best authors currently writing in my sub-genres of military and romantic suspense—including Susan Stoker, Lori Ryan, Dale Mayer, Geri Foster, J.M. Madden, Donna Michaels, Sharon Hamilton, Maryann Jordan, Becca Jameson, Elle James, and Becky McGraw?

It's been a thrilling ride, ladies! Love you all and thank you for including me!

OTHER SLEEPER SEALS BOOKS

All books in the Sleeper SEALs series are standalones and can be read in any order:

1) Protecting Dakota by Susan Stoker
2) Slow Ride by Becky McGraw
3) Michael's Mercy by Dale Mayer
4) Saving Zola by Becca Jameson
5) Bachelor SEAL by Sharon Hamilton
6) Montana Rescue by Elle James
7) Thin Ice by Maryann Jordan
8) Grinch Reaper by Donna Michaels
9) All In by Lori Ryan
10) Broken SEAL by Geri Foster
11) Freedom Code by Elaine Levine
12) Flat Line by J.M. Madden

OTHER BOOKS BY ELAINE LEVINE

RED TEAM SERIES

(This series must be read in order)

1 The Edge of Courage

2 Shattered Valor

3 Honor Unraveled

3.5 Kit & Ivy: A Red Team Wedding Novella

4 Twisted Mercy

4.5 Ty & Eden: A Red Team Wedding Novella

5 Assassin's Promise

6 War Bringer

6.5 Rocco & Mandy: A Red Team Wedding Novella

7 Razed Glory

8 Deadly Creed

9 Forsaken Duty

SLEEPER SEALs

11 FREEDOM CODE

MEN OF DEFIANCE SERIES

(This series may be read in any order)

1 Rachel and the Hired Gun

2 Audrey and the Maverick

3 Leah and the Bounty Hunter

4 Logan's Outlaw

5 Agnes and the Renegade

1

Zaida checked the clock. Again. Fifteen minutes after the hour…and still the room was empty. Where was everyone? Had this week's group meeting been canceled? If so, no one had notified her. A young woman in a pink headscarf and a long, flowered dress stepped inside Zaida's office. Hidaya Baqri. Zaida smiled at her, but the greeting wasn't returned.

The tension on Hidaya's face worried Zaida. She stood and asked, "What is it?"

Hidaya sent a look around the room, then closed the office door before approaching. Zaida instantly knew none of the other women would be coming that day for their weekly book discussion. Zaida took Hidaya's hand and had her sit next to her, frowning at her friend's pallor. "Are you unwell?" she asked.

"We have a problem," Hidaya said. She reached into her purse and withdrew a folded paper. She handed it over, then clutched her hands in her lap while Zaida read it.

The paper had a picture of a computer screen with a huge, red block of text that read:

∼

YOUR COMPUTER IS LOCKED!
All of your files have been encrypted and
moved to a hidden partition.
This is happening because you show
all the hallmarks of a
MUSLIM TERRORIST.
There's nothing you need to do…
except turn yourself in
(and you thought no one was watching).
All pertinent info used to make this assessment will be
sent to the government
unless you pay a ransom of $500 at this >>LINK<<.
You'll have control of your laptop one week after this
notice first arrived, but if you want your computer
back before the big black SUVs arrive,
click >> HERE << to pay the ransom.

Counter: 157:45:36:24

∼

ZAIDA READ IT TWICE. Her palms were sweating. "What is this, Hidaya?"

Her friend shook her head. "It showed up on some of our computers. If we don't comply, then some information—we don't know what—will be sent to the government. They might even plant information on our computers." She gave Zaida a pained look. "Whoever did this…maybe they already know everything about us. We will be exposed as apostates in our communities."

"Of course you can't comply, but not for any of those reasons," Zaida said. "You can't give money to terrorists."

Hidaya's shoulders slumped. "Some did try to buy their way out of the ransomware, but the links don't work." She tapped the paper. "They're calling *us* the terrorists. They're going to report us. It takes nothing, absolutely nothing, to be deported. There is no due process. Any suspicion at all is enough to end our lives."

"No. This is ridiculous. It's an illegal search and seizure—if the government is in any way involved," Zaida said, hoping her friend understood the dangerous path she was walking.

"We sometimes talk about forbidden topics in our group." Hidaya's voice was quiet and tortured.

"We talk about topics that interest us," Zaida countered. "Harmless things like recipes and family life…"

"And our sex lives. And stories with sex. Freedoms for women that fly in the face of Islamic law."

"There's nothing illegal about what we do. We

aren't plotting murders or planning sedition. We've done nothing wrong in our jobs or in our group. Here in the States, we're allowed to meet and talk. About anything. We're allowed to write and read fiction, even sexy fiction. We're allowed to contribute articles to a knowledge base of what we've experienced in our lives." She paused, studying Hidaya. "We are not allowed to fund terrorist groups."

"Some in our communities would consider our open discussion about intimate things immoral. Some consider it pornography and call it haram."

"But you're safe here to talk about anything, especially intimate things. If women don't understand about how sex affects their lives and relationships, how can they learn they have free will? We've talked about this. It is our Freedom Code."

Hidaya pointed at the paper. "Someone knows what we talk about. They're using it against us. My brother and the others' husbands will lose their jobs. They won't be able to feed their children. We will be ostracized in our communities and at the university. And when they find out the types of women I meet with, it will be even worse."

"Types of women?" Zaida raised her brows. "You mean our friends, Hidaya? We started as a simple readers group, but we've become so much more. We share our frustrations and dreams. We share tips about child rearing and dealing with husbands and boyfriends and parents. We talk about our health.

We've become a support group. We've become friends."

Hidaya's face went blank. She stood and straightened her skirt. "You don't believe me. It is already happening." She handed Zaida her phone. The screen was open to Hidaya's brother Abdul's Facebook profile, which was now full of horrible posts, including a jihadist manifesto calling for all Muslims in America to rise and destroy the Zionist enemy.

Zaida was shocked. "This isn't like your brother. Abdul is the kindest, sweetest guy. Just like you."

"It isn't him. They hacked his profile. It's all over his accounts—Twitter, Instagram, Facebook, and all the others."

"Who hacked him?"

"We don't know. He can't even access his accounts to take the messages down. I don't know what to do, Zaida. I only know that we can't come here. Not for our group meetings. Not for our work. At least for a while, but maybe forever." Hidaya walked toward the door.

"Wait. Hidaya, wait. What if I have someone look into this? I have a friend who might be able to help us. Would that be all right?" Zaida asked.

"You cannot go to the police. They will shoot Abdul and then ask questions."

"No, they won't. They have no cause to do that."

"We are Muslim. It is cause enough."

"My friend isn't with the police. He would help us without making things worse."

Hidaya nodded. "We only have days before whoever this is will carry out his threats and expose us."

"I understand. I'll text you after I talk with him." Zaida held up the paper. "I'm keeping this."

"All right."

"Don't do anything until then. Please."

"Let me know, Zaida. We are very afraid."

"Just stay at home. Keep your heads down, you and Abdul. We'll get to the bottom of this. In the meantime, have your brother work on getting his accounts back."

They hugged, then Hidaya left. Zaida emptied the coffee pot she'd brewed for the group meeting, dumped out the hot tea water, and packed up the cookies she'd brought. No one else was coming tonight.

She locked the office suite behind her, then went down the old brick building's three flights of stairs and out to the street. The late July evening was warm, with just a slight breeze. It was dark enough that the streetlights were coming on.

Zaida's office was only a couple of blocks from her apartment. It was a really convenient location. She'd lived at her current place for a few years now. She knew all the shops and many of the shopkeepers along the Old Town strip between her office and apartment. Some people she passed were familiar as well. Fort Collins, Colorado, was home to Colorado State University, whose students walked and rode their bikes everywhere; Old Town was one of their favorite haunts.

It was a beautiful place to live, and yet after Hidaya's visit, it took on a sinister pall.

Zaida looked around, feeling watched, trying to see if someone was following her, observing her. She quickened her pace. Though the area was well lit and heavily populated, she suddenly couldn't wait to get home and lock the doors.

Her apartment was on the second floor of an upscale development that took up a whole city block. The first floor housed an atrium-like space with plentiful greenery in the center and a big steel and glass skylight. The outer circle of the atrium had an eclectic mix of shops and restaurants frequented by those who lived and worked in the legal district at the north end of town.

Her parents had insisted she take the apartment they'd selected for her when she graduated from CSU seven years earlier. It was monitored twenty-four-seven and had the highest level of security of any apartment building in the area. Zaida liked it because of all of its amenities. There was a private parking garage for residents and visitors. A full gym. And all the restaurants that she could need. It even had a fabulous coffee shop.

She swiped her access card at the elevator, then took the short ride up to the second floor. Turning the corner to her apartment, she came to a full stop. Her front door was open, just a crack. A chill slipped down her spine. She froze, trying to decide whether she should enter her apartment alone or if she should call the police.

She pulled out her phone and keyed in 911 but didn't hit the send button. Proceeding cautiously, she inched closer to her apartment to peek inside. There was nowhere to take cover in the hallway. If a burglar saw her, she wouldn't be able to get away before they could get to her. But she couldn't very well involve a neighbor—especially if there was a criminal in there.

She crept forward until she was standing next to her front door. Her thumb hovered over the send button on her phone as she quietly pushed her door all the way open.

She couldn't see anyone inside, but she could hear someone in her kitchen…someone who was humming a tune that was all too familiar to her.

"Mother?" she called out.

"Hello, dear. I'm in the kitchen," Rayna Hussan called out. Pans clanked.

Zaida sighed. She shut the front door but didn't yet clear her phone screen. She set her purse down on a side table in her foyer. "Are you alone?"

Rayna frowned at her. "Your father had some work to do at the university. School will be in session before you know it. I thought I'd pop by and make a late dinner while we wait for him." She gave Zaida a dark look. "I am allowed to visit my daughter, aren't I?"

Zaida relaxed and erased the emergency number

on her screen, then went to kiss her mother's cheek. "Of course you are, but I've already eaten."

"Your father hasn't. He'll be here any minute. You can sit with us."

"I'd like that."

"I thought your group meeting would have run longer."

Tension shot through Zaida; she knew exactly how her mother would react when she asked for Mike Folsom's number. Their lifelong friend was a CIA agent. At least, that had been the running joke all the years she was growing up. He never fessed up to it, though. He had that edge in his eyes, a persistent situational awareness that wasn't normal civilian behavior.

"I forgot that everyone in my group was on vacation. My book has eaten my brain."

Her mother sent her a curious glance. "How is your story coming?"

An idea hit Zaida on the fly, and she went with it. "Pretty well. You know, I'm writing something different from my usual." She took a seat on one of the stools at her kitchen counter, feeling a little guilty for the lie. "It's a romantic suspense spy novel. Do you think Mike would be open to talking to me? I have some general questions."

"As it turns out, he's in town. In Boulder, anyway. Why don't you see if you can meet up for coffee? I'd go with you, but my schedule's booked getting ready for our vacation next week."

"What's his number? I'll call him now." Her mom called off the digits. Zaida dialed, but there was no answer. She left a message asking if they could meet. She desperately hoped Mike could make time for her. If not, she'd have to go to the police.

"Mom, you left my door open. I'd rather you didn't do that."

"And why not? Who's going to come down this end of the hall but you?"

"You never know. It's just not a safe practice. Fort Collins is getting very big. All sorts of people come here now. It scared me seeing it open."

Her mom looked worried. "Why would it scare you? I always leave it open when I'm here. I have to alert you before you barge in with a boy."

Zaida reached over and took a bite of tuna from the salad niçoise tray her mom was building. "I don't bring boys here. I bring men."

Rayna stopped what she was doing and glared at Zaida. "Men! My unmarried daughter brings men into her home?"

"Well, I can't do it once I marry, can I?"

Her mother's eyes went wide. "Zaida. You disrespect me."

"I'm teasing." She chuckled. "Just, please, close my door when you're in here."

"All right. I will. Do we need to discuss with your father the men you bring here?"

"No. We do not. I don't bring men here. Or boys. Or anyone."

Rayna shook a fork at Zaida. "It's time you did, though."

Zaida gave her mom a shocked look. "You just had a fit at the thought of it."

"Yes. I know. But you aren't getting any younger, and I want grandbabies. It's unfair to put such a burden on you, but I was only able to have you, so you must be the one who gives me a dozen grands."

Zaida choked. "I will not."

"One at least. *Masha'Allah.* Jamal is ready to settle down."

"Jamal is not my type."

"He will be when you marry him. You have to mold him, like I did with your father."

"I'm not marrying him, Mother. I'm not marrying a man I have to mold."

Zaida's front door opened, admitting her father. Both of her parents had their own key cards to her place.

Rayna leaned close to whisper, "We'll discuss this later."

"No, we won't," Zaida hissed.

Her father, Darim, took his shoes off in her foyer and set his briefcase down on the hall table. He came over to kiss Zaida and her mother, then went straight to the washroom to clean up for supper.

Her parents settled themselves at her table and talked about his day. Zaida watched them, letting her fear fade away. It all seemed so normal, like the world hadn't been turned on its side just minutes ago when Hidaya had visited.

Everything was going to be all right, Zaida told herself as she put the group's cookies on a plate for her parents. It was going to be fine. What Hidaya and her brother Abdul were dealing with was some kind of terrible cyberbullying.

It was all going to be fine. Really.

∽

ZAIDA WALKED down Pearl Street Mall in the heart of Boulder's Old Town. Her nerves had tangled on the way here until she was a bundle of knots. Mike Folsom was sitting at a bistro's outdoor table. He stood when he saw her, waving her over, giving her a hug and a kiss when she joined him.

He seemed even more uptight than usual. She hadn't seen him since his last visit to the area a few years earlier. He'd aged a little, and more lines creased his forehead, but his eyes were as alert as ever. He had that slightly unkempt look that he always had, with his scruffy beard and the baggy clothes he wore, but his broad, square face was a welcome sight to her. He'd been a big part of her childhood. He was who had helped her parents relocate from Iraq, years before she came along. He was, to her parents, an angel that looked out for them.

Zaida hoped he'd be her angel too.

They both placed their orders. She looked at

Mike, wondering how to broach the subject of her friend's problem, but he opened their conversation for her.

"You're actually why I'm here in the States, Zaida."

"I am? Why?"

"I've been informed that a *fatwa* has been issued against you from an ISIS terror group in Syria."

Shock didn't even come close to what that news made her feel. No, it was something much more explosive, like terror. She wasn't surprised that some in her community might push back against the stories she wrote and the freedoms she advocated, but to call a *fatwa* upon her was unacceptable.

"A *fatwa*? Against me?"

"I'm still investigating the whys, hows, and whos of this, but it appears that you sent a piece of code out into the world to identify likely terrorist threats. This code is technically called a worm, but it's also ransomware. It's self-executing and can jump from network to network. It's fast-moving—it took only a month to go from here to the Middle East and back."

Zaida's eyes widened. Ransomware? Was this connected to Hidaya's problem? She took out the paper her friend had given her.

Mike looked at it then at her, his eyes narrowing. "That's it."

"I'm not a coder or a hacker, Mike. I'm a romance writer."

"I know. But the worm was launched from your computer."

"How?"

"That's what I need to find out. Does the term 'Freedom Code' mean anything to you?"

"Yes. It does."

"And what is that?"

Zaida gave him a pained look. How could she say this so that he would understand? Men took their individual freedom for granted. Women still had to fight for theirs, especially in areas under stringent Sharia law.

"It's my belief that when women own their own sexuality, they can't be oppressed. I call it our Freedom Code. It's one of the reasons why I write what I write."

Mike tucked his chin in and looked at her over his glasses. "So women having sex sets them free?"

"No. Women having proprietorship over themselves gives them freedom. Sex is the most elemental freedom they can have. It has nothing to do with code or worms or international terrorists. Or even men. It has everything to do with independence and self-determination."

Mike held up his hands. "Just being a devil's advocate here…can't women already say no?"

"If they could, then men wouldn't still be sexually harassing them, they wouldn't be forced or sold into marriages—often while they're still underage, they wouldn't be assaulted in war for the purpose of genocide, and they wouldn't be subjected to genital mutilations. All these atrocities still occur. A woman having control over her own body is about much more than just sex. It's about freedom."

"Okay." Mike's gaze lowered to the table between them as he considered what she'd said. "Sure. But it can't be a coincidence that the worm was called that."

Zaida shook her head. "I don't know why the worm appropriated that term. I don't know anything about this worm."

"So, would you call yourself an activist?"

None of this conversation was going the way she thought it would.

"What does that even mean, Mike? Am I stirring the pot? Yes. Am I empowering underprivileged women? Yes. Am I financially supporting a half-dozen women's literacy organizations around the world? Yes. Am I writing stories with characters that act as role models and do I get them in front of the very women who most need to read them? Yes."

"That's propaganda."

"What isn't? TV commercials, restaurant ads, news media, blogs, magazine articles. Everyone has a bias. Mine is to show women how to assert their rights and advocate for their needs and desires."

Their food arrived. Mike went silent until the waiter left.

"You are your mother's daughter," Mike said, smiling.

"I am."

"I can see you feel strongly about all of this. Are you at a point in your mission that you would hire muscle?"

Zaida stared at Mike, shocked at the ease with which he slipped that question into their conversation. What was he getting at, exactly? "I have hired help."

"And…have you armed them and had your own *fatwa* ordered?"

"No. I hired translators. English is my first language. I do speak, read, and write Arabic, but it's not my natural language. It's easier for me to write in English and pay for a translation. I also have my work translated in Pashto and a few other languages. I have no idea how one goes about ordering a *fatwa*, or why I would anyway. I'm a pacifist, Mike."

"I think we're talking about two different forms of activism. I was trying to understand how you came to the attention of some serious bad guys and how you could have garnered enough attention from our enemies that a religious edict was set against you. I'm sorry you've gotten caught up in this. All I know is that the worm seems to have started in one of your computers. Would you be willing to let my company examine your machines?"

"Of course. Am I in danger?"

"Yes." He gave her a hard stare. "I've tracked communications from the terrorist group Tahrir al-Sham to some of their adherents here in the U.S., a sleeper cell, if you will. They've been called up and appear to be on their way here. To you."

Zaida's eyes and mouth went wide as she wrapped her arms around her stomach. "What do I do?"

Mike sighed. "I'm going to have some agents cover you. I can't actually do anything here on U.S. soil, so we have to keep this on the down-low. When we figure out the facts and the players, I'll turn it over to the FBI. I gotta get the case put together."

So, her parents' family angel *was* CIA, since he admitted he couldn't act in the U.S. "I'm scared, Mike."

"I know, honey. I ain't gonna let anything happen to you. I'm sorry for the tough talk—you know I love you and I love your parents. You're the only family I have. You're like a daughter to me. I have a few things to do here, then I'll come up and stay with you until backup arrives."

They ate more of their meal, then Mike asked, "Why did you call me?"

Zaida pointed to the paper with the ransomware text. "My friend's Facebook and social media accounts have been hacked. I'm afraid someone wants to harm the Muslim community where we live."

Mike sighed. "I get that your Freedom Code means the world to you, but is it worth dying for? Is it worth the destruction of your community?"

"Are you asking me if we women shouldn't shut up and put up and get on with life? Are you really asking that?"

"Look, I'll admit I don't understand your stance, but I'm not a woman, and I've lived too long in a world where keeping the peace is almost more important than challenging the status quo. If this is a battle you believe in, then it's a battle I believe in."

Zaida's eyes watered. "Thanks, Mike." She sniffled. "I never thought it would be a battle. I thought it was a philosophy, a matter of education. I know, in some cases, I'm pushing back against religious doctrine, but that's still an intellectual endeavor, not a feat of war."

"When a challenge like yours undermines the foundation of power—and what you're doing is driving a power shift—then those whose foundation is crumbling will have to fight. In case you didn't know…that's how wars are started."

They finished their meal, then made small talk, catching up on family news. Mike walked her to her car in the parking garage, which she was very grateful for.

"I'd rather my parents didn't know about this," she said as they had a last hug.

"If I can keep it contained, that's fine by me. I'll come and stay with you until this whole thing is done. You still have that swanky apartment in Fort Collins?"

"I do."

"It might be late, but I'll be up there tonight."

2

Some nights were easy. Some weren't. This one wasn't.

Retired Navy SEAL Levi Jones jerked awake. His hands were wet and sticky with blood. He splayed his fingers even before he opened his eyes. Slowly, he realized the arms holding him back were no arms at all, but the strong legs of his black shepherd. He looked at his hands, his fingers still spread wide.

They were clean and dry.

He slumped back on the sofa, keeping his hands aloft as his dream world gave way to the real world. Beau pawed him again. Levi took another deep breath and closed his eyes, letting the dream go…and Jules with it.

He supposed there'd be a fair reckoning when he joined her on the other side. He'd lived to see life outside the service; she hadn't…because of him.

Beau whined and nudged his way up Levi's chest to lick his face. Levi couldn't hold back the tears. And why should he? It was only he and Beau here. He wrapped his arms around the shepherd and buried his face in Beau's furry neck. As far as Levi knew, Beau had never received PTSD service training, but the retired K-9 dog knew just when Levi most needed him.

Levi hadn't thought of Julia in a long time, hadn't let himself think of her. Damn Mike all the way to hell and back for conjuring her up again.

Levi shoved free of Beau and walked barefoot across his living room to his front door. It was just five a.m., his favorite time, when anything was possible for the day ahead…and nothing had yet gone FUBAR.

CIA Special Agent Mike Folsom had called yesterday, asking to see him today. Mike had been the intelligence asset on the op Levi and Julia were working under the auspices of DEVGRU's Black Squadron two years ago. That probably explained why Levi had had the dream—hearing from Mike again brought everything to the top of his mind.

Levi's phone rang. Who was calling him this early in the morning? He took the call, recognizing the number. Commander Greg Lambert. Only one reason he'd be calling. "Jones here."

"Morning, Levi."

"Commander."

"Got a job for you."

Levi had taken one other job for Lambert since

his discharge in January. He was beginning to see why Lambert was running this shadow op business; there were too many threats for regular law enforcement to handle.

"I'm listening."

"Your friend, Mike Folsom, has been tracking the activity of the Syrian terrorist group Tahrir al-Sham."

"Odd that you mention that. We're meeting later today."

"He's dead, Levi. He was found beheaded in an alley in Boulder a few hours ago."

"Shit."

"Yeah. Like I said, he was tracking some activity coming here to the U.S. He said participants in a Tahrir al-Sham sleeper cell had been activated and were on their way to your area."

"Why?"

"A woman who lives in Fort Collins appears to have started a worm called Freedom Code. It was brilliant. And powerful. The worm burrowed through tens of thousands of computers, starting in Fort Collins and circumnavigating the globe. It hit a Tahrir al-Sham outpost in Syria. Their tech guys reverse-engineered its code and hacked into a database the worm was sending info to."

So that was what Mike was working on. Levi knew Mike worked cybercrimes in the CIA—it was how they met on the Tbilisi, Georgia op.

"What kind of data?" Levi asked.

"The worm's sole function was to analyze the

footprint of every computer it infected, profiling the user as either a terrorist, a potential victim of terrorism, or a non-threat. The Tahrir al-Sham group were, of course, identified as terrorists. It stole some critical info from them."

"Why would this woman do that? What did she get out of it? Big money?"

"No. As far as we can tell, no money changed hands. Her profile doesn't fit a potential recruiter, and she doesn't come from a tech background, but she is an activist in women's rights."

"Then why involve herself in this?"

"That's what I need you to find out. She claims to be innocent."

"But you don't believe her."

"Haven't met a terrorist yet who didn't claim to be innocent. Mike, however, did believe her. He knew her and her family. She and Mike met yesterday. I'll be sending you a recording Mike made of their chat after this call."

"So what's the mission, exactly?"

"Take out the Tahrir al-Sham guys coming for her. And keep her safe until we can determine her level of involvement."

Keep her safe... That was all he'd had to do with Julia, but he'd failed—on too many fronts. He hated cybercrime ops. He really should turn this one down.

"I'm in."

"You know the drill: keep this shit quiet," Lambert said. "We don't need the public stirred up and calling for the government to raise the threat level. It's already high. We got to do what we do so it doesn't get higher. All our enemies need is the window of opportunity that mass panic would give them."

"Copy that."

"As with the other op you ran for me, this can't come back to the government. You need something, you call me, but otherwise, you're on your own."

"Roger that."

"A packet will be delivered to your house shortly. In the meantime, have a listen to the interview Mike recorded with the woman. Her name's Zaida Hussan."

"Yes, sir."

"I'm out."

The call ended just as one of Levi's motion sensors was triggered. Someone was driving onto his property. Levi picked up his pistol from the coffee table. A knock sounded on his front door. Beau barked. Levi motioned for him to lie down. He instantly complied, taking a tense crouch as he watched the door.

No one was at the door when Levi opened it, but a subcompact foreign car was leaving his driveway.

Levi looked down at the package leaning against his stoop. He picked it up and went back inside, giving Beau a nod to release him. He spread the packet's contents across his kitchen counter. It was a mix of photos, documents, and other media. And a security key card. There were satellite images of the Tahrir al-

Sham tech camp in Syria, pics of suspected members of a sleeper cell based in Michigan, transcripts of unencrypted convos activating several of their men here in the U.S. Mike's notes on the woman Levi was to contain and a dozen images of her, were also in the packet.

Ho-lee-fuck was Zaida Hussan hot. No, not hot —beautiful.

She looked like Middle Eastern royalty. Her hair was shiny, brown-black, and long, sometimes curled, sometimes straight. Her skin was a pale olive color. Black brows, carefully shaped in an almost straight line, stretched out over big espresso-brown eyes. Her lips were neither thick nor thin but the perfect feminine shape—the bottom a little wider than the top. Her nose was thin, but the tip of it was lower than her nostrils, giving her an arrogant air. Her cheeks were high but not exaggerated. Her narrow chin was well defined. Her oval nails had a white band across the tips. It was hard to estimate her height since no one was near her in the photos. She had a nice rack, slim torso, hips that were wide, and thighs that were all female on legs that tapered down to slim calves and narrow ankles.

She was a siren. A woman like this could take a man to his knees with just a smile.

Levi let Beau outside. The recording from Mike hit his phone. Levi played it while he cooked his breakfast. Damn it all. Zaida's voice was lush and evocative. She spoke eloquently and passionately.

And Mike loved her like a daughter, which was clear.

That was all Levi got from his first listen. He played it a half-dozen times. Her fear sounded real. So did her belief in her cause…and wasn't that the making of all great terrorists? Finding a cause greater than one's self, one's community, or anything else in the world?

A person like her, with her beauty and charm and erudite ways, could easily wreak untold havoc just to leave her stamp on the world.

Levi didn't buy her innocence act. Not for one second. He opened his laptop and started a web search on her as he ate his breakfast. She was a published author. Looked like she had hit a few of the big-time bestseller lists—*New York Times*, *USAToday*, *Wall Street Journal*. Hell, Levi hadn't even known the WSJ had a bestsellers list.

Why would someone with such a high profile, such a successful life, take an active and dangerous stand against terrorists? Levi let his dog back in the house, then went for a shower.

Time to meet the siren herself and get some questions answered.

~

DAYLIGHT FILLED Zaida's living room when she opened her eyes the next morning. She was still in the clothes she'd worn the day before. She was momentarily disoriented by waking up on her sofa, not her bed, then remembered she'd fallen asleep while she waited for Mike.

He'd never called and never arrived.

She yawned and stretched. She needed to get cleaned up so she could go downstairs for her morning coffee. She had a coffeemaker, but she'd never actually used it. Her mom made coffee with it when she came for a visit. Zaida didn't think she even had coffee beans in her kitchen. Maybe she should call her mom and ask—she smiled as she thought how that would infuriate her mom.

She switched the TV on. A picture of Mike showed on the screen. Zaida had the sound way down. She turned it up as she read the ticker across the bottom of the screen: *Middle-aged tourist found beheaded in a Boulder alley.*

Zaida's phone rang, making her jump. "Did you see the news?" her mom asked.

"Yes." Zaida's answer was barely a whisper.

"You saw him yesterday."

"I did." She couldn't tell her mother what they'd discussed. No way.

"I can't believe this. This is terrible news. Our angel. Gone."

"I'm so sorry, Mom." Much sorrier than she could even admit. Mike had died because of her. What now? Did he report their conversation to anyone? Who could possibly help her if the men he was tracking had done that to a guy like him?

This was awful. And it was all her fault. *Is your Freedom Code worth the destruction of your community?* His question floated through her mind. At the time he'd asked it, it had been rhetorical. Now, not so much. What was she going to do?

~

Levi had been watching Zaida Hussan for the day, confirming that her patterns of movement hadn't changed since Mike's notes that were in the packet of intel he'd been given.

She was a creature of habit. Her apartment building was in the heart of Fort Collins' legal district. The pricey condos where she lived were owned by the town's elite—lawyers, judges, CEOs…and writers, apparently.

Mike's notes reported her usual schedule. At nine a.m., Zaida came down to the public atrium to buy coffee and a breakfast sandwich. At one p.m., she went to the gym, then stopped at the juice vendor for a healthy blend. At seven, she came down for dinner. She favored the French bistro. She'd stayed with that schedule while Levi had watched her, too.

The woman always looked perfect—he'd seen that in the pictures of her. Even after a hard workout, her skin glowed. Her dark eyes were fringed with thick lashes. Her thick black brows were perfectly trimmed. Her shiny hair slipped over her body like a silky mink, settling itself on one shoulder or the other.

Her lips were lush, forming the perfect bow shape. The red shade she wore now made him wonder what they'd taste like. Her nails weren't overly long. The polish she wore complemented her lipstick. He could almost feel those nails in his back, digging into his shoulders as he pleasured her.

Not the most original thought, considering the look in the eyes of every other man watching her right now.

His gaze moved lower. She was of average height, though she seemed taller. Maybe it was her innate elegance. Or her straight posture. She wore heels, moving in a sleek and easy way, like a model, always aware of the looks she garnered from any man nearby —and many of the women, too.

Her breasts were large. Her clothes showed her generous cleavage, but never in an obvious way. Levi knew from the pictures of her that she wore designer outfits that seemed tailored just for her, like they were fucking sewn right on her. If she moved just so, and you happened to be looking, you'd catch a glimpse of the bounty her blouses covered.

He and every other man watched for that glimpse.

From Mike's notes, Levi knew he'd never seen her with anyone. No boyfriend—or girlfriend—ever accompanied her. She had an easy smile and a deep-throated laugh that made Levi think of other things she could do with that mouth.

The vendors all seemed to love her. She chatted with them easily. They fell over themselves to put her at the right table, hand her a bouquet they'd made just for her, or have her coffee ready before she even asked for it. Fawning, really, all of them.

Such an exquisite and charming terrorist.

He hated her already.

Levi sighed inwardly. He shouldn't have taken this op. He was tired of war. Though he was only forty, his soul felt twice that age. Why couldn't humans find a way to get along? Why did the motherfucking Tahrir al-Sham have to bring war here, to his country, his town, his people?

He should have told Lambert to call up someone else. He'd worked with the CIA before, not just in the previous gig he did for Lambert, but in posts overseas, sometimes pairing with female operatives from the Black Squadron—the only unit that admitted females. The forward operations he'd been part of had laid the groundwork for numerous successful raids, netting considerable intelligence.

He should have known his CIA connections would come back and bite him in the ass. This wasn't the commander's fault. The war on terror wasn't over, and it wasn't a thing that respected national boundaries or peaceful college towns. It was everywhere.

And so were men like him…in sleeper cells of former SEALs activated as CIA contractors licensed to work wherever they were needed against an international enemy making incursions into the U.S. The higher-ups in Defense and State felt retired spec ops guys like him, still of able mind and body, were national assets that were being wasted after they left the teams when they could be put to good use in the quiet war that was being fought on lean margins.

He wondered if retired Rangers and Delta Force guys were being activated as well. That hadn't been a question the commander had been willing to address.

On this op—unlike his work on the teams—he was a lone wolf. If he screwed up, he'd take the fall as a citizen acting on his own behalf. There could be no blowback hitting the CIA or any other part of the government...

His time with the Black Squadron had shown him firsthand just how capable and deadly a female could be, especially a beautiful, lethal operative like Zaida Hussan.

That was probably the reason he lived alone. Easier to sleep when you could close both eyes.

Tonight, Ms. Hussan did something different, yanking him from his thoughts. She came downstairs at nine p.m. and left the atrium to go outside. He followed her, watching her from across the street. It was a late July weekend. Kids were already returning to town in preparation for school starting next month. And they were all over the place, barhopping, reuniting with friends. It was a warm evening. And even though the sun had set almost a half-hour ago, there was still a little pale light in the sky. The streetlights had come on, making it easier to watch Zaida's reflection in storefront windows.

A man approached her. Tall. Swarthy. Middle

Eastern or Latino. Was this guy who she'd come out to meet? They stopped and talked. Levi moved to stand under a tree, watching Zaida's body language. The man was all smiles, but she was not. She even drew back a few steps, but the guy closed the gap between them.

Levi started across the street. The guy grabbed her wrist. She pulled free. The streetlight shining on her hair showed the vehement shake of her head.

Levi had had enough. It was time he made contact with her, anyway. He inserted himself between them and gave her a light hug, letting his body block her confused reaction. "Zaida. God, it's been a long time. Mike said he ran into you recently." At the mention of Mike's name, her expression shifted from fear to interest.

Levi turned to her companion and thrust out his hand. "Johnny Smith, nice to meet you. Zaida and I go way back. Went to college here, in fact."

When lying, it was always best to keep things close to the truth. Zaida had gone to Colorado State University. Of course, his name wasn't Johnny Smith, but no need to make this guy's homework any easier.

"I'm Jamal. Zaida and I were leaving."

Levi's brows lifted. He looked over his shoulder at Zaida, whose eyes were big and frightened. She gave a slight shake of her head.

"Well, I guess you got that half right: you're leaving. She's not."

Jamal stared at Levi, then looked around him at

Zaida, who was still parked behind his back. "Zaida, it's time to go. We don't want to keep our table waiting."

"You want to go with him?" Levi asked.

"No."

Levi grinned at Jamal. "Sorry, pal. Guess she's done with you for the night."

Jamal's eyes narrowed. "Get out of the way."

"No means no." Levi's eyes hardened. "Take a hike."

"She's not your concern."

"True, that. I just like the word 'no.' It's such a clear, short, sweet directive. But if you aren't able to grasp its meaning, then maybe you need my fists to explain it? They can talk short and sweet, too."

The guy's rage tightened his whole body. Levi braced himself for whatever would come next, but nothing did, other than a hissed sigh.

"Zaida," Jamal said, "we will finish this later."

Zaida held her silence.

The man glared at Levi, then pivoted and headed off in another direction.

Levi watched him walk away. A black van turned the corner then sped in their direction. Levi saw Jamal make a gesture toward it, just a simple flattening of his hand and a wave against his leg.

Levi moved Zaida closer to the building, using his body to block her from the road. The van moved past them. Levi noted its license plate.

"What are you doing?" Zaida asked a little breathlessly.

Levi didn't answer her. He was too busy looking around them, checking for someone, anyone, who was watching them. It was hard to tell in the dark; the open thoroughfare of the Old Town strip was like a death gauntlet. Threats could be anywhere.

When no other ones showed up, Levi turned to Zaida. She was watching him with that artful expression of hers, her exquisite eyes full of dark promises and tightly held secrets.

What was her game, getting the Tahrir al-Sham stirred up?

"Did Mike really send you?" she asked.

"Yes." Levi didn't hesitate. It was because of Mike that he was here.

She sighed. The tightness in her posture eased. Had she called Mike…or had Mike summoned her? The former would explain her ease with Levi; the latter would give the lie to her posturing.

"We need to talk," Levi said.

"Yes, we do." She looked around them. "We can go to my place. It's near here."

"I know. I've been watching you."

Her lips parted and her eyes moved from his eyes to his mouth and chin, shuttering herself from him. "I'd been feeling watched."

Levi's whole body tightened. Visions of her fluid strolls through the atrium popped in his mind. Had she been performing the whole time? Sowing a harvest of lust she could reap when it best suited her? He'd lapped it up like a panting dog.

And fuck if all the lessons he'd learned the hard way didn't fail him when he most needed them.

"Let's go," he said.

They started toward one of the entrances to the atrium in her building. The restaurants were still going hard. He knew they would pull down their gates on the atrium side by eleven p.m. For now, everything was wide open. He wouldn't put it past Jamal to be waiting for them somewhere between there and Zaida's place.

She sent him a sideways look, then stopped. "I should have asked for proof that you are who you say you are."

"Yes, you should have. But it wouldn't have mattered. I have none. We're going to have to go on trust, you and I," Levi said.

"What agency do you work for?"

"I'm a ghost, Zaida. No government agency will acknowledge me. But right now, I'm your only hope."

3

Zaida felt a shiver cut through her. This man, "Johnny Smith," looked about as American as they came, with his deep blue eyes, rough beard, reddish-brown hair, and height. He was a foot taller than her, maybe more. She remembered the feel of his body pressed to hers after Jamal left. He was as solid as the brick wall he'd pinned her against.

What did an American look like, anyway? She was born in this country and was as American as he was, but they looked nothing alike. Why was it even an issue for her?

Maybe she was just being sensitive about her ethnicity. The ongoing wave of lawless actions by people with backgrounds like hers painted them all with similar brushes. She feared for herself and her family because of the actions of others, but that had never hit home as it did now. Perhaps Johnny blamed her for what happened to Mike. Maybe she was to blame. She'd begged Mike for help…a request that had gotten him beheaded.

Johnny had stepped between her and Jamal without a twinge of fear—something she could never have done. Maybe she should have gone to her parents instead of Mike—maybe then he'd still be alive. The terrible truth was that she feared Jamal, the son of her father's old friend, was somehow part of everything that was happening.

"Show me your driver's license," she said.

He did. His name wasn't Johnny, but Levi Jones. She took her phone out and snapped a photo of is ID.

"While we're at it, let's swap phone numbers," Levi said. She gave him her digits so he could dial her. When the call went through, he hung up. "Now, we need to talk."

"Come back tomorrow. We'll talk then."

"Thinking of researching me?" he asked. She nodded. "You won't find anything on me. I told you I was a ghost."

"What kind of person doesn't have a digital profile?"

"I guess one who doesn't want to be found." He grinned. His teeth were white and straight. The expression might as well have been a grimace for all the humor it held, which gave her another shiver.

She was handicapped by the fiction she wrote. Romance was her genre of choice. Reading and writing it was cathartic in times like these. She wrote emotional contemporary stories set in small towns;

unlike the ruse she'd used on her mom, she never ventured into the edgier stuff of romantic suspense or thrillers. But no matter what subgenre, in the world of romance fiction, good always won…as did love.

Sometimes, her fictional worlds were more real than reality. But this was the real world—right here, right now—and it never quite worked out as it did in her stories.

"You aren't going to save me, are you?" Her words were barely a whisper. She'd leaned a little closer to say them. His eyes darkened as he watched her lips move.

"Do you need saving?" he asked.

"Maybe."

"From whom?"

"I don't know."

"What makes you think you're in danger?"

"Besides Mike being cut in two?"

"Yeah."

"Someone's using me to get to terrorists. Or rather, using me to infiltrate my network of Muslim readers, putting me—and all of them—in jeopardy."

Levi grunted. His eyes narrowed as he puzzled through that revelation. "We shouldn't be talking about this here."

She nodded. They headed toward the elevators. She swiped her badge in the reader. Levi held the elevator door for her, then followed her inside. The next floor was for the regular apartments. The upper two floors held the penthouse apartments with their luxurious rooftop decks. She'd been up there recently when one was for sale. One day, perhaps, she could afford one for herself. For now, she was content where she was.

Her apartment was large and modern with a crisp, open floor plan. The white of the walls, big kitchen counter, and cabinets was alleviated by her dark wood floors and the rich red colors of the Middle Eastern textiles that hung on the walls and the beautiful Persian carpets that were in every room.

"Nice place you have," Levi said.

Zaida smiled. "Thank you. I spend all of my time here, since I work at home, so I filled it with things I love."

"Why Colorado?" he asked.

"I grew up in Denver, but came up here for school. After I graduated, I just stayed. My folks helped me get this place, but I only agreed under the condition that they hold the mortgage instead of buying it outright for me." She set her purse down. "I knew they'd use it as leverage against me if I accepted this condo as a gift."

He frowned. "What kind of leverage?"

"They want me to get married and settle down, have a bunch of kids."

"And you don't want that?"

She shook her head. "I'm having too much fun right now. I own my life. If I were to get married, especially to someone they chose for me…well, everything would change." She looked at Levi. He was a complete stranger. She rarely had men up here—she never brought strangers up. "Jamal was one of their choices. He's the son of a man my father knew a long time ago."

Levi's expression hardened. "What makes him right for you?"

"Other than they vetted him?"

Levi nodded.

"I don't know. He's the founder and CEO of a tech company and an adjunct professor of computer science at CSU. They like that he's got his life in order. But he's too much of a traditionalist, too conservative for me. He is too enamored of the old ways—the very traditions that forced my parents to come here in the first place back in the eighties."

"Parents are funny creatures. Why did he scare you?"

"He can be overbearing." Zaida went into the kitchen. "Would you like something to drink? Coffee, tea, wine?"

"Got any beer?"

"No."

"Water would be great."

She was relieved he didn't ask for coffee. She really should learn how to make it. She filled two tall glasses with ice water.

"What about your parents?" she asked as she handed him his glass. They were only minutes into their acquaintance and already he'd dragged a lot of personal stuff out of her. She didn't like that.

"They're gone. While ago. Big pile-up on a frozen interstate. Took them both."

"Oh, how awful. I'm so sorry."

Levi shrugged. "I was in the service. It was a long time ago." He set his drink on the big island that separated the kitchen from the living and dining rooms. "Mind if I check your place out?"

"Check it for what?"

"Terrorists. Bugs. Bad things."

Icy fear knotted in her stomach. She nodded. "Sure. Do you think they could get in here?"

"I could."

"How?"

He shook his head. "My secret." He took out his phone and walked around the place, opening every door. Her apartment was spacious—three bedrooms, two bathrooms. One of the bedrooms was her office. Everything in her life was exactly as she wanted it. The perfect apartment in the perfect town. Perfect furnishings. A schedule that was of her own making. The independence to work when she wanted—where she wanted. The self-discipline to meet her goals.

Everything was just great...until this terrible wrinkle in her life. A friend of the family murdered, possibly because of her. Her parents pressuring her to settle down. And now a stranger walking through her home, a stranger who might have come straight out of one of her books. Rough, manly, and mysterious. But unlike a hero she'd write, Zaida had no idea what this man would say or do...or if he even was a hero.

She followed him from room to room, turning on lights for him, then shutting them off behind them. Her bedroom was the last stop on the tour. As he had in each room, after a physical sweep, he did an electronic one. Zaida was glad he was focused on his task and not on her, but that didn't last long. He glanced up just as he came to a stop next to her Kama Sutra sofa. It was a long, elegant lounging couch in the shape of a stretched-out S. A girlfriend had gifted it as a joke, given the erotic nature of some of Zaida's stories.

Levi stared at it a moment, then looked at her, a single brown brow lifted.

She felt heat rise up her neck. Did he know what it was? Most people didn't. Her parents didn't. They'd mentioned it once, but she was fond of modern furniture, so she shrugged it off as being a comfortable place to read and put her feet up. She gave Levi an innocent smile.

He looked around her bedroom once again, then at her. The heat in his gaze almost melted her knees. She wondered if he'd be good in bed…or if he was a get-it-done-and-have-a-sandwich kind of guy. He stepped closer to her. Her breath quickened. She wanted to fan herself.

Never had she reacted to a man this way.

"Got something on your mind, Ms. Hussan?"

"Um…so no bad guys, huh?"

"Looks like." He followed those two words with a slow grin, apparently not intending to back down.

"Great." She walked out into the hallway and returned to the living room, forcing him to follow her. "Glad we got that resolved."

Crazy that she felt spent just having him in her bedroom.

~

Levi followed Zaida down the hall, watching her hips move with each step she took. She'd taken her heels off at the front door. He wondered now whether he should have removed his boots.

"Tell me what you told Mike," he said.

"I run a weekly salon."

"Salon?"

"A women's group. We talk about everything, including my books and ones by other authors in different genres, but also our lives, what help we need. I've been doing it for almost a year. The group's getting large—I may soon break it out into a second group. I learned a couple of days ago that some of my readers have gotten a ransomware message."

She handed him her phone with a photo on it. It was the same message that had been found in Mike's hotel room. Levi had already cloned her phone when they exchanged numbers downstairs; it was good she'd brought this to his attention rather than leaving it to him to find.

He looked at her as he handed her phone back. "Did you call Mike or did he call you?"

"I called him. The women who received this threat have stopped coming to my groups. They have no one they could turn to. Not their husbands, not their families. They're scared."

"Are they likely to comply?" he asked.

She gave him a wounded look. "No. Of course not. They love their families. They don't want them to come to harm by sending money to terrorists." She gestured toward her phone. "This is anti-Muslim, just as it is anti-Christian…anti-anyone with a thinking mind or half a conscience."

"This threat has been popping up in communities in the Middle East as well. Did you know that?" he asked.

Her eyes went wide. "No. Mike said that it had shown up on the computers of a terrorist group, not that it was widespread." When Levi didn't appear to accept her innocence, anger took over. "If you think that I'm a party to any of this, then you can just get out right now. I write romance fiction. Talk about rose-colored glasses." She gestured toward her phone. "I want the world to be perfect, full of love and joy and happily-ever-afters. Not this ugly hate." His silence further infuriated her. She walked over to her front door and opened it for him. "Get out."

Levi walked over to her door and shoved it closed. "Like it or not, we're stuck with each other. I don't know whether you're a victim in all of this or if you're up to your neck in it through your own actions. I aim to find out. But to do that, I have to keep you alive.

Jamal would have kidnapped you tonight if I hadn't been there."

"No."

"You didn't see the black van speeding toward you?"

Shock filled her expression. "When you pushed me against the wall—"

"Yup."

"What makes you think it wasn't just a black van using the same street we were?"

"Because I saw Jamal wave it off."

"Oh my God." She gripped his arms. "What about my parents? Are they in danger? If Jamal wants me but can't get me, will he take them?"

"I'll get them some security. But right now, we need to get out of here."

"And go where?"

"Someplace that's not here. I suggest you pack for a more rugged existence. We may be gone more than a few days."

"I have to call my parents."

"No."

"I can't just disappear."

"That's exactly what you have to do. The less they know, the safer they'll be. Unless they're involved in all of this…if so, they can kiss their asses goodbye."

She released his arms, but still stood close. Too close. He could smell the fragrance she wore. Something exotic and faint, heated by her skin. A spice and flower blend—cardamom and geraniums, with just a hint of vanilla?

"How could they be involved in all of this? They don't do anything with my books. I don't think they even like that I write them."

That gave Levi pause. Maybe sabotaging her work was the goal of this whole deal. Before he could insist she pack, her phone rang. She answered it as she stepped away from him. "Hi, Mom… Mother? Slow down." Zaida's brows knitted. "Mother? What's happening? Are you safe?"

The line must have gone dead. Zaida lowered the phone as she stared at nothing for a moment.

"Talk to me, Zaida," Levi said.

Her eyes met his. Panic covered her face…until it didn't. She drew a breath, then her features settled into a calm mask. "Thank you for helping me tonight. I'll be more careful of Jamal." She took Levi's arm and turned him toward the door.

He put the brakes on. "Hold on. What just happened?"

"Happened?" She blinked. "Nothing. My mom often does that."

"Does what?"

"Safety drills. Really, I'd like you to leave now."

Under any other circumstances, he'd have complied. "They got to your parents," he said.

"No. I just forgot that I promised I'd meet with my mother in the morning. I need to hit the sack. She worries so if I show up with bags under my eyes."

Shit. They didn't even have time for her to pack. "We have to get out of here."

"I'm not going anywhere with you. For all I know, you are the problem."

"I'm not going to hurt you. Dammit, Zaida, I'm trying to keep your beautiful head on your hot-as-fuck body."

Just then, someone began fussing with the lock on her front door. There was no other way out of her apartment—he'd seen that on his tour. "Go into your room. Lock your bedroom door, then go into the bathroom. Lock that too. Do you have a gun?"

"No. No, I don't have a gun. I write romances for a living. It's not exactly a dangerous career path."

He took out his XDM40, chambered a round, then handed it to her. "Hold it like this." He adjusted her hold so it covered the grip safety. "Don't give a warning. Just pull the fucking trigger if you see anyone who isn't me."

She nodded toward her front door. "What if it's the cops?"

"It's not. They would have announced themselves." He shoved her toward the hall. "Go. Now."

Levi was glad she had a cover on the peephole in the door—kept the bad guys from seeing into the room with a reverse peephole viewer. It disadvantaged him, too—he had no idea what kind of weapons the bad guys were carrying.

He moved to stand behind the door. The guy fussing with the lock finally got it. The door opened—

just a crack at first, then wider. Levi let them all get inside. They didn't close the door.

"Hurry, get the girl," the last man through said in hushed Arabic. "Be fast and quiet."

"But we have time to—" the second man never finished his sentence. He saw Levi as soon as he turned to speak.

Levi grinned. "Something I can do for you, gentlemen?"

The man closest to Levi rushed him. The middle guy hurried to help the first. Levi ducked their punches and slammed his fist into the diaphragm of one guy, following it with a blow to his throat. As that guy started to bend over, gasping for breath, Levi put a hand on the guy's shoulder and hoisted himself into the air, kicking the second guy in the face, cracking his jaw. The guy's head hit the wooden arm of one of Zaida's side chairs, breaking the chair and snapping the guy's neck.

The first guy straightened and grabbed for Levi. Turning, Levi yanked his hand forward, straightening it over his shoulder, then slamming downward, breaking the man's arm at his elbow. He cried out.

The third man, who'd barely made it to the hallway, rushed back to help his friends. He pulled out a pistol with a suppressor and waved it around, trying to get a straight shot.

Seeing him, Levi turned again, pulling the guy whose arm he'd just broken in front of him as the guy fired. The man Levi was holding slumped in his arms.

Levi shoved him aside, knocking a lamp off a side table.

The guy with the gun was only a couple of feet from Levi now. Levi lurched forward, ducking as he shoved the guy's gun up and aside. The guy squeezed off another round. It hit the wall. Keeping a hand on the gun, Levi kneed him in the groin. A quick twist of the fist holding the gun, and Levi took possession of it. He stepped back and fired a round into the guy's chest.

As fast as it happened, it was over. Three men were down.

Levi locked the door again. He cleared the weapons from each of the intruders, then checked to see if they were alive. They weren't.

He collected their identification. They had regular driver's licenses…and passports. Their passports showed they were from Turkey, but who knew how valid any of their IDs were? Their names weren't ones he'd been given in the packet, but he had to assume they were from Tahrir al-Sham's crew.

He dragged them into the kitchen, away from Zaida's carpets, wondering how many more were waiting for them downstairs, or already on their way up.

He and Zaida had to clear out of there. Fast.

Levi went to get her. Her bedroom door was locked. He grabbed the lock probe that one of the other bedroom doors had over the doorjamb and let himself into her room.

"Zaida—it's me, Levi. You're safe. For now." No answer. "Zaida, I'm coming in. Don't shoot me."

"Levi?"

"Yeah."

She fumbled with the lock, then stood back as he opened the door. His gun was in her shaking hands. Black streaks of makeup ran down her cheeks. She looked behind him, watching for someone else, but didn't resist when he reached for his pistol. He slipped it into his holster.

Zaida's face was pale. Her whole body was shaking. He pulled her close. Wrapping his arms around her, he lost a few precious minutes waiting for her panic to recede. "You're safe. For now."

"Did they come in? I heard a shout, but nothing else."

"Yeah. Three men came in. All are dead. My people will come clean up. We need to get out of here." He leaned back and checked her over. Catching her face, he forced her to look up at him. "I have a safe place for us to go. Grab some things. Be quick about it. We have to get out of here." He left her, but called over his shoulder as he walked away, "Bring your laptop. And pack for rough accommodations."

Back in the living room, he took snapshots of the intruders and their IDs. He sent them to Lambert and got a call right away.

"What am I looking at?" Lambert asked without preamble.

"Three guys who broke into Zaida Hussan's apartment. Not clear if they would have taken her alive."

"You take them out?"

"Affirmative. I'm leaving them for you. There was an attempt to nab Zaida off the street earlier tonight by a man she thought was a friend. Some guy named Jamal. I'll text you the license plate on the van. Our enemies want her…so we want her. I'm taking her to my place. We need to get to her parents ASAP. They called her with some kind of warning just before these guys broke in here. Not sure if or how they are involved, but either way, we want them too."

"Agreed. I'll handle it. Get out of there." Lambert hung up.

4

Levi waited for Zaida to come out of her room. Didn't take long. She brought out a leather satchel, stuffed to the brim, then went into her office to get her laptop. When she came out, her messenger bag was stuffed with papers, cords, supplies, and a laptop in a pink case.

"Got everything?" Levi asked.

"Probably not." Her gaze snagged on the three bodies lying side by side in the kitchen. "Oh my God."

"Don't worry about them. Like I said, my team's coming in to clean up."

"How will they get in?" she asked.

Levi tilted his head. "Security—here or anywhere—just keeps out the less determined. Let's go." He dropped her satchel strap over his head, leaving her to carry her laptop bag.

"Wait—I want to call my parents before we go. They must be worried sick."

"Not now. When we get where we're going, you can. Leave your phone here."

"I can't. It has all my information." She turned panicked eyes on him. "I don't even know their phone numbers. I did, but they got new numbers a year ago when they moved closer to me and I haven't bothered to memorize them. I just put them in my phone."

"Shut your phone off and leave it here. I don't want anyone tracking you. I have your contacts. I have all your vitae."

"How?"

"I cloned your phone."

"When?"

"When we were downstairs swapping numbers. And you can bet if I did it, your enemies did too." They went to the front door. His boot crunched on broken glass from the lamp. "Hope that wasn't valuable," he said.

"No, but it was one of my favorites."

"Well, if you don't go to jail, I'll buy you another one." He threw out that jab to distract her from the fact that she was running from her apartment in the middle of the night, heading someplace she'd never been with a man who was a stranger, leaving behind three dead guys on the floor in her kitchen. Anger was better than fear.

She took the bait and stopped in the hall outside

her apartment, furious. "Why would I go to jail? I haven't done anything. I haven't broken the law."

He met her angry gaze. She'd washed her face and fixed her makeup. The shaking, crying, terrified woman she'd been just minutes earlier was gone. She'd changed into a crisp white cotton blouse with three-quarter-length sleeves. The shirt's collar was turned up. It was fitted at the waist then flared slightly over her hips. She wore a pair of tight jeans and high-heeled boots that went up her calves.

So much for roughing it.

"Your innocence hasn't been established yet," he said.

"What about being innocent until found guilty?"

"Nice sentiment, until you start hanging with terrorists."

"I'm not a terrorist. I wasn't 'hanging with terrorists.'"

"Okay. Let's get out of here so we can prove it."

"If you didn't think I was innocent, why'd you give me your gun?"

"Because no one gets to you on my watch. Let's go."

Her door locked behind them. They took the elevator down to the resident parking level. A man stood outside the elevator when the door opened. Levi was already standing in front of Zaida, but he blocked her from leaving. The man met his eyes. His dark brows lifted. Levi laughed and stepped out of the cab, drawing Zaida with him.

He held a hand out. "Kelan Shiozski. How the hell are you?"

"Good, Levi. You?"

"Not bad. Been better. What are you doing here?" He noticed Kelan was wearing wide leather cuffs on his wrists and couldn't remember him doing that before. Maybe they were a peculiar fashion choice now that he was a civilian.

"I have an apartment here. My girlfriend's on again, off again at CSU. What about you? Heard you left the teams."

"Yeah. Retired this year. Starting a second career growing organic herbs and veggies for local businesses and a huge crop of sunflowers. You still in the service?"

"No. Got out this year, but same shit, different boss."

Levi wondered what he meant by that. Maybe it was the same type of situation he was in. "Kelan, this is Zaida Hussan. Zaida, my friend Kelan. He was in the Army while I was in the Navy." Kelan and Zaida shook hands. "You here because of your girlfriend?" Levi asked, remembering that Kelan had said he lived in South Dakota.

"No, a few of us are working a case up in Wyoming."

"No shit. Who's up there with you?"

"You know Max Cameron. Not sure if you met the others. Maybe Kit Bolanger? Angel Cordova? There's a bunch of us."

Levi nodded. "You gonna be there a while?"

"Yeah, why?"

"Curious. Zaida's a client. Things are getting hot here. You and your girlfriend may want to avoid the building for a little while." He grinned. "Least until they get the bodies out of Zaida's apartment."

"Shit, Levi. Who are these guys?"

"That's unclear. Just know they aren't good."

"Roger that. You working alone? Got a team?"

"Alone. Feels a little odd," Levi said.

"Well, if you need something, we aren't that far away." Kelan handed Levi a business card. "Zaida, nice meeting you."

Levi was glad he'd run into his friend. If he'd seen anything suspicious as he came through the parking garage, they wouldn't have stopped to chat. Didn't mean one of Zaida's enemies wasn't there, waiting for them. Just meant it was less likely.

They went to Levi's Jeep. He put her satchel in the back seat then opened her door for her.

"How did you park in here?" she asked.

"You mean how'd they let a lowlife like me in here?"

She looked irritated. "This is residential parking only."

"I may be working alone, but I do have friends in high places." He showed her his key pass.

"Does that go to my apartment?"

"Yes."

"Have you been in there before?"

"Not until tonight."

"How long have you been watching me?"

"Long enough." No need to tell her that her friend Mike had been watching her for a while. Her world was already taking on water as it was.

THEY DROVE out of the parking garage, into the dark night and busy street of the downtown area. Zaida watched around them nervously, wondering about the threats that might be out there, lurking, waiting for them. Levi was on edge, too—he kept checking his mirrors. She watched the cars in the rearview mirror on her side, but none of them seemed to follow them and their crazy, zigzagging route through town.

She tried to distract herself by thinking of the conversation Levi and his friend had. There were bits of good information that she should tuck away.

"So you were in the service?" she asked.

"I was in the Navy, until earlier this year."

"And now you're a farmer."

"An urban farmer." He flashed her a grin, then returned his attention to the road. "I like the way that sounds."

"You don't want to be a regular farmer?"

He shrugged. "Either way. I dreamt of becoming one for years before I got out. I took some ag courses. I bought some land out east of here. It came with a little farmhouse that I spent my off time refurbishing."

"Why did you get out?"

Levi's face tightened. She watched him in the light coming off the dashboard. "I guess I aged out. I could have shifted from an active team to a teaching or desk job. A lot of guys do. But I was done. You become addicted to the adrenaline each mission demands. I didn't like the thought of watching the young guys head out while I held the fort down."

"You're not very old. You're not much older than I am."

"I'm forty."

"Oh. You are old. I'm twenty-nine."

"I know."

"So now you're back in the adrenaline game?"

"I guess. I don't mind getting called up now and then. The government has a lot invested in its spec ops guys. Looking at it from their perspective, we're valuable commodities that should be used not wasted."

"But you wanted out."

"Yeah…but when the threat's here in my own country, guess that's when you know you bleed red, white, and blue."

"I'm not a threat, Levi."

He glanced at her. In the shadowy light, she thought he almost believed her. "I hope not. We'll be safe where we're headed. We can take some time to figure things out."

"Can I call my parents?"

"Not yet. Don't think I want you using my phone.

I have one I can give you at my house. I can set it up with your cloned data."

"Have you gone on many of these missions since you've been home?"

"One, before this. The pay's good. My farm could use the infusion of cash."

"So the government's funding this? You said you were too valuable a resource to waste."

"They are, but if shit hits the fan, I'm out cold. No one will ever acknowledge me, which is why I said I was a ghost."

"And yet they clean up the dead bodies you leave behind."

He grinned at her. "It's easier to disavow me if there's no evidence."

She turned and faced forward, watching the painted lines on the road zip past. "I thought the world was different. I thought things were what you see is what you get."

"It is. But the devil's in the things you don't see."

"Will you help me, Levi?"

"I am, aren't I? We'll figure out what's going on, then we'll decide what to do about it."

"Will you help my parents?"

"I already asked my contact to send someone out for them. We'll call them when we get to the house."

"What does your family think of your moon-lighting?"

He shrugged. "Nobody to answer to. I already told you my parents are gone."

"No wife?"

"No. I was married once. Very briefly. Came close a second time. But they weren't the forever kind, I guess. I'm not exactly good at picking spouse material."

Zaida sighed. "Me either. I write about love and couples finding each other, but I've never found it myself. Don't tell anyone—because it would wreck my career—but I'm starting to believe happily-ever-after is a myth."

She peeked at him to see his reaction. His smile seemed a little sad.

"So what does your perfect mate look like?" he asked. "How would you know him if you saw him?"

"Beyond the physical stuff?"

Levi waved a hand over the wheel. "No. All of it. Build your husband avatar."

"Well. I guess he'd be taller than me. Around my age."

"Is he a desk jockey or does he do something interesting? Does income matter?"

"I never thought about that."

"What do your parents do?" he asked, though he already knew the answer from the dossier Lambert had sent over.

"My dad's a professor of political science. My mom's an ob/gyn. I guess my perfect guy could be a doctor. He'd be well-educated and make a good income. Writing is a feast or famine kind of trade. His income could help level that out."

"Okay. What nationality is he?"

Zaida thought about that for a bit. "I guess it doesn't really matter, but it would be good if he were American. I don't want to be an expat. And I would like to set down roots."

"So there you go. A short American doctor."

"I didn't say short."

"Well, you said taller than you. Same thing." He laughed when Zaida gasped.

She wanted to punch him, but caught herself before she did something so hands-on. They were strangers, she and Levi.

"Maybe your mom could introduce you to a couple of young docs."

Zaida groaned. "No. She tried. Come to think of it, let's not do a doctor."

"Okay. So we're back to short, American, and able to provide a steady income."

"Right. No—"

He laughed. "So put yourself in one of your books. Who would you pair a character like you up with?"

"I'd never be in one of my books. I'm too boring."

Levi snorted. "You, an elegant, sexy, somewhat affluent modern young woman living in a highly desirable condo development—"

"Well, it was desirable until people started getting killed there. Bad for property values." She paused and flashed a look at him. "Wait…you think I'm elegant and sexy?"

He hooked a brow as he looked at her. "Have you looked in a mirror lately?" He waved a hand. "Don't worry about your apartment; it'll be cleaned up in no time. No one will even know it happened."

"What about you? What would your perfect wife be like?"

Levi looked at her and grinned. "I'm a simple man. Just give me a sex kitten."

"For real?" She glared at him. "You don't want a wife. You want a consort."

"Okay."

Zaida stared at the road. Why was it so easy to talk to Levi? She never gave away so much of herself to a stranger...especially not a man. Talking to him made her feel less off-kilter, as if the night's terrible events hadn't happened.

"Did you ever think about having kids?" she asked, wanting their conversation to continue.

"Sometimes. Never was a good time for it, not with me taking missions, being gone for irregular amounts of time."

"And you're still doing that."

"Yeah, but at least the missions are local now."

Zaida sat up and looked at him in shock. "Are there that many terrorists here?"

"It only takes one crazy-ass bastard to cause a lot of damage and spread terror."

"The cops can't deal with this stuff?"

"No. We keep what we can well away from them. They don't have the intel we have. And they don't have the surgical precision to get in, neutralize the threat, and get out without a big public production. They have a lot of higher-ups to answer to. Far too much visibility for the work at hand."

"What is the threat, Levi? What is it you have to neutralize? And why am I involved?"

Levi sighed. "Mike was tracking a group of bad guys who were doing some heavy recruiting throughout the Middle East. Beyond the clichéd promises of virgins and honor, these recruits were being offered a chance to strike back at the vulgar and oppressive Western influence being spread around the world by America. And then the Freedom Code worm stole info from them, which they blamed on you."

"Freedom code." Zaida couldn't hide her annoyance.

He shot her a couple of quick glances. "You've heard of it?"

Zaida felt her throat go dry; this all circled back to her, but she still didn't get why she was involved. "I always felt writing romances was like giving women the code to their freedom. I've even called it Freedom Code in some of our circle chats."

"How do you figure romance fiction is freedom for women?"

"Women writing fiction for women that's about women is just about the most feminist thing I can do. People read to understand how to deal with life. Storytelling is something the human psyche is wired to do. Stories help take the edge off our worries by shortening learning curves. Readers know so much more about life and handling choices through the stories they read; they're important stuff. In romances, women learn they are important, that they can stand up for themselves, that they can build a life they love, no matter who they are or where they live. Romance says a lot about the good side of life and surviving dark times and hard trials and winning. It talks about finding your way in a complex world…finding your way to love."

"Huh. Romances aren't just about a lot of sex?"

"Well, sex is an important part of life, isn't it? For some reason that I will never understand, sex is this secret, taboo thing." She lifted her shoulders and gave a little shake of her head. "Why shouldn't we talk about it, share stories about it, learn that it can be a fun and healthy thing in adult lives? Why are we constantly sex-shaming things? Shining a light on it brings it out of the dark, which is good, because when things are kept in the dark, then dark and ugly deeds can be done there. I firmly believe that when women own their own sexuality—when they can say yes or no, and have no taken for an answer, then they can never be oppressed because no one has a say over their bodies but them. You see? In that way, romances are a freedom code for women."

"So you're a rebel."

"Yes. I am a rebel. I want to empower women. I

want to see them be joyful. The world needs a whole lot more love and kindness than it has right now."

"And sex."

"Healthy, consensual, adult sex, yes."

Levi fell silent. Zaida looked out her window. They really were driving way out to the east. The city lights were tiny sparkles behind them. Civilization was still scattered here and there, in little collections of farmhouses, outlier neighborhoods, and distant towns, but the longer they drove, the fewer there were of those.

"Where are we going?"

"To my farm."

"Where is it?"

"Another half-hour east of here." Levi shot her a quick look. "So tell me about these gatherings you have with your readers. Who comes to them? How often do you hold them? What do you talk about at them?"

"I started them when I first published. I still had a lot of friends in the area that I knew from my CSU days. The group grew organically over the years. The ladies brought friends, sisters, mothers. We're actually surprisingly diverse—people from different religions come; a few have no religion that they formally adhere to. We have women in their twenties and in their seventies. We have U.S. citizens and non-citizens. People in the group speak English, but also Arabic, Pashto, Spanish, and others." She looked at Levi. "Of all the things I've done so far, my group makes me the happiest. Getting such a diverse people together to talk about life and their challenges and triumphs in a safe place is magical. A lot of what I write about revolves around ethnicities and love that crosses those boundaries, how families deal with those challenges. I am intensely curious about the human condition."

"I hate to ask this, but you understand I have to, could any of your friends have infected your computer or your work with a virus? You said it was spreading among your network of Muslim readers. I'm trying to understand how that could happen."

She shook her head. "The people in my group—they're my friends. They would never do something that would hurt others or me. Never. It's the antithesis of what we are."

He nodded. "I'm not arguing with you, but someone you know did this to you. We need to figure out who."

Zaida fell silent. Tears distorted the world outside the Jeep. "I don't want to. If I find out, I know I'll be hurt. And I love every one of them."

Levi sent a glance her way. He frowned. "Well, being hurt's a helluva lot better than being dead, so we're gonna have to dig into it."

5

Zaida was getting sleepy by the time they pulled off the country road. The dark was complete...or, rather, different from how it was in town. The moonlight was brilliant. It was almost as if they could have driven without headlights. Strange how streetlights seemed to make things darker than they were.

They turned onto a dirt road, and then a few more dirt roads before Levi slowed as he approached a final turn. The drive was through a dense growth of sunflowers that rose at least seven feet from the ground.

"I don't like this place," she whispered.

"Why not?"

"It's eerie. And dark."

"It's nighttime."

"You live on a sunflower farm?"

"Yes, I do. Wait until you see it in the daylight."

"What if they come alive and kill me while I sleep?"

Levi grinned. "So is that a guilty conscience speaking, or did you eat some magic mushrooms while I wasn't looking?"

She focused on him. "I have nothing to be guilty about."

"So it's the mushrooms."

"Levi. Jones. I don't partake of illegal substances."

He parked, and they got out of the car. No lights came on outside his house, leaving them to stand in the naked moonlight. So much nature made her nervous.

He took her hand and led her up the stairs to his front porch. The view gave her a little perspective of how extensive his sunflower fields were—and they looked infinite. "I've never seen anything like this."

"So I gathered from your comments." He looked over his field. "I've heard stories about kids"—his gaze swiveled toward her—"and city dwellers getting lost in fields like this for days. Not a good thing."

Zaida crossed her arms and held a hand to her throat. "Why? Do they starve to death?"

"No. The rattlers get them long before that. These fields are full of rodents…and the predators that hunt them."

"That's horrible." Zaida shivered.

"Why? They eat the mice that eat my crop. Nature has a beautiful sense of balance that works perfectly—when humans don't muck it up."

Her eyes narrowed. "Are you just saying that to scare me into not running?"

"Is it working?"

"Yes."

His grin was enigmatic. She didn't like it one bit. Didn't help that it was a very male expression, and it made her more aware than ever of all their physical differences—his height, his broad shoulders, his lean, muscular build. His hand was big and warm and a little calloused. She shivered, feeling a pull between them that she hadn't felt in a very long time with any man.

"Let's go in. I'll get you settled. Tomorrow, I'll show you around, and we'll work on figuring out what's happening."

"And I need to call my parents."

"Right." He unlocked his door and pushed it open for her. She stared into the black space behind him, wondering if it was a good idea to go in there, alone, with a stranger. No one would ever find her out here. They wouldn't even look for her here. She never did nature—unless it was walking to one of her favorite coffee shops outside the atrium where she lived.

She sent Levi a worried glance. His face was blank. He did nothing to alleviate her fears. "If you harm me, I will fight you. And I fight dirty."

Levi smiled. He caught her hand and held it up, showing her nails. "These nails have never hit anything other than a keyboard."

"Because no one has ever dared harm me."

"Well, princess, let's keep that streak running." He flipped the lights on in the house.

She stepped inside, sending a fast look around the place, half expecting to see women chained to walls. Instead, she saw a lovely, cottage-like farmhouse that could have been decorated by Martha Stewart herself. The walls separating the public rooms were gone, making the tight space seem larger than it was. The kitchen took half the open space. The living room had pale green walls, white linen drapes, a taupe L-shaped sofa with a coffee table, and a big TV on one wall. Another wall was covered by a long bookcase. The kitchen had a huge white quartz island, gray Shaker cabinets, white subway tiles on the backsplash, and top-grade steel appliances.

Whatever she was expecting, it wasn't this. A black German shepherd sat up from the sofa and stretched, then jumped off and hurried over to them. Zaida stepped behind Levi. That dog was huge.

Levi looked at her over his shoulder. "Dogs not your thing?"

"No."

"Sorry. Should have warned you about him. That's Beau. He retired from the K-9 unit in Fort Collins. He's pretty much a couch potato now."

"Yes." She gripped a fistful of his shirt and pressed closer.

"Beau's not going to hurt you, unless you've been building bombs or are transporting contraband."

"I haven't and I'm not."

"Perfect. Then you've got nothing to fear—except now you've shown you're afraid of him, and your fear's going to make him nervous about you. Nothing's spookier to a dog than a spooked human. Here's what you've got to do." He turned so he could see her, which meant that she had to let go of him. "Hey, look at me." She did. "Pretend he's not there. Now that you've introduced fear between you two, he's going to mirror it back to you. He will never bite you, but he isn't certain you won't bite him. So you two have to take the long way toward getting along. That means ignoring each other and respecting each other. Got it?"

"Why do you have a dog?" she asked.

"Who doesn't have a dog?"

"I don't. My parents don't."

Levi bent over and rubbed Beau's ears. "I knew when I got out of the service that I wanted a dog. Took me a while to find the right one. Beau's been a good friend. I think he's happy to have a place he can chill. And he still has an important job to do when I'm not here."

"Which is?"

"Protect the place."

"Protect it from what?"

"Dunno. Things that make me nervous. Like your friend Jamal."

Zaida stared at Levi. Jamal had always had that effect on her too.

"How about I show you around?" Levi offered.

"Not much to see. There's only one bedroom, so I'll take the couch. There's a full bath in the bedroom, and another off the porch. I have my exercise equipment out there. The laundry's in the guest bath, if you need to wash anything." He looked around the house. "The maid was just here, so the place is still kinda neat."

"You get maid service way out here?"

"A neighbor's wife does it to make extra cash. Mrs. Nolan comes once a week. She just changed the sheets, so they're fresh for you. I'll go bring your stuff in."

Thankfully, the dog followed him outside. Zaida walked around the rooms. The little house was tidy.

When Levi came back in with her satchel and computer bag, he took her things straight to her room. "You got any weapons in here?" he asked.

"If I did, I doubt I would admit it. And if I did, I could probably have taken care of Jamal myself."

Levi grinned. "How? By shooting him? You can't just go around offing people you don't like."

"You did. At my apartment."

"In all fairness, I have no idea if I would have liked them or not. Probably not. But I have a license to kill."

She folded her arms. "There is no such thing."

"Yeah, princess, sadly, there is. Get yourself settled. I'll get your phone set up so you can call your folks."

Get yourself settled. What did that mean? How long

was she going to be here? She put her toiletries in the bathroom, next to his shaving supplies, which she was surprised to see he owned, since he didn't seem to use them. She looked at herself in the mirror. Touching her cheek, she wondered what his rough beard would feel like against her skin. No sooner had she thought it than a molten heat slipped through her skin. Most of the men she'd dated were clean-cut, not like Levi. There was an edge about him. Something rough and uncivilized.

When she came out of her room, he handed her an older iPhone and a piece of paper. "I moved your info over. That's your new phone number. For now. When this is over, we can reset your old phone and restore it. Just have to make sure the baddies are no longer tracking you."

She nodded. "Thank you. But when this is over, of course they won't be tracking me."

"We'll never get them all, Zaida, though I will get this batch. The people driving them from outside the country will just run to ground and hole up for a while. When they come crawling out, I don't want you to be a target again."

She opened the contacts and found her mom in her favorites, then hit the number. It rang. And rang. No answer. She gave Levi a worried look, then tried her dad's number. No answer. She lowered her new phone and stared at it. "One of them always answers."

Levi took out his phone and called Lambert. "Go, Levi."

"You get her parents?"

"The team I sent hasn't checked in."

"How about cleaning out her apartment?"

"Someone got there ahead of us. Bodies were gone. We finished the cleanup. I'll text you what I find out about your Jamal guy and that van." Lambert hung up.

Levi sighed as he looked down at his phone. Lambert was a mystery. The guy had retired from the teams four years ago with a stellar record. How many ops did the man have in flight? It was a resource-intensive and logistically difficult undertaking the commander carried. He was well connected in D.C. and obviously could name his price for each mission.

"No news from my contact, either." He pocketed his phone. "I'll get my things out of the bathroom and grab a few blankets, then the room's yours." He did that, then paused at her door. "Night, Zaida. If you need me, I'll just be out here. Me and Beau." He smiled at her.

"Night, Levi. Thank you. For everything."

"You bet."

Zaida closed the door behind him. She was glad he wouldn't be far away, which was interesting, because had they met on the street, she probably wouldn't have given him the time of day, and yet…he was so much like a hero she would write. Handsome, charming, funny, brave. Her stories weren't romantic suspense, though—they were mostly new adult college or small-town stories. Maybe she should write a romantic suspense and explore a whole new set of characters and challenges.

She changed into a silky tee and a pair of knit boxer shorts, then washed her face and brushed her teeth. She got into Levi's bed. He must not have women out here—his bed was just an extra-long twin. That made her happier than it should have. He'd brought her to this place that was so special to him. Granted, he hadn't had many other options. He had a dog and a farm to care for. She shouldn't let any of this go to her head.

She looked at her phone. A half-hour had passed since she last tried her parents. She called them again, but neither picked up. She didn't want to think that it wasn't safe for them to answer her call. They might have been forced to leave their phones at home too.

She could hear water running. Maybe Levi was taking a shower. She sat up and leaned against the wall, replaying the day in her mind. Everything had been normal until she met up with Jamal. He'd scolded her for disrespecting her parents, reminding her that they had selected him to marry her and that it was time they got serious about planning their wedding.

None of which had rung true. Yes, her parents had approved of him—and even selected him—but they had never forced her to accept their choices. Nor had they ever felt disrespected when she hadn't liked someone they had, which was every time. She knew they were all about wanting her to settle down and have kids. They told her that quite often. You'd think it was their biological clocks ticking fast, not hers. But without a doubt, she knew they wanted her happy, first and foremost.

The floors creaked in the living room.

Zaida started to cry. She'd never been this scared in her life. She got up and pulled the quilt from the bed. Wrapping it around her shoulders, she went out into the living room.

Beau's head popped up, the tags on his collar jingling. It was cold in Levi's house. Zaida was shivering.

"What's the matter?" Levi was barefoot and barechested, wearing only a pair of jeans. He pulled on a fresh T-shirt.

Zaida drew a shaky breath. What she needed, no one could provide. But that didn't stop her from wanting it. "I-I just…I just really wanted someone to tell me everything would be all right. And a hug."

LEVI WALKED over and looked down at the woman who'd appeared so confident and indomitable when he'd watched her stroll through the atrium at her apartment building. Now her shoulders were slumped, her eyes held no joy, and her face was pale. Those bastards had stolen all her vibrancy and sass.

For that alone, they deserved what he was bringing to them.

He touched her cheek, struck by how soft her skin was. He wished he wasn't such a poor judge of women. He always felt protective of them, and it was no different with Zaida. God help him if she was another Jules, 'cause he could fall hard for her.

He pushed those thoughts out of his mind and wrapped his arms around her, pulling her against him. He would soon enough learn her truth. For now, her head fit nicely against his chest, and it was nice to not be alone.

Her arms were folded between them, so he couldn't feel much of her curves, but her shoulders were slim. She really was such a petite thing.

"I can't lie to you, Zaida. The guys we're up against are sneaky and desperate—a bad combo in psychopaths. I can tell you that you aren't dealing with this on your own. And I'm damned good at what I do. I've been doing it for more than two decades… just not on U.S. soil. Put it out of your mind for a few hours. Get some sleep. We'll hit it hard in the morning."

Zaida wrapped her arms around him, returning his hug. He felt her—all of her—pressed up against his body. It was exquisite torture. She probably felt his reaction too. Not much he could do about that, except ignore it.

He wasn't in any hurry for her to pull away, so they stood there, in the middle of his living room, with Beau watching them, for long, delicious minutes. Why couldn't he have a girl like her? She was fun to talk to, sexy as hell, and living an exciting life.

He'd thought the same of Jules and look where that led him.

No, he damn well better keep his heart separate until he knew whether she was or wasn't venomous.

He pulled back. She sent a quick look at his eyes, then stared at his throat, then nodded and went back to her room.

6

Zaida had just shut her eyes when the most ungodly commotion started up in the living room. She looked around, startled that her room was so bright. What time was it? She looked at the phone Levi had given her: nine thirty a.m. She flopped back on her bed with a sigh. She hadn't even been aware she'd gone to sleep, and here it was, morning already.

What was that noise in the living room? Someone was singing. Someone and…a dog. Geez. Levi and Beau were howling their way through "Werewolves of London." She giggled when she realized Beau could hold a tune better than Levi.

And then she smelled coffee. And something sweet and cinnamon-y. Her stomach growled. She rolled out of bed and plodded over to the bathroom. She brushed her teeth, washed her face, and lathered on some lotion and sunscreen. Levi's house was still freezing, so she slipped into a loose cotton pullover and put on a pair of socks, then went out to greet him and his one-dog show.

She took the coffee mug Levi handed her. It already had cream and sugar and tasted like heaven. "Could you be any louder?" she grumbled.

"Oh, I'm sorry, princess. It's not like we have murdering terrorist thugs to track down. Or anything pressing in the real world at all…" He grinned at her.

"Beau sings better than you do."

"I know. He thinks I just need practice." Levi shook his head just slightly so the dog wouldn't notice.

Zaida laughed. Levi froze in place, staring at her. "What?" she asked.

"Sorry. Forgot what I was doing. You look so pretty. I don't usually have visitors out."

Zaida raised her brows. "I don't even have my face on. I haven't brushed my hair. I'm not dressed. And I'm grumpy and hungry and still scared."

"Hmm. Three of the seven dwarfs."

She laughed. "I don't think Scared was one of Snow White's dwarfs. I don't think Hungry was either."

"No? Then there should be a lot more of them. Humanity is far more complex than six adjectives and a doctor."

She shook her head. "You talk a lot for first thing in the morning."

"First thing? The morning's almost over."

"It smells good out here," she said.

"Good thing I can cook. You've been under observation long enough for the record to show you don't."

She gasped. "For real?"

He nodded.

She shook her head. "What did you make?"

"Monkey bread. Egg soufflé. Fresh fruit. And coffee. I don't know what you like yet, so I figured I better cover all the bases."

"I like eating."

Levi grinned. "My kinda girl."

While he got some plates out and did a few dishes, Zaida took her coffee outside. It was about a hundred degrees hotter outside than in. Felt wonderful. She looked up and came to a full stop. This was the first time she could actually make sense of where they were. Last night, the huge sunflowers had looked ominous. This morning, they were glorious. As far as she could see, there was an ocean of yellow and green.

Levi had a small patch of lawn, which was neatly trimmed. Pavers led the way from the driveway to the house, and from the front steps out to a big patio with a huge picnic table. Another path led off that to a fire pit area with four Adirondack chairs sitting around it. Still another path led from the side of the house to a row of greenhouses. She couldn't wait to look in them to see what he was growing.

His place here was a bit of heaven…even for a city girl.

The screen door behind her banged shut. She

looked at Levi as he came to stand next to her. "What do you think? It's a work in progress."

"This is amazing. It's a forest of flowers."

He nodded then went down the steps. "You should see them from the other side of the house. They face the east in the morning and the west in the evening, then during the night, they turn east again."

"It's like they know—things."

"They do. They're sentient, I'm certain of it. Come here." He walked over to the picnic table, which was on the far side of the lawn. He climbed on the bench then held a hand out to her. "Climb up here and look west."

She set her coffee down, then took his hand and followed him to the top of the table. They turned toward the big field of sunflowers that were facing them. "Wow. How can plants move?"

"It's heliotropism. Some scientists argue it doesn't exist in sunflowers, but I have a video of them doing it. And you'll see tonight that they are facing the west. Want to eat out here?"

"Yeah. It's freezing in your house."

"Sorry. It's a swamp cooler. No thermostat. It just runs. Trust me, by this afternoon, you'll be glad for the break from the heat." He helped her back down to the ground. "Hey, while I bring out our breakfast, why don't you give your parents a call?"

Zaida put her fist on her heart. "Do you think they'll answer?"

"I know they will. I talked to them earlier."

"They're safe?"

"They're fine. Someplace safe. Pissed as hell about it, too." He grinned.

Zaida threw her arms around his neck and hugged him, standing on her tiptoes to do it. His body was solid. He acted like he wasn't sure where to put his hands. His fingers were spread wide, like a boy in a china shop who was told not to touch anything. She laughed, then caught his face and kissed his mouth. "Thank you!"

Zaida rushed into the house. She grabbed her phone from the nightstand and called her mom, putting it on speaker so she didn't have to hold it to her ear.

"Zaida!" her mom said, her voice a little breathless.

"Hi, Mom. You okay?"

"I'm fine, honey. Your father and I are both fine. Last night was a little scary, but everything's fine now. Did you heed my warning last night?"

"Yes. A lot's happened since then."

"I know. I'm glad we had that emergency protocol in place. Jamal called us; he wasn't making sense. So I called you. Then some other men came to our place. They took our phones away but gave us new ones this morning. Are you safe, honey?"

"I am. Where are you, Mom?"

"I don't know. And even if I did, I don't think I'd be allowed to say. It's a safe house of some sort. Your father's here. Say hello to him. He needs to hear your voice."

"Hi, Daddy."

"Zaida," her dad said with a big sigh. "Are you well?"

"Yes."

"Where are you?"

Levi had come into the house. He was leaning against the doorjamb in her room. She covered the microphone and asked him, "Am I allowed to tell them?"

"Sure. I'll write it down for you," Levi said.

"Just a minute, Dad. I'm getting the address. It's somewhere way out on the plains, east of Fort Collins." Levi handed her the address, which she read off to her father, along with a phone number next to Levi's name.

"You're with a man." Her dad's statement was filled with concern. "Did you know him before this?"

"No. I just met him last night. Don't worry about him. He's very nice."

"He's respecting you?"

"Yes, Daddy. You know I'm twenty-nine years old now."

"I know you're my baby. I know that we've kept you sheltered and protected from so much that I don't think you're ready to deal with a mercenary, male or female."

"That's true. He's a farmer. He has a sunflower farm."

Her father's next words sounded irate. "How can a farmer protect you?" It seemed he turned his head from the phone when he said to someone near him, probably her mom, "Why would they send her off with a farmer? What good is he going to be for her?"

"H-he"—she paused, flashing Levi, who was grinning, a glance—"killed some men who broke into my apartment last night."

"Why were there men in your apartment?" Zaida's mom said from a little distance back.

"I don't know. I don't know what's happening. They think someone was using my network of contacts to recruit for some terrorist activity."

"This is terrible," her father snapped. "First, we were accosted in our own home by men with huge guns with suppressors on them. We were given five minutes to pack and get out. How can you pack a lifetime in five minutes? They said someone would be watching our apartment, but I don't know what that means. I had to call the university and take emergency leave. Apparently, my presence there endangers everyone. Your mother had to cancel her appointments for the next week and hand them off to other doctors for coverage. These things aren't easy to do without sufficient notice. At least for me, school hasn't started yet. But for your mother, it's not so easy. And if it gets out that we're involved in any way with a terrorist plot, our careers are over. Yours as well."

"Yes, Papa." Zaida only called her father Papa when he was very angry. She sent Levi another quick look. He wasn't amused any longer. He came over and took the phone from her.

"Dr. Hussan, let me assure you, no one is accusing any of you of being part of this plot. As far as we know at this point, the three of you were just easy victims. Right now, we have more questions than answers. Zaida's friend, Jamal, tried to kidnap her last night. I was afraid that he might come after you when he couldn't get her. You're currently in protective custody, as is your daughter. We're going to try to get this resolved as fast as we can. In the meantime, I need your cooperation. I'm not overstating the situation when I say that your lives are in jeopardy. Am I making myself clear?"

"You are. But we have our lives, our reputations, things that we must tend to," Darim said.

"And Jamal would never do that," Zaida's mom protested from the background.

Levi let that go. "The people you're with can provide you with secure internet connections that can't be traced to your location. Come up with a cover story, stick to it, minimize your exposure. Do not leave your current location. Not for any reason. Even if you hear Zaida is in danger. I assure you, she is not."

"How long will we be in this untenable situation?" Darim asked.

"I don't have an answer to that yet. But I will do what I can to shorten it, sir." He handed the phone back to her.

"Zaida, have you done something that your mother and I don't know about?" her father asked.

Zaida was silent. She swallowed hard. There were a lot of things in her life that her parents didn't know about. She looked at Levi, who was still standing near her. At her hesitation, his curiosity intensified. "Nothing that is illegal, Papa." At least, not in this country.

"That isn't a very reassuring answer, daughter."

Zaida sighed. "You know how I feel about women expressing themselves."

"Yes. We've had many discussions about it."

She drew a breath. Once some things were said, they couldn't be unsaid. She'd vowed to protect the women in her circle. She couldn't expose them now. Instead, she diverted to a tangential topic. "I've been writing a less risqué version of my stories for Middle Eastern markets. They deal with women making their own choices about their lives…not necessarily in conformance with Islamic law."

She didn't tell her parents—or Levi—that she had women she hired to translate the stories into various Middle Eastern languages; that was work that could get the women in a lot of trouble within their families and communities.

Her father was quiet for a long moment. Zaida could sense he was building up a head of steam. "Have you not heard what happened to other Muslim authors who advocated secular views? Did you not see what happened in France when comics were published that disrespected Islamic beliefs?"

"But Papa, how can we show people to take responsibility for their choices and behaviors if we don't discuss any of this?"

"Zaida. You cannot change the world."

"I don't believe that, Papa. I think I can."

"Harming people is not the way."

"Mine is a peaceful rebellion."

Levi squeezed his eyes shut and hissed, "Shiiiit."

"Your rebellion has us all in hiding. *¿Que coño estabas pensando?*" her father growled in Spanish. "I did not expect my own daughter to become my enemy." This he said in Arabic—for her and her mother's ears alone. "Mr. Jones, I expect you will deal with this."

"On it, sir. We're out for now." He took the phone and shut it off then tossed it on her bed. Levi sent her a tense look. "Why don't you get dressed? I'll warm up breakfast. We can talk while we eat."

Zaida folded her arms around her waist and bent over, rocking back and forth. "I did this, didn't I? This is all because of me. My father never uses Spanish unless he's very, very angry."

"I need more info before I answer that."

"Levi—"

"Get dressed and come out."

He closed the door as he left her room. Zaida had a horrible feeling in the pit of her stomach. She'd known going in that what she was doing could totally blow up on her. She thought it would only reflect on her, but she'd done terrible harm to people she loved, putting her family, her friends, her community in danger. Because of her, people had died. Like Mike—and the men who broke into her home. Yes, those were thugs, but still.

She rocked some more. This was bad. This was so bad. She covered her face and wept, hearing her father's voice over and over. *I did not expect my own daughter to become my enemy.*

A few minutes later, Levi knocked on her door. "Hey…you coming out?"

"No." She wiped her tears away.

"Why?"

"I can't do this. I can't face what I've done."

"Are you decent?"

"No. I'm a horrible human being. My father can attest to that."

There was a thump on the door roughly in the area where Levi's head would have been. "Okay. But are you a human with clothes on?"

"Yeah."

"I'm coming in."

Zaida unfolded slightly to look at him.

He crouched in front of her. He put his hands on her knees. They were warm hands, a little scraped from the fight at her apartment. She ran her thumbs over his knuckles. His touch was a kindness she didn't deserve.

"Hiding isn't going to help," he said. "The sooner we dig into this, the sooner we can get it resolved. And

Freedom Code

there is a ticking clock."

She nodded. She needed to warn her group. How could she do that while she was here with Levi? She couldn't even use the phone she'd been given—he would know everything.

"Look at it this way. You started this…and you can end it, too," he said.

Zaida sighed. Anger slipped in through a crack in her shame. She hadn't started it. This was just another nit in the litany of injustices women had experienced for millennia. It likely wouldn't end with her, either. But she could contribute to the ripples of resistance, ripples that could become waves that might build into tsunamis. Nothing less than a sea change would ever stop her. Not even her father's disapproval.

He watched those thoughts march across her expression. His eyes hardened. "You don't know what you're dealing with." He stood. So did she.

"I do know, Levi." She felt sad. "We've always known."

"We?"

"I have to go," she said.

"Go where?"

She kissed his cheek. "Thank you for helping me last night." She began gathering her things. "I have to do this alone. I'll call for a ride share."

Levi put his hands on his hips. "And that, princess, ain't gonna happen. From here out, until this is resolved, we're joined at the hip."

7

Levi returned to the kitchen, his blood was buzzing. *Mine is a peaceful rebellion.* Zaida's words made him rethink her role in this whole affair. This had echoes of Julia all over it. He knew how it all would play out. The op was all that mattered—any and all lies were fair game, whether or not they hit the heart.

He wondered if Zaida's parents were really her parents—or were they just hosts for this gig of hers?

He looked over at her room. She'd shut the door. Maybe she was finally putting herself together. The meal he'd made had definitely seen better days. If he warmed it up one more time, it would be unrecognizable from what it once was.

He texted Lambert, asking him to send everything he had on Zaida and her parents. He wanted their full dossiers, an accounting of every event in their lives, every step they'd taken in this country. If a psych analysis was available, he'd take that too.

My rebellion is peaceful. Every terrorist believed the same—short-term violence could net an eternity of peace. What he didn't know was why she was doing this. What was driving her? Why take a stand now, here?

What was really at stake?

It was time to dig in and get some answers.

His phone buzzed with a text from Lambert. *Want me to do your fucking job for you?*

So you got nothing on them? Levi texted back.

I gave you everything I had.

Fucking A.

BTW, Lambert texted, *that black van from last night was a rental used by your Jamal guy. His last name is Abd al-Mukhtar. Looks like a regular guy—businessman and adjunct prof of computer science at CSU. We're looking into him further.*

At least that matched up with what Zaida had said last night.

Lambert continued, *And your hit men from last night are confirmed Tahrir al-Sham.*

Tahrir al-Sham. That group was a new incarnation of an older al-Qaeda group. Bad motherfuckers, for sure.

Levi responded, *Well, three down. Ran into a former Red Team guy yesterday. A group of them are working an op in WY. Could use some of their tech guy's time. You know Owen Tremaine? It's his team. Can you clear it with him?*

I do and I will. I'm out, the commander texted.

Levi looked up as Zaida came out of her room. Though her face was pale, she was fully composed. She'd showered, dried her hair, put on her makeup. She wore a purple cotton-blend shirt that showed a sweet column of honey-toned flesh pointing down to her cleavage and up her neck. The shirt was fitted at her waist, accentuating her generous breasts and curvy hips. Her shirttails weren't tucked in, so they hung down to the top of her thighs, leading his gaze down her decadent legs to a pair of wedge sandals. Her toenails were painted the same deep red that was on her fingernails.

All of it, all of her, made everything deep inside him quicken, as it was no doubt meant to do. He was grateful for his time with the Black Squadron. They'd taught him feminine wiles were as deadly as a KA-BAR.

He dished out a portion of the now-flat soufflé, cut a piece of the monkey bread, and scooped a spoonful of the fruit for her. He pushed those dishes across the wide island so she could sit on one of the stools to eat. He made a plate for himself, then ate standing up, facing her, the island between them.

He thought about and discarded a half-dozen tactics. The only one that was going to work with her was an empathetic approach. Hard to do when he was so angry, but he had to keep emotion out of this if he wanted to survive her.

"He was wrong, you know—your dad," Levi said.

"You can change the world."

Her eyes met his. "Do you believe that?"

"Absolutely. Every change that's ever happened in humanity started with the determination of a single person."

She lowered her gaze to her plate. She ate all of her soufflé, half her monkey bread, and all of her fruit. He poured her a fresh cup of coffee, deciding to switch tactics mid-stream.

He was too pissed to play games, so he hit her with a direct question. "How long have you known the Hussans?"

Her eyes widened before her face settled into a frown. "Since I was born. Why ask that?"

"Just trying to get to the bottom of things. That little convo with your 'parents' has made me re-evaluate some things." He used air quotes around the word *parents*. He could see she was taking offense. If it weren't so critical that he break her open, he might have found it amusing. "Why would Jamal want to kidnap you?"

"You'll have to ask him that."

"I would, but he's in the wind. No one from his company or the university knows where he is. I checked this morning." Levi sipped his coffee. "Did you know that one of your manuscripts showed up in a Syrian camp along with that ransomware message?"

"That message is why I met with Mike. It was showing up on computers belonging to some of my friends. I don't know how or why that worm was called Freedom Code. For me, it has a very specific meaning, which I explained to you. You were right. It means everything and…nothing." She shook her head and said, "As far as my manuscript, I don't know. My books are published in print and ebook all over the world. It wouldn't be hard to download a copy. Maybe a reader in Syria likes my work."

Levi gritted his teeth. "I don't have infinite patience, Zaida." That got him nowhere. "Talk to me about your Freedom Code. Pretend I'm one of the women in one of your group. Tell me what I need to do to be in your rebellion."

"I can't. That's not how it works."

He huffed an irritated sigh. "I need to know specifics."

She left her stool and went into the living room, pacing the short length to the porch and back. Facing him, she waved her hands in sharp movements, as if she were arguing silently to herself. "No. My rebellion means 'no.'"

Levi frowned. "Pardon me?"

"No, I won't have sex with you. No, I don't want to marry that man. No, I don't want to be a stay-at-home mom. No, I want to be a stay-at-home mom. No, I can't do whatever—I need to work on my degree. No, I don't want children right now. No, I don't want to wear a head cover. No, I will wear a head cover because I choose to. No, I won't participate in female mutilation to satisfy your insecurities."

Levi came around the island and leaned on one of

the stools. "I'm not following."

"Freedom Code is the ability to say no without repercussions."

"That's it?"

"Yes."

"Is your rebellion worth dying for?" he asked. Mike had asked the same thing. Her big brown eyes looked wounded. Levi almost wished he hadn't gone there.

"Yes. But how can I teach 'no' if I'm dead?"

"Is it worth having others die on your behalf?"

She slowly shook her head. "You so don't get what our Freedom Code is."

"I don't. I'm trying to understand. If it's okay with you, I'd like to keep asking questions until I do."

"Women are half the human population. Humanity ceases to exist without us. And yet we have no parity with men."

"So you're a feminist. And an activist."

"Yes. But I'm not a terrorist. I'm not advocating anyone harm anyone. I'm simply advocating that we stop harming ourselves by not pushing back. We need to be asserting our right to choice in our lives. It's like an honor code, but about freedom. Our freedom."

Levi bowed his head and rubbed his palm over the edge of his hair. What Zaida was up in arms about was stuff he thought the general U.S. population had already come to terms with. She mentioned the different cultures represented in her group meetings. Perhaps this was a bigger issue for them. Or perhaps he just wasn't seeing the whole picture because it wasn't one that affected him. She was clearly passionate about it, so it behooved him to keep trying to understand.

Lives were at stake. A lot of them.

"Levi, women here in this country are being denied access to birth control based on the religious beliefs of their employers, while male enhancement drugs are still covered. That's not okay. Women make seventy-five cents to every dollar of their male counterparts. That's not okay. Women in some parts of Africa and South America are brutally raped as a means of destroying entire cultures—full-on genocide. That's not okay. Being forced into polygamy, here or abroad, is not okay."

Levi held up a hand. "So how is saying no in a violent rape situation going to help those women?"

Zaida looked away as she blinked against her tears. He saw them roll down her face. She swiped them away before they hit her shirt. "This is bigger than that. I thought if we could help women stand up for themselves, if we could influence healthy populations to honor our freedoms, it would spill over into the more at-risk populations. It would become a worldwide behavioral norm."

"So you're seeking to impose your worldview on others? That's your rebellion?"

"No. This isn't a value judgment at all. I don't care how many spouses you have if you choose to be in that situation. I don't care how many children you do or don't have as long as you were part of the decision about those children. I don't care if you do or don't use birth control, if you've exercised your right to make that decision. I'm not advocating living a certain way, only that you consciously know you have choices. In everything, every aspect of your life. I don't care what your beliefs are as long as you believe in yourself."

Levi sighed. "That's it? That's your Freedom Code?"

"Yes. It isn't a view my parents espouse. They're live-and-let-live people, like Mike was. But that isn't enough for me. Ignoring a problem only lets it grow. We have to pull together and fight for the lives we want. I know that I can only influence the people I interact with, and then, only some of them. But my group meetings give us an outlet to reinforce those beliefs. We support each other in learning about and exercising our freedoms."

He looked at her. She was trembling. Her eyes were still watering. Even the women from Black Squadron hadn't summoned such a depth of emotion. She couldn't be faking it, could she?

He went over and gripped her shoulders. "I think I get it. At least I'm beginning to. But it still doesn't answer the question about your ties to Syrian terrorists and their cells here."

She sighed and leaned her forehead against his chest. He couldn't help but wrap his arms around her as a fierce need to protect her pierced his shell. It was hard to imagine these slim shoulders, this beautiful, vibrant woman being a tool for terrorists.

But, as ever, he'd slipped back to his pre-Black Squadron days, when he still believed women were soft creations to be protected. He had to find the answers. If Zaida was innocent, then he needed to clear her name. And if she was guilty, then he needed to figure that out before the whispers being reported on the dark web became fight calls.

"Can I meet your group? When's the next one being held?" he asked.

She looked up at him. "Is that the only way?"

"Yes."

"Please don't make this a witch hunt through my friends."

"I'm not looking for a scapegoat. I'm looking for a terrorist. Big difference. You can tell them I'm a new member."

She shook her head. "They won't believe it. Your eyes are too intense."

That wasn't something he'd expected her to say. Had she noticed his eyes because she found him attractive or because she was reading him...as an operative would?

Geez. Why did women have to be like a two-sided blade with no handle?

"Then tell them I'm a new boyfriend."

"They'll know I'm lying."

"You don't do men?"

Warm color deepened the tone of her face. "I've

never brought a boyfriend to our meetings."

"Have you dated anyone since you started the group?" All right, fine. That was for his personal edification, not the op.

"No."

"Well"—he grinned—"maybe you finally fell for someone."

She gave him a caustic huff and pulled free. "Of course. That makes total sense. I would fall for the man about to tear my life to shreds."

"You could look at it that way. Or maybe I'm here to help you hold your life together."

"Why can't I follow my own advice and say no to this?"

"Because you aren't selfish. There's more at stake than just you. Gather your friends for one of your salons tomorrow."

She nodded. "I will. It's not one of my regular meeting nights, but I should be able to get some people there. I have to tell you, though, most of my Muslim friends won't come, not after getting the worm and its ransomware."

"Try anyway. I need to talk to them. We can go visit them individually, but bringing them to a familiar environment might put them more at ease. I need to ask you something. I know it looks as if I'm still focused on you, but I have to follow the leads. The bad guys are expert at shifting blame and covering their tracks. We'll get them, but only if you're open and honest with me."

"Go ahead." Zaida sat on the back of his sofa. Beau came over to sit next to her. He nudged his head under her hand. That, more than anything she'd said or done, gave Levi confidence in her innocence. She carefully ran her hand over his soft fur, touching him absently while she focused on Levi.

Levi had to hide his smile. "You said you called Mike, right?" Maybe starting back at the beginning of all of this might help them find the missing pieces.

She nodded. "Mike's an old friend of the family. *Was*, I mean. He always checked in with my parents when he was in town. They go way back."

"So he contacted your folks. How was it you met with him but they didn't?"

"Their schedules conflicted, so I went without them. We had a good conversation. I told him about that ransomware message. We talked about my Freedom Code. He said that was what the worm that spread the ransomware was called."

Her dad had pretty much thrown her under the bus earlier, Levi thought, wondering if he was focusing his investigation on the wrong Hussan. "And Jamal is really a friend, not part of all of this?" It was a point of note that Jamal was capable of writing and releasing this worm. But if he had done so, why did things point to Zaida?

She shrugged. "My parents want me to settle down. He's their best candidate. They want grandkids. It's the whole circle-of-life thing. You know."

He didn't, really. His parents hadn't survived long

into his adulthood. "So are you not interested in Jamal? Or just you're just completely rebelling against your folks?"

"Jamal and I are not a fit. He's too overbearing."

"And apparently a criminal," Levi said.

"And that. I'm not opposed to marrying someone and having kids, though I have no intention of settling down."

"So you're living the arc of your stories."

Her raven brows lifted. "Have you read my stuff?"

"I listened to part of an audio version."

"And?" She bit her bottom lip.

Cripes, that was sexy. He could imagine her nibbling the sensitive skin of his cock. He cleared his throat. "Definitely chick stuff. But I enjoyed it."

She smiled. "Did you jump to the sex scenes or skip them?"

"You mean some scenes weren't sex? I guess I just heard the good parts."

She huffed an exasperated sigh. "No. You missed all the good stuff. Everything that led up to their intimacy…and came out of it."

He grinned at her. "I'll have to do another listen."

"A full one this time."

"Do you gals really spend so much time on emotional thinking?"

That seemed to take her aback. "Well. Yeah. That's the important stuff in relationships. Guys don't?"

"No."

"So what fills your mind, then?"

He shrugged…and couldn't hold back another grin. "Food. Sex. Sports. Guns. Weather. Cars. Terrorist machinations. The usual stuff."

This time she smiled as she crossed her arms. "So food before sex for you?"

"Food's certainly been more plentiful than sex. Lately, anyway. I try not to think about what I can't have."

She walked toward him, slowly, her eyes holding his. His dick tightened. Fuck. The damned thing didn't even have eyes and it knew she was near.

"Why no sex for you?" she asked.

He bent his legs, opening them, easing the pressure on his groin. "I guess sex was widely available. But I was looking for more. I want something permanent. Or, at least, longer lasting than a supercharged weekend."

"I know some single women." She walked into the open space between his legs.

His gaze lowered from her eyes to her mouth, then back. "Do you?"

"Yeah. What are you looking for?"

"If I knew, I probably wouldn't still be single."

"Maybe it's like any other subjective thing. You'll know it when you see it."

"Damn straight." What if he'd already seen it? What if it was standing right in front of him?

He leaned forward. She did too. He loved the way she smelled. Exotic and familiar. Sweet and spicy. He wondered if her skin was that fragrant all over her body.

Jules. Remember Jules, he warned himself. "There's something we have to do today."

"What is it?" Her espresso eyes were dilated and unfocused. Her voice was rough. There was a new sweet scent coming from her heated body that did nothing to disarm his persistent hard-on.

"We need to get your computers up to Wyoming to have a friend check them for viruses."

She pulled back fast. Her eyes were confused at first, then angry, then blank. "Do you trust this friend not to plant something on my computers?"

"I do. They're on the same team as Kelan, the guy we met in the parking garage at your place. I trust them; we go back a long way. Our teams ran into each other on some missions. We need to go back to your place and get your desktop."

"Do you think it's safe to go back to my apartment?" Zaida asked.

"I've been told it's clear," Levi answered.

"Will Beau be all right without you?" she asked, looking back at his black shepherd.

"He's got his couch, food, and water. And he has open access to his dog run through the doggie door. He's good until we get back." Levi tilted his head as he looked at her. "If I didn't know better, I'd think you were starting to like him."

She gave him a closed-lipped smile. "He is very soft."

8

Zaida looked over at Levi, who was calmly holding the steering wheel. He seemed a fair investigator. He certainly was a phenomenal cook. She glanced back out her passenger window. His home was magical. She was surprised to regret leaving his property. She wondered how many other women had been there… but then she remembered his narrow twin bed and smiled.

She turned to him again. "Are you lonely, Levi?"

He sent her a measuring glance, then faced the road again. A half-smile curled one side of his mouth. "What makes you ask that?"

"The romance author in me, I suppose."

"I have a job that exhausts me. A dog that loves me. A fridge full of food waiting to be cooked. All the coffee I want. Life's pretty good."

"And a very narrow single bed."

"When I meet the right woman, she can pick out the bed she wants. That room's big enough for it."

"So you're waiting, like a spider in a web, for her to come to you?"

There was that half-smile again. "Sounds serendipitous."

"Is it working?" Zaida asked.

He looked at her again. "You tell me."

What did that mean? Was she the one he'd been waiting for? 'Cause it was entirely possible he was the very kind of man she'd been holding out for. When he gave her his full attention, it was sometimes hard to breathe. Instead of answering him, she just watched the road, but inside, she was screaming that, yes! it was working.

And yet all they had was a forced intimacy—not one either of them had chosen.

They were silent the rest of the ride. Zaida felt her tension deepen as they entered the Old Town portion of Fort Collins. The drive into town didn't seem nearly as long as the drive out had been.

Levi used his badge to get into her parking garage, and picked an open guest spot. He locked the Jeep as they crossed the garage. Both of them looked around cautiously as they made their way to the elevator. Before the doors opened, he moved her slightly behind him. Fortunately, no one was coming out. He did that again when they hit her apartment floor. He pressed his key card to her door's security pad. The door unlocked.

He took her hand and drew her in behind him. She glanced around her space, looking for signs of the violent struggle they'd had to walk through on their way out yesterday, but all of it was gone. The blood. The shards of her broken lamp. The bullet hole in the wall.

She sent Levi a relieved glance. He gave a brief nod, immediately understanding what her look meant. He motioned her to silence, then whispered, "I'm going to clear your apartment. Wait here."

He moved rapidly through the whole space, opening doors, dipping into rooms. As soon as he went down her hallway, she hurried into the kitchen to the drawer where she'd left her old phone. Fortunately, it still had power. She quickly texted the group of women who worked on her translations, telling them that she couldn't explain fully, but that all of them should take the next week off and not come to the office. She said some trouble was afoot and they should make themselves scarce until it was figured out. She'd written her message in Arabic, making it a little harder for Levi to read just in case he looked at her phone. Of course, he could always use a translator tool, but maybe he wouldn't think of that.

No sooner had she sent her message and stowed her phone than Levi had finished his walk through her apartment. He holstered his pistol as he came back to her. "We're good. Let's get your stuff and get out of here."

Zaida followed him into her office. She shut her

Mac down, then gathered it, the keyboard, and a mouse.

"Just bring your machine. The guys have the rest of the stuff they need. Also, are there any flash drives you've used in the last year? Tablets? Other devices? Other computers? They could be the source of the problem. Bring them too."

She collected them. He found a nearly empty bin in her closet that he'd dumped and was loading everything into. "What about my ereader?" she asked.

"Bring it. Any of these could be the source of the problem that showed up in Syria." He looked at her. "You know what I can't understand? The manuscript that was in that ISIS encampment wasn't one you've published."

"What was it?" she asked. He hadn't mentioned that before. She'd just assumed when he'd said "manuscript" that he meant one of her stories.

He told her the title. "I don't recall seeing that in your catalog. Is that something you have on your hard drive?"

"I did publish that, but it came out with a different title. If that's what they had, then they somehow got a draft of my unpublished work. I don't give those out. Not to anyone. Was I hacked?"

"That's what we're going to find out today."

∼

LEVI WAS quiet on the ride up to Wyoming. Zaida

tried to puzzle through that. Did his silence mean he was uneasy about where they were going? Or was he worrying about what he'd discover on her computers? She was a little miffed herself. If those terrorists in Syria had her information, what other personal identifying information did they have? And what would happen if they decided to use it?

Their drive took close to two hours. At last they pulled off the highway into a little town called Wolf Creek Bend, which they drove straight through. A few minutes out of town, they turned onto a long dirt drive that led up to a huge monstrosity of a timber frame house. A mansion, really. She looked at Levi, but didn't ask to confirm if this was the place or not. His tension was even worse than when they'd been driving. She followed him up to the front door, which opened before they could knock.

Standing there, blocking almost the whole entrance, was a huge, wild-haired man with a scar through one dark brow and a big grin full of white teeth. He hooked hands with Levi then pulled him close for a shoulder-to-shoulder hug.

"Max Cameron," Levi said, grinning. "Looks like they let just about anyone into Wyoming."

"I was thinking the same about you. Aren't you usually slapping around in some ocean somewhere?" Max said.

"Got out of the Navy. Retired at the beginning of the year. Guess someone still had a way to make me feel useful," Levi said.

"Can't wait to catch up. That her?" Max nodded in Zaida's direction.

At his hard glare, Zaida had an overwhelming desire to turn and run. She could wait in the car. Or maybe have Levi drop her off at the diner she'd spotted in town.

Levi reached a hand out for her, which she only very tentatively accepted. Why had she trusted him so completely? Look where it had landed her. Standing face to face with some horrible gang enforcer-type guy.

"Yeah. Zaida Hussan. Max. He's going to look into your computer," Levi said.

Zaida's brows lifted. "This is your computer guy? For real?"

"Best hacker I've ever met. If something's going on in your systems, he'll find it."

Zaida gave Levi a meaningful look, but he didn't take the hint. This Mr. Cameron looked like he'd just eaten a small child and was thinking she'd do for his next meal. She cleared her throat. "Is he our only option?"

Max threw back his head and laughed. Levi grinned and said, "Yes."

"Come on in, Ms. Hussan." Max stepped back from the front door. "I'll show you where you can wait." His deep voice rumbled round the big foyer.

"Great. I'll go get her stuff," Levi said, leaving her alone with the monster man.

Max led her from the foyer into a massive living

room, one so big it needed two full suites of furniture. It had a bar in one corner. A few French doors led outside to a long patio. Stairs led up to a second-floor bridge that connected the two halves of the house. Another wide set of stairs led up from the sunken living room into a long dining room.

"Help yourself to anything in the bar," Max said. "If you get thirsty or hungry, go see the guys in the kitchen. They might keep you company while I do my thing."

"And…what is your thing, exactly?" Zaida asked.

Max grinned, slowly and without humor. "Gonna dig around and see what you've been up to."

"I haven't been up to anything."

"Of course you haven't. I'm gonna enjoy this."

Levi came back into the house carrying the bin with her things. He gave her a curious look, which she couldn't interpret. "You okay here?"

"Yes." No. Not at all.

"I'll come check on you in a bit." Levi nodded at her. "Call me if you need me. Don't wander off."

"I won't."

~

Levi followed Max down a long hall. Man, this place was huge. They passed a wine cellar, a kitchen, some stairs up to another wing, and then stepped into a den, which was occupied by a single man. He was in his mid- to late thirties with blond hair and blue eyes so pale they looked like a blue shade of white. He stood up from behind his desk.

"Owen, this is Levi Jones," Max said. "Owen Tremaine."

"Commander Lambert's guy," Owen said as he reached his hand out. They shook.

"Thanks for making Max available," Levi said.

Max nodded toward the door. "He left his terrorist in the living room."

Owen's brows lifted.

"I don't think she's a terrorist," Levi said, "though I can't rule out her being used by one."

Owen pressed his comm unit. "Selena, I need you to keep a woman company in the living room. Be aware she may not be a friendly." Owen looked at him. "Better to be on the safe side."

They started toward the open closet, but Max stopped. "Hey, boss. Is Remi here today? Maybe she could get a read on Ms. Hussan."

Owen nodded. "Not a bad idea. Ask Greer to make it happen."

"Greer's here with you too?" Levi asked, surprised.

"Old war dogs like us have to do something when we get out of the service," Max said.

"Yeah, but Greer is, what, twelve?" Levi said.

"No. Our baby's grown up. He's thirty."

"Huh. Who's Remi?" Levi asked.

"Dr. Remington Chase is an associate professor of

sociology at the University of Wyoming," Owen said. "She's also seeing Greer."

Levi grinned. "Still can't believe he's old enough to date."

Max laughed. Owen almost cracked a smile. Bastard reminded Levi of Commander Lambert.

"The bunker's down here," Max said, leading Levi into the closet to a hidden door that opened to reveal a steel staircase. They went down two flights. Max opened the door at the bottom landing. They stepped out into a huge conference room with a long table. Two smart screens were on one wall. Several men sat around the table, reading through stacks of papers. Some Levi knew, some he didn't. Max took the bin from Levi and made the introductions.

First one up was another tall blond that Levi knew from their time in the service. He had been a sniper in the Army. His eyes were a warm Caribbean blue. "Valentino Parker. This is awfully country for a city boy like you," Levi said as they shook hands.

"Right? I've been telling the team I can work long-distance from Denver, but they're not buying it," Val said.

Levi greeted everyone. He knew about half the team from the times his unit and theirs crossed paths on assignments in Afghanistan and other locations. "So is it true the Army's shutting down the Red Team?"

"It's true," another blond guy said. Kit Bolanger.

Levi learned he was this group's team lead. "We've all gotten out ahead of that. You left the Navy?"

"Yeah. Twenty-two years in was enough for me. I'm a farmer now. And I work the odd case here and there. What are you guys doing here in Wyoming?" Levi asked.

"Chasing down a nasty cult," Kelan—the man Levi had seen in the parking lot at Zaida's—said.

"I'm going to dig into Zaida's stuff. Come make yourself useful," Max said.

"Be right there." Levi looked at Rocco, the team's polyglot. Levi took his phone out and opened it to the Arabic text that Zaida had sent from her phone this morning while they were at her apartment. "Any chance you can translate this for me?"

"Sure." Rocco read the message, then gave Levi a dark look.

"Read it aloud," Levi ordered.

Rocco did.

"Great." Fucking peachy. He'd gone to bat for Zaida, then she did something like this, even knowing he'd cloned her phone. Maybe she didn't grasp what that meant. She'd done it in a sneaky way, too; she could have sent that message at any point from the phone he'd given her. But no, she'd waited to send that message until they got to her apartment and she could use her old phone, probably thinking he wouldn't know about it. And she'd communicated in Arabic, which he could understand some of, but couldn't read.

He had to fight the urge to go ask her about it right then. He'd find out soon enough. Tomorrow they were going to one of her group sessions. He wondered if whoever she'd been texting would show up at the meeting. And where was this office she mentioned? It hadn't been included in the vitae Lambert had provided on her.

Levi followed Max down a short hall to an ops room where Greer was sitting at a bank of computers. The kid got up and gave him a fast shoulder bump. "Kit told us this morning we'd be assisting on one of your missions. Didn't know you were back in Colorado. I hear you're out of the Navy."

"Yup. Got a big farm of sunflowers and the odd op here and there. It works for me for now." Levi nodded at the technology in the room. "Looks like you guys have a serious gig."

Greer and Max exchanged looks. "That's one way to look at it."

"So what are we looking for?" Max asked.

"The Freedom Code worm."

Max shared a surprised glance with Greer. "What makes you think that came through her systems?"

"It's a theory I'm running down. Hacked content believed to have come from a database on the server the worm communicates with had info on Zaida. The hackers were in a terrorist camp in Syria." Levi turned a chair around and straddled it. "The CIA had been following the worm's trail through the Middle East. When one of their guys saw Zaida's stuff, he came back to talk to her and her family. He was murdered in Denver a few days ago. They cut off his head. Zaida's in this up to her neck, but how or why, I don't know. There were two attempts to kidnap her last night."

Max looked impressed. "Then let's see what we can find."

~

Two hours later, Levi leaned back, then stood and rubbed his neck.

"There's no evidence of malware existing on her systems," Max said. "If the Freedom Code worm had come through any of her stuff, it would have left markers. If it came from her, then it didn't come from these machines. Does she have other computers?"

"Not that I've seen."

Greer was packing Zaida's things back into her bin. He handed Levi a flash drive. "If you do come across other computers you need us to check, use this. We can connect remotely to them. You don't have to come back up."

"What's really going on up here?" Levi asked as they escorted him from their ops room into a weapons room, to an elevator. "You've got a lot of muscle here for a little cult action."

"Not so little," Greer said. "It's a big group full of homegrown terrorists doing some nasty stuff." Greer looked at his phone, then texted someone. "Looks like my girlfriend is waiting upstairs to have a word with you." He glanced at Levi. "Guess she had a chat with Zaida."

Good. Levi could use all the insights he could get. He sure didn't trust himself when it came to Zaida. She'd gotten under his skin and, like a true poison, was working her way right to his heart.

The small elevator from the bunker opened into a bedroom on the main floor. A woman with straight reddish-brown hair and deep forest-green eyes was standing there. Levi looked back to see Greer closing the gates and sliding the wall panel back into place, hiding the elevator from untutored eyes.

Levi set the bin down and shook hands with the professor as they were introduced. "So, I guess you've had a chat with Zaida," Levi said.

"I have. I like her."

So did Levi.

"She's in a difficult spot."

"Yes, she is," Levi said. "I can't quite make out how much is her doing, and how much is just a wrong place, wrong time type of deal."

"There is a growing cultural fear of Muslims. While many of her people, like her parents, are educated and upper class, even more are not—life's a struggle for them."

"None of this is news to me," Levi said.

The professor's lips thinned. "You're going to have to build rapport with her if you want her to trust you enough to let you in. You cannot get your questions answered from the outside. Give her the benefit of the doubt."

"I'm not sure I can. She warned some people away because of me—people who might have critical knowledge."

"And wouldn't you do the same to protect people you love?" Remi asked.

"Love wasn't involved."

～

Zaida held her silence as they left Levi's friends' house. It had been an odd day. She'd had a nice chat with Remi, the sociology professor. Remi knew about the women's charities that Zaida favored. She also seemed to have a sense of what was at risk, which must have come from her work with cult survivors. And yet the professor's advice ran counter to Zaida's instincts.

Trust Levi.

She'd said it several times. Zaida looked at him now. They were driving south, back to Colorado. The summer evening's sun was warm on his hard features. He'd been super quiet the whole day, laughing only with the monster hacker guy who'd crawled through her systems. She was glad they'd given her computers back.

"Levi, who cleaned up my apartment?" she asked.

"My team. I guess."

"You guess? You don't know who was in my apartment?"

"I don't." A muscle bunched in his cheek. "Our roles are highly segregated. Sometimes, the less we know, the safer we are."

Zaida squinted into the sun streaming through the passenger-side window. Maybe that was her answer. The less he knew, the safer her women would be. The safer they all would be.

9

Levi's silence continued well into the evening. They'd eaten sandwiches for dinner, then he'd withdrawn to his exercise room. Zaida had retired to her room with her laptop. The world might be collapsing all around her, but she still had a deadline to meet.

She worked well into the night. Sometime close to midnight, she heard an odd clatter outside her window. She swept the curtains aside to have a look, and was surprised to see a ladder.

She slipped on a pair of flip-flops, then went to investigate. No lights were on outside, so she turned them on. She didn't get any farther than the front stoop before Levi shouted down to her from up on the roof, "Shut them off."

"What are you doing up there?" she asked.

"Watching my crop. Shut them off."

Watching his crop? Was that a farmer thing? She

reached inside his front door and flipped them off, then went outside. The moon was high in the sky, just a few days into its waning phase. It illuminated the area round Levi's house with crisp relief, casting sharp shadows from the tall sunflowers. She followed the pavement that surrounded his home around to the side where the ladder was.

"Why are you watching your crop?" she called up to him.

"Because of the magic." He came over to the ladder. "Come up."

"Is it safe?"

"Is anything we do safe?"

Zaida frowned at that cryptic answer. Levi wasn't an easy man to figure out. The heroes in her stories were simpler, but maybe that was because her stories were generally more centered on her heroines. Perhaps she'd given short shrift to her male characters.

Maybe she should write one from a male POV just to explore that half of humanity.

She started up the ladder. Levi reached down to steady her as she stepped from the ladder to the roof. It was cooler out than she'd expected, and utterly…magical. Silvery light spilled across the sea of broad sunflower heads. They shimmered in a way that was more mystical than their daytime brilliance, like something fairies would conjure up, more fantastical than real.

"Levi," she whispered. She didn't want to be

jarred out of this reverie. In this ethereal place between dark and light, anything was possible. All of her dreams could be true in a blink of the eye. Even the nightmare she was in had ceased to exist in the here and now.

"I've never seen anything like this. They're facing us again."

"It's the heliotropism. They turn during the night so they're facing east in the morning."

Zaida crossed her arms and looked up at Levi. "Why do they do that?"

He shrugged. "Not sure it's really known. One theory is that facing east—and following the sun—warms the flowers, activating their scent, which stimulates bees to get busy pollinating them. They'll do this until the flowers are mature, then they stiffen into one position." He looked down at a blanket he'd spread on the roof. Another one sat folded nearby. "Do you want to sit with me for a minute?"

"Sure." She smiled, wondering if his pique was over.

He grabbed the folded blanket and wrapped it around her shoulders. His eyes bored into hers as he adjusted the blanket near her neck. "I can't believe you came up here in flip-flops."

"I wasn't expecting to climb a ladder." She could feel waves of heat coming off him. His eyes said so much more than his mouth did. She realized she wanted to know everything about him. Had he ever been married? *Probably*, she thought, answering her own question. He was older than she was.

His eyes in this silvery moonlight held hers just a little too long, as if he was seeking something from her. He looked lonely. Was he? Or was he just a loner who wished to have his home and life back to the way it was before she'd gotten mixed up in it?

"Do you think this will be over soon?" she asked.

"It could be. The more you let me in, the faster I can resolve it. Remi said that I need to establish a rapport with you so that you'll trust me. But it's really much less complicated than that. I'm supposed to find the terrorists who are using you and end them. If you're working with them, then I'm supposed to contain you. You have the information I need to do that. Truth is, I don't think you're the bad guy here."

Now Zaida knew why he'd called her up here on the roof. It wasn't for the magic of his midnight sunflowers; it was because he had her cornered. There was nowhere for her to retreat to.

Zaida looked away from him. Professing her innocence right about now would just make her look guilty…as would her continued silence. The truth was that she had people to protect, people who were innocently doing a job she'd hired them to do. She couldn't give them up or cast doubt on them. Their family and community situations were too tenuous as it was.

"I am not working with terrorists, Levi."

"Then why do I have the persistent feeling you're withholding information from me?"

"I'm only trying to protect some people in my community."

Levi waved her over to the blanket he'd laid out. He sat when she did. "Okay. That's exactly why I need you. Your community has a healthy distrust of outsiders. An understandable one. If the people you're protecting are innocent, you have no need to fear for their safety from me."

"You aren't the one who causes me anxiety. These women do my translations. Their husbands and brothers think they do administrative work for me, not that they translate my work."

Levi leaned back on his hands. His legs were stretched out in front of him. The silvery light made talking to him easier somehow than it was in the daylight. Maybe because she couldn't see the little expressions that crossed his features, indicating his approval or disapproval.

He sighed. "Some high-profile, highly erotic fiction was widely distributed in Middle Eastern countries recently, making bestseller lists there, as it did here. Is your stuff like that?"

"No. Big names can get away with a lot, like that author. I'm not at her level. I wouldn't be granted as much freedom as she was. Nor would my translators. I write a line of fiction better suited to women living under Islamic law. The bedroom door is often left open, but only when the characters are married to each other, and even that's still considered very risqué. These stories really aren't anything like Western romantic fiction. They are very conservative…but in a conservative world, they're also quite edgy. A gentle rebellion of sorts. Young women who aren't married need to have an understanding of what will be expected of them. I often portray young couples that eschew the practice of polygamy and husbands who help their wives achieve success in their education and professional endeavors. It's progressive stuff—not here in the West, but it is in some Islamic countries."

"This is more of your Freedom Code."

"Yes. I have women who translate the stories I write for the Middle Eastern markets. Their families here would not like them being exposed to these radical feminist ideals. It's part of the work I do with several literary foundations. The women who do these translations strengthen their English skills. It also helps them find their own voices. I often see them going on to tell their own stories about their lives— before and after immigrating. Those are the most important stories for them to tell. The foundations I work with collect and share those stories.

"And it isn't just immigrants I work with, but women in impoverished communities here in the U.S., women on reservations, homeless women." She looked at him, wondering if he got the importance of what she was saying. "Having a voice is a freedom and a right. It's a step up from invisibility and oppression. One step closer to being empowered. These are the women you want me to expose. Most of the money I make in the Middle Eastern markets I donate to these foundations."

"And all of that can be traced and accounted for properly?"

"Legally, you mean? Yes. All of it is properly handled through legitimate distribution services."

"It was these women you warned to stay away from work because of me this morning?"

Zaida frowned. "Yes. How did you know?"

"Because I cloned your phone. I can see everything that your phone sees."

Zaida covered her mouth as her eyes widened. "I thought cloning my phone meant you copied my contacts and such. Not that you were spying on me."

"In all fairness, I did tell you I cloned your phone."

"Wait…do you read Arabic?" She'd purposely written that text in Arabic so he couldn't read it.

"No. I had Rocco translate it for me when we were in Wyoming. I want to meet these women."

"No."

"Zaida, I need to meet them. I need to rule them out. What if one of them is working with the bad guys? What if she's a weak link, potentially exposing you and the others for her own gains, or maybe just for her own protection? If they are as vulnerable as you say, then they need my help too."

Zaida lowered her forehead to her knees and thought about it. What choice did she have? "All right.

I'll call them into the office in the morning." She turned to face Levi, her cheek still resting on her knee. "Jamal hated that I worked with them. He wanted me to abandon the work I was doing with them."

"Why?"

"Respect. Safety. It was another reason why I could never accept him."

"Do your parents know about this?"

"No." She stared out at his field. "I'm really getting afraid, Levi. My father wasn't exaggerating when he said this might ruin all of us, perhaps even our entire community, if people from the outside world learn of it and twist reality to suit their beliefs."

"I know. Which is why the faster we can figure this out, the safer everyone will be." He stood and offered her a hand. "Let's hit the sack for tonight. Tomorrow, we'll make some more progress."

She nodded and accepted his help to rise. He didn't immediately let her hand go. Zaida's heart started a rough beat. What would it feel like to be kissed by him? Not the fast peck she'd given him this morning, but a passionate embrace?

Inadvertently, she licked her lips, watching him track the movement of her tongue.

"I'll go down first," he said.

Whoa…had she heard that right? "You'll what?"

"The ladder. I'll go first."

"Oh. Okay."

He bent and swooped up the other blanket, dropping it over his shoulder. A few steps down, he waited for her to join him on the ladder, then they descended together. When they were on the ground, he stowed the ladder on the side of the house.

Zaida walked to the back of the house and stopped at the base of the stairs, giving the sunflowers a last look. Heat lingered in her body from their near kiss, which she still craved.

When he returned to her, the moonlight showed the resignation in his face. He caught her hand in his, then pulled her into his arms. "Tell me no. Right now."

She shook her head, her eyes locked with his. "Yes."

He ran the fingertips of both hands up her neck then into her hair. He looked like he was about to devour her. She shivered and moved her hands up his hard chest.

He leaned down and set his lips to hers. One of his hands cupped the back of her head, the other slipped around her waist. He lifted her, moving her up a step to ease the differences in their heights, then deepened the kiss, turning his head to get a better angle.

Never had Zaida been kissed so savagely by a man starving for her the way Levi was. He moved closer, wrapping both arms around her. She ran her hands up to his broad shoulders, then hooked them behind his neck. His hands went to her face, holding her as he broke their kiss, then he started it over, his mouth wide open. She wanted to feel his hard body against her soft one, but the stupid blankets over their shoulders buffered them.

She tugged at the blanket, but it didn't budge. Levi pulled back, a frown wrinkling his brow. He tossed his blanket down and followed it with hers, then reached for her again. She pulled his T-shirt up, baring his ripped abs…and his holster. He finished removing his shirt, yanking it over his head then dropping it on the ground.

She had already begun unbuttoning her shirt, wanting it off before he thought to rip it off her. It had a lot of buttons. So damn many. Her fingers were shaking, as if contact with his body was a fix she needed desperately. He pushed her hands aside, but his big fingers weren't suited to tackling her buttons, so she took things back over.

He spread the top of her shirt wide, baring her chest and all of her bra. He smiled as he looked down at her, then pulled her to him, his hands on her back under her shoulder blades. He kissed her bared skin, nipping and sucking. She wondered if he'd given her a hickey. Whatever he was doing, she wanted more of it. When he bent his head to the crook of her neck and moaned, her panties were instantly wet. His beard was prickly against her skin, tantalizing her.

He wrapped his arms around her, lifting her up the steps to the landing. When he joined her there, he was once again too tall for her short frame. He backed her up to the house and reached over to open the porch door. She stepped up into the house, but he pinned her against the doorjamb. Inside, the house was shadowy, but moonlight still illuminated half his face, clearly showing the war he fought with himself.

"What is it?" Zaida asked.

He leaned his forehead against hers. "I can't do this."

"Do what?"

He didn't immediately answer her. When he did, his words came out in a low growl. "I've had fast and easy. A lot of it. Now I want something different. Deeper. Permanent, even…if that really exists. Anything we do now will be tainted by this case."

Ice poured through all the secret places inside Zaida that had been burning just seconds ago. She'd told herself this was nothing, a fling. That giving herself to Levi did not bind them in any permanent way.

But that wasn't how he was looking at it.

She wanted to laugh at the pickle she was in, but for the life of her she couldn't.

He fisted her hair, forcing her head back as he stared down at her. "If you're not after the same thing I am, then leave. Now."

"Levi—" her voice was whispered. Even she didn't know if she was urging him on or begging him to stop.

His nostrils flared and his cheeks bunched. He made the decision for her. "Take off your clothes," he ordered her. Her body grew chilled as he pulled away, disappearing into the house as he unfastened his belt.

She stared after him a long second, filled suddenly with doubts and a wretched desire that still burned. Could she really sleep with him, a virtual stranger?

He was barefoot when he came back to the porch. His jeans were unfastened and rode low on his hips. His belt was open and dangling lazily. His holster band was gone. Where had he put his gun? He leaned against the big opening from the house and folded his arms. "You're not naked."

God, were they really going to do this? She'd met him, when—two days ago? She licked her lips. He arched a dark brow. She removed her shirt, then opened her jeans and slowly pushed them down her hips, wiggling out of them—not because she was giving him a show, but because they were tight and had to be coaxed off her legs.

Standing in her panties and bra, she stared at him, almost like a girl who didn't know the next steps. That was ridiculous. She wrote about this all day long. But the truth was that a lot of time had passed since she'd been with anyone.

"Come inside," Levi said, slipping into the shadows behind him.

She folded her lips between her teeth, pinching them, running her tongue over them. How many times had her female characters indulged in this type of wild behavior—pure carnal exploration? A lot.

And yet...she never had.

Until now.

She followed him into the house. He stood near

the sofa. She looked across the space to her room. She could run there. Lock her door. Hide from him, from this…from herself.

But God help her, she didn't want to.

She walked up to him and put her palms on his chest. It was nicely furred in the area over his pecs, then narrowed to a thin line that ran down the center of his chest, widening a bit below his navel, disappearing into his black boxer briefs.

He cupped his hand under her chin, then his long fingers slipped into her hair, sending tingles along her spine. He lifted her face as he bent to kiss her. This kiss wasn't as hard as his first. He held himself back, letting his tongue gently enter her mouth. It stroked hers. Zaida shivered at his gentle exploration, then began doing to him what he did to her. She wrapped her arms around his waist and ran them up his back, feeling the power of his muscled body.

All too soon, he pulled back. Before she could complain, he lifted her into his arms. She caught his neck with one of her hands, holding herself up. For a long moment, he stared down into her eyes. Then he said, "Let go of me."

"What?"

"Lie back in my arms. I've got you."

"Levi—"

"Do it."

She eased her hand away from him.

"Relax. Completely," he ordered her.

"Levi—"

"Now, Zaida."

She tried to do as he requested, but it was awkward holding her head up.

"Go limp."

She took a deep breath, then finally relaxed in his hold. Her head was draped down over his arm. The room spun in upside-down shadows and shapes. And then his lips were on her neck, his tongue, too. Her nipples hardened at the contact. She arched up against his mouth, feeling his hot breath as he kissed his way down the side of her neck. He lifted her body to his face, kissed her collarbone, let his mouth move over the lacy edge of her ruby bra.

He lifted and turned her body toward his face as his mouth moved toward the center of her ribs, down to where her belly was soft. His tongue dipped and swirled in and over her belly button. He buried his face in the tender skin between her navel and her panties.

Zaida sucked in a sharp draw of air as his hot breath heated her mound. There was nothing she could do to participate. This was his own private feast that she was the beneficiary of. She did cry out, in pleasure and yearning, when his chin ground against her folds. And then his teeth were on her thigh—one, then the other.

Never had she been so ready for sex as she was at that point.

She closed her eyes, wondering how long he meant to torture her this way. Suddenly she felt the room shift. They were moving...toward the sofa. He set her down on the long side of the L-shaped sofa, then shooed Beau off it, ordering him to his dog bed. Straightening, Levi dropped his jeans and stepped out of them.

Zaida reached up to run her hand over his strong thighs, up even more to cup his balls. Levi hissed and widened his legs, giving her all the access she wanted. She found the hardened length of him and followed it to its wide tip.

He knelt on the sofa, between her legs, then settled himself over her, rocking himself against her core.

Zaida sighed, loving the feel of him over her, his strength, his weight. "Levi—do you have protection?"

"Of course."

"Where is it?"

"Under the cushion here."

Zaida's eyes popped open. "You keep condoms in your sofa?"

"Well, yeah. Don't you?"

"No. I have two condoms in my bathroom."

He grinned. "Two? You only stock up for half a night of fun?"

Her lips parted even as her body quaked at the thought of needing more than two condoms. "What else do you have in this sofa?"

Levi kissed her neck, her chin. "Guns. Knives. A fucking armory."

Zaida pushed him up. She stared up into his face,

but couldn't make out the finer nuances of his expression. Maybe he wasn't kidding. What was she doing having sex with a mercenary? Was she out of her ever-loving mind? She didn't do casual sex. And things with Levi were never going to go anywhere. "I have to go."

Levi sat up. "Go where?"

"To my room."

"Briefly? Or for the night?"

"The night."

He caught the corner of his lips in his teeth and nodded. "Okay."

LEVI WATCHED HER SWEET, rounded ass as she edged past him and went to her room. He'd been surprised that she hadn't stopped him sooner. He was curious to see how far she was willing to go, and couldn't help wondering if she was doing it to get under his skin. Did she think to control him by offering him her body? That he couldn't shoot someone he'd fucked?

Hadn't been an issue with Julia.

Levi went to the fridge and pulled out a beer. Twisting off the cap, he went back and sat at the end of the sofa nearest the grate blowing cold air from the swamp cooler. His body was hot as hell and needed to cool the fuck down.

Unfortunately, neither the beer nor the cool stream of air stopped his thoughts from going where they always did in his still moments…to the real reason he left the teams when his latest tour had ended. *Jules*. Sweet Julia Rickers.

He sat forward on the sofa and banged his beer down on the coffee table, then dropped his head in his hands. Two years had passed since that terrible day, and still it was as fresh as when it happened.

Levi polished off his beer, then called Beau over and settled in for a few hours rest. Tomorrow was going to be harder than today was, and he was going to need his mind functioning.

Jules was gone. Zaida was not—would never be—a replacement for her.

So why did he feel a crazy seed of hope when he saw her? Why did he find himself wanting to make her laugh? Wanting to hear her stories and her hopes and dreams? Why was he torturing himself with what would never be?

10

The next morning, Zaida was up, showered, and dressed by eight a.m. She hadn't stepped out of her room yet, though the smell of Levi's freshly ground coffee was a sore temptation.

She was nervous about what to expect from him… and embarrassed by the fact that her body still burned for him. He hadn't tried to dissuade her from leaving last night. She knew he'd been fully aroused—she'd felt the evidence of that. Had he been playing a game?

Well, it had worked. She was fully discombobulated today. And on this, of all days, when she needed her wits about her. They were going to meet her translators. Somehow, she had to convince Levi to respect their privacy. She had to get him to understand the fine balance these women walked between what their families thought they did and what they actually did.

When she did open her door, Beau charged toward her, happy to see her after the long night. She set her purse on the sofa, then sat down to rub his ears.

"Looks like you figured out he's not going to eat you," Levi said as he handed her a coffee mug, the rich elixir fixed just how she liked it.

"I've never met a dog I liked before Beau."

"He's not a dog. He's my best friend. My only friend, really."

Zaida looked at Levi, saddened by his admission. She was not a loner like him. She had a ton of friends —she made them easily. But the truth was that none of her friendships were very deep. She wondered if she did that on purpose, building a wall between her and the outside world through light friendships that were never very taxing.

Maybe she and Levi weren't so very different after all. She looked at her coffee, suddenly realizing this was the second time he'd made it how she liked it, but she'd never told him how that was. "How did you know I liked my coffee this way?"

"Lucky guess." He shrugged.

"I texted my translators," she said. "They'll be in the office around ten this morning."

"Where's your office?"

"In Fort Collins. It's just a small suite on the third

floor of one of the Old Town buildings. I can walk to it from my apartment."

"Have them bring their computers. I'm still looking for the origin of that worm."

Zaida texted that directive from her phone. She frowned as she looked at Levi. "How do you know the worm originated from one of my computers?"

"Not sure how that conclusion was drawn. I wasn't given that info. Just that it had come from one of your computers." He set some plates out and started dishing out breakfast. "I made us omelets. Let's eat, then we can go."

Zaida took up a fork and pulled her plate closer. She looked across the wide counter to the mercenary whose hands and mouth and body she still craved. His eyes were hard as he returned her stare. He finished before her, then switched his focus to washing the dishes, banging around more than was needed as he filled the dishwasher and scrubbed the pans.

She ate her food, tasting little of it. "Levi, about last night—" she said as she brought her dishes around to him.

He looked over at her. "Forget it. Won't happen again."

"What if I want it to?"

His brows lifted. She actually stepped back. Still, he closed the space between them. "Next time we're in our skivvies together, I will bury myself in you. Have no doubt about it. There won't be another time when we come close but stop. You strip in front of me again, you're mine."

Zaida stared at the hard lines of his mouth. "You're the one who told me to strip."

He caught her hands and lifted them against the wall, spread-eagled. "And if I told you to now, would you?"

Zaida felt heat all through her core. She knew her breathing was ragged, but there was little she could do to calm it. *Yes*. Yes, she would. But she didn't want a fast coupling. She wanted a long interlude. She wanted to be *sated*, mindless and numb after their time together, something they simply couldn't achieve now, when they had the meeting with her translators.

He took her silence for a negative and let her go. Her legs were like noodles. She doubted she could stand on her own if she tried to move away from the wall before gathering her composure.

No man had ever made her feel this way. He busied himself doing some things with Beau, which gave her a few precious seconds to pretend her entire body hadn't just betrayed her. She left the kitchen and went to her purse to check that she had everything she might need for a day away from the house. She wasn't bringing her computer, so she didn't need her messenger bag.

"Ready?" he asked, standing by the front door, keys in hand.

She followed him out the door and down the steps

to his Jeep. It was nice that he held the car door for her.

"If you get thirsty, there are some water bottles in the cooler behind my seat," he said as he got settled in the driver's side.

They drove in silence for a while, then Levi started asking her questions. "Tell me about your translators. What do they do for you? What do you do with their translations?"

"My books are available in English in dozens of countries, some of them in the Middle East. In the more conservative countries, the stories that I tell here don't resonate with readers because they don't reflect the morals and traditions of those countries. So I write a line of romances geared toward Islamic readers. Those stories deal with issues that matter to the women reading them—finding love, of course, but sometimes, in the framework of a polygamist society, women finding employment, contributing to the economics of their households, pressures of new- and old-world cultures, globalization, war. My stories can make readers question things in their lives. For their environment, they are edgy because they give women a voice. Many women have to hide the fact that they read them." She looked at him. "Did you know that some libraries in Afghanistan won't loan books to women? These books have an entirely different distribution channel—but still all through legal channels."

"You speak Arabic yourself. Why don't you do your own translations?"

Freedom Code

"Because I work through a handful of women's foundations that do work like this for hire. The women who work for me are technically employed by one of those groups using a grant I fund. The work helps them with their language skills, gives them employment outside the home, a safe place to work, the tools to do their own writing when they have no translations to do. They are an important part of the ecosystem. It helps them have a voice. It helps them realize their own value."

"Your Freedom Code again."

"Exactly. As they develop their language skills, their comfort expressing and supporting themselves grows. They, in turn, reach out to the community to help other women who don't have voice…or don't have a safe way of expressing themselves."

Zaida looked over at Levi. "The first part of healing a society is giving it a voice. Silence is the language of the disenfranchised. It translates easily to fear and anger, fists and guns. When we feel heard, then we feel we have value. That doesn't only apply to immigrants, but also to undereducated and forgotten pockets of American society—and there are more of them than you think. The women you'll meet today are at risk in their community. They are allowed to work because it's known I'll provide them a safe environment where they can work in tandem with their religious beliefs. We have a room dedicated to prayer."

"What if one of them was secular and doesn't pray?"

She smiled at him. "Like me?"

"Do you do the prayers?"

"Sometimes. It's peaceful. Most times, no. Sometimes I use the prayer room for meditation or just a quiet space."

"You know, this office space of yours was not in your dossier."

"You have a dossier on me?"

"Of course. You're at the center of this investigation."

"I'm not doing anything illegal. Writing romance and helping women is not shady stuff."

"True enough. I'm not here because of either of those activities. I'm here because of your role in a stream of international terrorism."

"Which I'm also not a part of. Nor would I be."

"Perhaps not knowingly."

She huffed a frustrated breath and turned to face her passenger window.

"It's why we're checking out every possibility," Levi said.

"I'm telling you, the women you'll meet will be terrified of you. Your very presence in my office puts them at risk. It will bring suspicion upon them and their families. If their men find out you were investigating them—or me—they will be forced to quit. So please, go easy with them."

"I will be respectful, but I will not pretend women are incapable of dastardly deeds."

Zaida held his hard gaze as long as she could before he returned his focus to the road. He said that as if he had personal experience in the matter. Had a woman betrayed him?

"So back to your offices…how is it that it didn't show on the info we have for you?" Levi asked.

"I'm subletting them until the end of the year. Having an office was an experiment the sublet let me explore."

"And after the new year?"

"I'll take over the lease. The income I make from the stories I've had translated funds my translators and other things. It's working, so far. One of my translators has started at the university. That's huge."

Levi nodded, but said nothing more. They'd reached Fort Collins, so Zaida directed him to the building where her suite was. It was on the third floor of the building. Access to the building was done via a security card. Outside the actual suite, Zaida entered a code into a keypad.

He was glad she had some security, but either was pretty easy to crack…or share. Looked as if she hadn't been there in a while. There were a couple of packages outside waiting for her to bring in. A stack of mail was spread out over the floor from the mail slot in the door. While she went through her mail, he looked at the boxes.

"Anything about these boxes look suspicious to you?" he asked.

She gave him a scolding look as she reached for one of them. He caught her wrist. "Zaida, now is not the time to be overly comfortable. I wouldn't be here if you weren't in the middle of this—in some way we don't yet understand. And because we don't, we have no idea how far things have progressed. Those who are using you—or who are after you—may well have reached the end of their need for you. A bomb in a package could be an easy way of eliminating you."

Zaida's eyes got big. "Let me see them. If I don't know who sent them, I won't open them."

"Good. Make that a habit."

"These are fine. They're from my printer. I frequently order print copies of my books."

Levi nodded, leaving her to her mail as he checked the space for bugs. Besides the front reception area, there were two more offices in the suite, along with a smaller east-facing prayer room. One of the offices was small, with a single desk and two side chairs, the other larger, with four desks. The smaller office had only a single, narrow window. The back office had several large windows that let in lots of light. There was a steel door that exited the back office and led to fire escape stairs.

Levi went to the front reception area where Zaida was still going through mail. The outer walls in the office were exposed brick. And because the suite was on the top floor, it had cathedral ceilings. It was a nice place to do some quiet, creative work.

"Zaida, when I asked if you had other computers, you didn't tell me about the ones your employees use."

"They aren't my computers. Well, technically. I bought them, but then donated them to the foundation. And I'm not exactly the employer of these women. More like their client."

Levi shrugged. "That's all semantics."

"These women aren't guilty of any illegal activity."

"We'll see. Give me their full names and home addresses."

"What are you going to say to them?" Zaida asked as she began writing down the info he'd requested.

"Only that you've asked me to help you find someone who is stalking you. That's not far from the truth. And, hopefully, it will make them want to help you."

"Okay. We'll go with that."

Levi grinned. "What's harder to accept, that I'm your friend or that we're trying to resolve a mystery?"

One of her beautiful raven brows lifted. "Can you be friends with someone you might have to shoot?"

As soon as she said that, it was clear she wished she could unsay it. Her face flushed a warm rose—a color that, apparently, his groin understood too well.

His smile widened. "I've never made friends of a known enemy, so I can't answer that."

Zaida returned her attention to her mail, once again ignoring him. He leaned against the wall behind the door and waited for her staff to join them. He didn't have long to wait. He soon heard a handful of women coming up the stairs, talking quietly among themselves in Arabic.

Zaida sent him a nervous glance, then stood as the women entered. One look at her face, and they all fell silent. Fortunately, they made it all the way into the room. When the door shut, they saw him. He regretted the fear that entered their eyes as he moved to stand between them and the door.

Zaida introduced him as a friend who was helping resolve a problem, that someone had been threatening her, and she feared they might become targets of this stalker. She told them not to fear him, that he would not harm them or trouble their families. He got all of this from following her lilting Arabic. He could speak it fairly well, but couldn't read or write it worth shit. He realized how much he admired her bilingual capabilities.

"Is he the Fed you warned us about?" one of the women asked, sending him a sidelong glance.

"Yes, but I now know he's here to help, not harm us," Zaida answered.

Zaida led them back to their offices. Levi texted Max in Wyoming that he had the contents of a few more computers headed his way. When he went into the back office, he realized one woman was missing.

"Who uses the fourth desk?" he asked. Zaida had listed four women on the paper she gave him.

Zaida frowned. She asked the others about the missing girl. They passed a nervous glance between them, then one of them said that she was home with a sick brother and couldn't come in.

Yeah, that fired off all Levi's well-honed alerts.

"Ask them to open their computers and sign in, please," Levi directed Zaida. He knew the women could speak English, since their jobs were to translate Zaida's English manuscripts, but it seemed they preferred to talk to her directly.

Zaida did as requested.

"What is he looking for?" one of the women asked, still in Arabic.

Zaida translated that for him. He didn't tell her he'd understood the question. He had little enough edge in this investigation. If there was a chance that something would slip, since they believed he couldn't understand them, it was a benefit to him.

"I'm checking to see if their computers have been hacked, since your stalker seems to know a lot about you and your movements through the day. If so, that info could endanger your team here."

After he used the flash drive he'd been given on each of their computers, he asked, "Are these the only computers they use for work?"

"Yes," Zaida said. "I needed to provide them with

laptops because they didn't have access to ones at home, and I didn't want them doing my translations on library computers."

Levi nodded. "Then we're finished here. I'll wait for you out front." Once there, he did a search on his phone for the girl who hadn't shown. There was nothing of note to be found about Hidaya Baqri. Her social media was almost nonexistent. But there was a link to her brother on Facebook, and what Levi saw there caused every warning system he knew to sound off.

The women came out of the back, ignoring him as they left. Zaida stopped beside the receptionist's desk. "Are we finished here?"

"Look at this." Levi handed her his phone. Her face went pale as she looked at the Facebook post of her friend's brother, which included a jihadist manifesto, and post after post of hate and death wishes to America and its people.

Zaida's hand shook as she handed the phone back to Levi. "I saw that a while ago. It's one of the reasons I wanted to get Mike's help."

"Unless he was hacked, he made those posts himself."

"He was hacked. They locked him out of his accounts. It's on all of his social media. But you don't know Abdul. He is the gentlest, kindest man I've ever met. He's curious about life and people and open to all philosophies. He is not a terrorist. I *know* him. You don't. He's a pacifist."

Levi scoffed at that. "A pacifist who wants to terminate our country and all of its sinners, which is just about every fucking adult in it. Maybe pacifist doesn't mean the same thing to you as it does to me."

"Levi, I'm not kidding. Something is very not right. I'm scared for Hidaya and Abdul. Neither of them are ever sick. She never misses work."

Levi took his phone back, but didn't take his eyes from Zaida. If he were to believe her, and he was seriously leaning in that direction, an innocent kid was being framed as a jihadist. Why? And by whom?

They needed to get to him fast, before any other faction did. "Where does he live?"

"He and Hidaya share an apartment on the west side of town."

"Let's go. Can you call her? Maybe if you can talk to her, we can stop this before it goes too far."

"I texted her while we were in the back office. She didn't answer. I'll try again."

They locked up the office and hurried down the stairs. Levi was glad the university wasn't in session. That was at least one positive in a string of bad breaks they'd faced. If this progressed to an explosive situation, then it was good a large percentage of the population wasn't yet back in the area.

It took less than ten minutes to get across town. The apartment the kid and his sister shared was in an older unit. Children were riding bikes around the parking lot. Levi followed Zaida to the stairs, but stopped her so he could go up first. "I'd really rather you waited in the Jeep," he said.

"I can't. They know me. They won't answer the door for you, if they're even still there. The others will have warned them by now. Hidaya hasn't answered my texts or calls."

Levi frowned. Nothing looked untoward…yet. If she could get them into the apartment with the least amount of fuss, great. "You follow my lead. For all we know, he's rigged his place with bombs. I go in first. And if I tell you to get your ass back to the car, you do it. Read me?"

"Yes. Yes. Just let's go."

On Abdul's floor, the apartment doors were closed; no one had come out to stare at them. Levi took a set of lock picks out of his wallet. He fitted them to the locks and tinkered with them just a second until the lock clicked open.

"What are you doing?" Zaida hissed.

"Giving us options. Knock on the door. Call out to your friend."

She did as he'd ordered. He moved in front of her, waiting briefly to hear sounds from inside the apartment. There weren't any. "Wait here, Zaida. Don't come in until I'm sure it's safe."

He looked over his shoulder at her. Her eyes were big, and searched his. Damn it all, he wished he could give her some assurance, some promise that her world wasn't crumbling at her feet.

Then he did the most illogical thing he could have

done: he kissed her. He turned just slightly and caught her chin in his hand and pressed his lips to hers. His jaw opened, as did hers, letting him inside. His tongue stroked along hers. When he broke the kiss, he stared into her eyes and said, "We'll figure this out. I promise that. Wait here." He gave her his keys. "Hold on to these for me."

Levi cautiously cracked the door, checking it over for trip wires. Seeing none, he stepped inside. The apartment was trashed. Someone had ransacked it. Everything had been turned over, slashed, trampled. Levi made his way through the entire apartment. There was no laptop or desktop or tablet to be found. And given the state of the apartment, it was also impossible to tell what might have been taken.

ZAIDA WAITED outside Hidaya's apartment, trying not to call attention to herself. A neighbor across the way had spotted her with Levi. Zaida had seen the neighbor's door open a sliver as Levi had gone inside. When the neighbor caught Zaida watching her, she slammed the door shut.

Great. Zaida hoped the woman didn't call the cops. What was taking Levi so long? It seemed like minutes had passed. He hadn't come back to tell her it was safe to go in. Maybe she should wait in the car. She looked toward the stairs and saw a face that shot dread straight through her: Jamal.

A couple of his men were coming up behind him.

She couldn't escape. She didn't want to rush into the apartment for fear of bringing trouble to Levi. She stepped back, pressing herself against Hidaya's door.

"Finally. I found you," Jamal said.

"Leave me alone, Jamal," Zaida said.

"I can't. You have to come with me. I need you to trust me. Zaida. Please. You know me."

Zaida shook her head. "I don't know you at all."

"I'll explain everything to you. I promise."

"Explain it to me now."

He looked around the breezeway of the second-floor apartments. Curious onlookers had come out to see what the commotion was. "This isn't the time or place. I need to get you to safety. I have Abdul and Hidaya."

Zaida gasped. "Levi! Levi. Hurry."

"No!" Jamal growled. "Obey me!" He grabbed Zaida's arm and started dragging her toward the stairs.

Zaida screamed for Levi again, then kicked Jamal's shin, briefly freeing herself. She ran to Hidaya's door just as it was yanked open and Levi came out. By then, Jamal had gathered his guys and was hurrying down the stairs.

Levi wrapped an arm around Zaida and led her into her friends' apartment. As soon as the door was closed, Zaida leaned against Levi, taking strength from him. And then she remembered what Jamal had told her. She fisted Levi's shirt.

"He has Hidaya and Abdul," she said, staring up at Levi's worried face.

"Okay." Levi nodded. "We need to get out of here."

Zaida looked around and saw the trashed living room. Gasping, she asked, "Did you do this, Levi?"

"No. It was this way when I got here."

Zaida knew she looked unconvinced.

"I haven't even been here five minutes." Levi shook his head. "I couldn't find any computers. We have to go. No doubt the neighbors will be calling the cops. When we get outside, move calmly and with confidence. Don't look anxious. This is your friends' apartment—you had every right to be here."

There were only a couple of neighbors still in the breezeway when they left. The woman from across the hall was not one of them. They went down the stairs and got into Levi's Jeep without any issues. In fact, they were halfway down the block before they passed two cop cars heading toward the apartment buildings. Apparently, no one had reported their Jeep to the cops, so they weren't stopped.

11

Zaida looked stricken as they made their way to her apartment. Levi considered taking her back up to Wyoming so she could stay with his friends while he worked the case. He reached over and took her hand.

"Hey. It's going to be all right. All of this will be a distant memory in a few days."

She looked over at him. "I don't think it will ever be over."

"We're just dealing with a lot of unknowns at the moment. Once we have answers, we'll understand how all of this came to be."

"My friends are innocent. Jamal said he was keeping them safe. Safe from what? How can he think he can keep them or me or anyone safe?"

"He also said for you to obey him."

Her eyes widened as she watched him. "So you do speak Arabic."

"Some. I'm nowhere near as fluent as you are. I've learned the words a sailor needed, little more. Enough to do some light interrogations, find my way around somewhere, ask for help. That's it." Levi faced the road as he asked, "What did he mean by demanding you obey him?"

Zaida sighed. "His parents and mine have been friends all my life. He was like an older cousin I was pretty much raised with. I told you they all believed we would eventually marry. Jamal's nearly forty now. He's been angry with me for a while that I would not settle down. But he's like a brother to me. And like an older sibling, he thinks he knows what's best for me."

"That the real reason you aren't into him?" They'd talked a little about that, but there had to be more to it than Jamal simply not being her type.

"Yes. He honestly thinks I should obey him. For real, for fuck's sake. That's been his attitude toward me my entire life."

Levi grinned. He'd never heard her cuss before. It was actually kind of cute.

"Where are we going?" she asked as she focused on the road.

"Back to your apartment. Thought you might want to rest or recoup a bit while we wait to go to your group meeting tonight."

"We're still doing that?"

"Yes."

At her apartment complex, they pulled into the residents' parking area and selected a visitor spot.

Zaida still looked awfully lost. Levi took her hand and led her to the elevator. They went straight up to her floor without encountering any threats. Once in her apartment, Levi did a quick check. The space was clear. Zaida had taken off her ankle boots. Without her heels, she was super short, probably five three. He was six four, taller in his steel-toed boots that he was still wearing…boots he had no intention of taking off, just in case they needed to make a fast exit.

Zaida was sitting on one of the stools by the big counter in her kitchen, leaning against the counter, watching him. "Why did you kiss me? At Hidaya's."

"I wanted to." He tilted his head. "And I wanted to distract you from being afraid."

"I'm terrified."

"I know." Levi shoved his hands in his pockets. "Want me to rustle up some food for us? You hungry?"

"I don't have much here. Help yourself. I think there are some cans of soup. Or we could order something from downstairs."

"You really don't cook, do you?"

She shook her head, looking even more dejected. He went over and scooped her off her stool and carried her over to the sofa. "What are you doing?"

"Thought we'd have a cuddle."

"You can't carry me around like a doll."

"Why not?" He set her on her sofa just off to his side with her legs across his lap, then began rubbing her feet.

She moaned as he worked her feet. "Do you cuddle all your enemies?"

"Are we still enemies?"

"You make it sound like we are." Zaida leaned back against the cushions. "Do you really think this will be over soon?"

"Yeah." He looked at her and grinned. "Either everything will go back to normal very soon, or half the town will be gone."

"Levi! That's horrible."

"But true."

She pulled her legs free and sat up, right next to him. "Then we can't stop, can't rest until we resolve this."

"No. We can…and we have to. Why not go to your room, now? Rest. Take a shower. Whatever you want. We have a little time before your group meeting. I need to check in with a few people."

She got up, but he caught her hand before she moved away. When she looked down at him, her brown eyes darkened. She straddled his hips, her slight weight so perfect right there. She caught his face in her hands and leaned forward to kiss him, then tilted her head to one side to get an even better connection to him. He kept his hands on her waist, even though he desperately wanted to press her body against his, bury his face in her breasts. He feared this…and wanted it with everything that he was.

Some part of him believed if they didn't do this, if they resisted the pull that was drawing them together, if they never gained carnal knowledge of each other, then when this was done in a few days, they could go their separate ways and forget each other.

But if they did do this, he wasn't sure he could let her go. She needed him. And he needed her. They were opposites, yes, but opposite in ways that were wholly complementary. Female/male. Short/tall. Urbane/country. Weak/strong.

It was selfish, his reasons for fighting this. He was a coward. He didn't want to get hurt. But Zaida needed this. His woman needed him. When he realized that, he was all in, giving what she needed, losing himself in her. He pulled her fancy purple shirt off, then leaned forward so she could help him remove his. He always wore two shirts—a T-shirt and a loose summer shirt—because of his concealed carry. He leaned back, scooting a little lower on the cushion. She moved with him, resting her chest on his. He felt the weight and heat of her breasts through the soft-scratchy texture of her black lace bra.

He was holding her face when their kiss broke. Their gazes met and locked. He had the crazy thought that he had one shot at her heart, and that was through their bodies. Like an audition. How many men had failed her, failed to satisfy her needs?

"Zaida…do you have any condoms?"

"I have two. Just a half-night's worth." She smiled. So fucking sexy. He rocked his hips under hers.

"We'll have to make do." He couldn't hold back the cocky grin that slipped out.

"I'll be right back." She climbed off his lap. Cold air replaced the heat of her body. She pushed her jeans off. "Take your boots off."

"On it." He caught her arm. "Take your bra off."

"Levi—"

"Do it."

Her chest and neck flushed a warm rose color as she reached behind her and unfastened the clasp. The large lace cups went slack as the straps slipped off her shoulders. Her breasts were gorgeous. The stuff of dreams, heavy, bumping against each other. Her nipples were large and dusky. He lifted his gaze from her tits to her eyes, but his eyes snagged on her amazing lips.

"Zaida…you're killing me. How fast can you get back here?"

She pivoted and rushed down the hall. He removed his boots and jeans, leaving his black boxer briefs on. He was not a small man, and Zaida was a petite woman—he didn't want to scare her.

He sat on the sofa as she came back into the room. She handed him a packet.

"Only one?" he asked.

She winced. "The other had expired."

He grinned. "No worries. I'll make it up to you tonight." He set it on the coffee table, then pulled her between his spread legs. Her breasts were right at face level. He did what he had wanted to do since the first time he saw her saunter through the atrium down below: he buried his face in her warm skin. Cupping either side of her breasts, he pressed her against his cheeks, groaning at her sweet, spicy scent.

"Zaida, God, your body is amazing. How are you not spending every hour of every day fucking?"

She set her hands on his shoulders and smiled. "Because some of us have serious things to do, like manage a writing career and help other women."

"Okay. But you need to take time for yourself, no?" He caught one of her breasts and brought its tip into his mouth. He rolled it around his tongue, then flicked the tip. She gasped a sharp breath as he sucked on her nipple. Her nails dug into his shoulders just slightly, stinging him in a way that set his whole body tingling. He repeated his attentions on her other breast, nuzzling, nipping.

Oh yeah. It was going to take a whole lot more than one encounter for him to satisfy all of his curiosity about her body and her pleasure. He leaned forward and kissed the bottom of her ribs. Her skin was deliciously soft and sweet. He eased her panties down her hips. She was naked now. Beautiful. Her feminine curls were trimmed to a neat column. He liked that she was still standing. He wanted to give her her first orgasm while she was in front of him.

He kissed her belly button. Her long nails raked through his hair as he ran his hands over her rounded hips, reaching around to cup her taut ass. He pushed his hands between her thighs, spreading them a little apart. He gripped her hips with one hand as the fingers of his other hand slipped between her sweet folds. She was wet. He wanted to taste her, but not this time. He rubbed her clit with his thumb. She gasped and her body jerked reflexively.

"I can't do this standing, Levi."

"No?"

"No."

"I'll catch you." He stroked her intimate folds, teasing ever closer to penetrating her with his fingers. He knew she was enjoying what he was doing because her eyes went a little unfocused, her nipples tightened, and she was wet and hot where he touched. His thumb massaged her clit, rhythmically, slow then fast.

"Levi…please…I can't…"

Levi wrapped an arm around her waist, holding her against him, sucking a tit as two of his fingers entered her. Her legs did give out as her orgasm broke free. He held her and worked her sensitive flesh as long as her tremors lasted. When they began to ease off, he steadied her as her legs took her weight once again, then stood and pushed off his boxer briefs. His cock was rod-hard, heavy and throbbing to be in her body. He sat back down and ripped the condom pack open, hurrying to cover himself.

Zaida knelt over him. Her body was hot and soft, and he could tell she still hungered for him the way her eyes stayed dilated. Her hips settled against his, pressing his cock between their bodies. He let her lead them, giving her a chance to feel the hard length of him, knowing she would tell him when she was ready for him to enter her.

Her breathing was as ragged as his. Her hips rocked back and forth. She kept her hands on his shoulders. Her movements were fevered. Levi wished he could feel her body without the condom between them, but that wasn't going to happen.

At last she lifted up, rising to her knees, and guided him to her opening. He caught her hips, slowing her. "Go easy, Zaida. You haven't been with anyone for a while. And I'm big for you. I don't want to hurt you."

The terrible result of that warning was that she slipped herself down over him in painfully small increments. He wanted to slam into her and thrust hard, but her body needed to slowly open to him. He groaned at the torture. She smiled then licked her lips.

He reached up and caught her face in one of his hands, bringing her forward to kiss him. His tongue thrust between her teeth, sliding against hers, back and forth. He released her face to hold both breasts in his hands as she continued kissing him. She was almost all the way down on him. Each little bounce of her hips let him in deeper. He smiled against her mouth, loving everything about her.

He reached between their bodies to massage her clit. She climaxed instantly, with him not all the way in her. He pressed his head back against the cushions of her sofa, fighting his own release. They only had one fucking condom—he had to make it last. Not an easy feat as he felt her small muscles tightening around him, grabbing and releasing as her hips jerked.

And then, without warning, she slipped all the way down on him, burying him deep inside her. Another orgasm took her. Jesus. His whole body went hard. He wanted to feel her in a hundred different positions…but that wasn't going to happen this time, not with her orgasms freely rolling and his so close to the surface.

Before her third orgasm had fully passed, he lifted her and moved her to her back on the sofa. He slipped his arms under her shoulders as he thrust inside her with hard, long strokes, extending her orgasm until she screamed and pushed up against him, banging into him, thrusting as hard as he did.

His release exploded from him. He gave himself over to pure sensation. Too soon it was over for him, though her body continued to have little ripples. Her legs were around his hips, holding him to her. He stayed buried in her until the very last tremor passed. Her arms tightened around his neck as she pressed her face against his skin.

After a long moment, he leaned up to look at her, worried he might have hurt her. She looked stricken. What did that mean? He gazed into her eyes, frowning, and gently stroked her cheeks with his thumbs. "You okay?"

She nodded. "Levi—what did you do to me?"

"What do you mean? Did I hurt you?"

"No. No. It's never been like that. Ever."

"In a good way or a bad way?"

"Good. I lost my mind. I only knew I needed more and more of you."

Levi smiled. "Your pleasure is what drives both of us to ecstasy."

"But no one else seems to know that." She brushed her hand over his cheek and smoothed her fingers across his lips. Even now, he could see she wanted him again. And they only had the one damned condom. "It isn't that I've been with a lot of guys. It's just that none of them knew what you do."

Levi grinned and kissed her jaw. "So you're saying I'm your best lover ever?"

"Ever."

"Fucking A." He raked his teeth over her chin. "Now you see why I need so many condoms."

"Let's go get a box."

Levi laughed. "Tonight. I'll take you home to my place and fuck you until you're spent." He pulled out of her, then eased the condom off. "Don't go anywhere."

12

Zaida watched Levi disappear down the hall on his way to the bathroom, then she heard water running. She had the strangest feeling in her gut, almost a panic. What was she going to do when this was over and they went their separate ways, which she knew they would do? They were from different worlds. They had different life plans.

The lingering warmth she'd felt before he left was rapidly disappearing. She got up, worried he'd see right through her, then laugh at her for being so needy. She gathered up her clothes and hurried to her room. He came out of the bathroom just as she reached that door.

"Hey." He stepped in front of her, blocking her with his beautiful naked body. "Where are you going?"

"It's getting late." She stared at his chest. "I need to shower before we go."

"Okay." He brushed a lock of hair from her face. He lifted her chin. Her eyes met his. "What's going on?"

"Nothing."

Had he really hoped they'd have more time together, just the two of them, before the world intruded? He looked disappointed as he dropped his hand and stepped out of her way. "All right. Want me to warm up a soup for you? Or get something from downstairs?"

"No. I'm not hungry."

"Okay. Well, come out when you're ready. I guess we'll head out, then."

An hour later, Zaida rejoined him in her living room, carrying another satchel and her purse. She was gorgeous as usual. She wore a cream-colored silk blouse that was tucked into a black and cream flower-patterned pair of loose capris. Her shoes were narrow, pointed-toe beige pumps with heels so tall and thin that he imagined she was really just walking on her tippy toes. Her silky hair shone like black glass. Her makeup was perfect, and yet something was off about her. She was quiet and her dark eyes weren't as sparkly as he'd come to expect from her.

She'd built new walls around her, separating her from him. It shouldn't hurt, but it did.

"We aren't coming back here afterward," he said.

"You have everything you need? I'm not sure when we'll get back."

She nodded. "I packed a few more things."

He opened her door and held it for her. It locked behind them. He had to respect her walls, even if it killed him. "Where do you hold your meetings?"

"At the office. We meet in the front room."

It was a short drive over to her office. Upstairs, Zaida made a pot of coffee and another pot of hot water in case anyone wanted tea. She looked over at Levi. He met her gaze. She broke contact first. What happened this afternoon had shaken her. She'd never been with someone like him, and that scared the hell out of her. Even now, though only a few dozen feet separated them, she wished he was closer, wished she had the right to stand next to him or hold his hand.

She felt as if she'd been steamrolled, and the worst was that she didn't know why she felt that way at all. Maybe because it was easier to be alone when you'd never been with someone you wanted to have in your life. But once you'd sampled paradise, not having it was torture.

When the coffee and water were brewing, she took a seat. He'd taken another pass through her office and now came back into the room. They exchanged looks, but didn't speak.

No one came early. No one came on time. No one came ten minutes late. No one came at all. This wasn't their regular night to meet, but Zaida had texted the group to come together tonight, that she had a conflict with keeping their next meeting date.

There was no RSVP system, though she had sent a reminder earlier about the changed date. Word had gotten out about Levi and his investigation. Finally, at a quarter after the hour, Zaida heard someone coming up the stairs.

One woman came in, carrying her large purse and wearing a hijab. Mina. She was one of Zaida's friends. She sometimes ran the groups. Mina gave Levi a quick look, then focused on Zaida. In Arabic, she said, "Hidaya gave me her laptop to give to you."

Zaida reached for it. "How did you get this?" She was torn about mentioning what had happened to Hidaya and Abdul. If Mina didn't already know, Zaida didn't want to scare her.

"She gave it to me this morning. She said you'd called everyone in, but she knew she couldn't make it —I don't know why. She asked if I was coming tonight." Mina looked at Levi again. "I wasn't going to, especially after hearing what happened here earlier. But then something happened to Hidaya and her brother. I don't know what—I've only heard rumors. I don't know what's going on, but I thought you might need this."

"Thank you. I do."

"What is going on, Zaida?"

"I don't know. Not all of it."

"Are we in danger?"

Zaida nodded. "Yes. Very possibly."

"Why? What have we done?"

"Nothing. Nothing at all. But that doesn't mean someone can't point the finger at us and blame us for things we haven't done."

"I'm tired of looking over my shoulder."

"Yes. We all are."

Mina nodded toward Levi. "Is he driving this?"

"No. He's trying to resolve it before it blows up into something much bigger."

"Zaida, tell your friend to keep her eyes open," " Levi said in English.

"For what?" Zaida asked.

"Anything. Anything at all."

Zaida relayed that info, though she needn't have. Mina was fluent in English. She gave Zaida a quick hug, then left. Levi took the laptop and plugged in the flash drive that his friend in Wyoming had given him. Zaida looked on nervously. What was he going to find? And what would it mean for Hidaya?

Levi's phone rang. "Go, Max... You sure? Okay... Uh-huh... I see... Thanks." He hung up, then sighed. "This is it. Ground zero for the worm."

"How do they know?" Zaida asked.

Levi shook his head. "Something about information it left behind. Stuff it harvested from your computer. He's following the threads to see what it did with that info. He said it was looking like a form of spyware. Was this your computer at one point?"

Zaida nodded. "I did some of my early writing on

it. Since it was just going to be used for translations, I thought it would still be fine for light usage."

"You let Hidaya work off-site?"

"Yes. She needed it for school. I didn't run this one through the literacy foundation that I did with the others. Hidaya and I have been friends for a long time. I just loaned it to her. Kind of permanently. Or at least, for as long as she needed it." Zaida crossed her arms. "What does all of this mean? Maybe Hidaya didn't know she released a worm."

"Maybe. What does her brother do?"

"He's a student at Colorado State."

"Majoring in…?"

"Computer science." She covered her mouth. "He didn't do this. He wouldn't, Levi."

"Okay. We can't jump to any conclusions. We know who and what, but not when or why. We only have a partial picture so far." Levi frowned at the computer. "You said Jamal said he had Hidaya and Abdul and was keeping them for their own safety, right?"

"Yeah. Maybe Abdul is one of his students."

"One of the things that I never understood was how an older version of one of your books was popping up in the terrorist camp in Syria. Was that version on this computer?"

"Yeah. I had some stuff on there that I never took off. Hidaya wouldn't have sent it to anyone. Why would she? Who would she send it to? I don't think she knows anyone from Syria. She and her family came from Iraq when she was a kid."

Levi's phone rang again. "Hold on, Max. I'm putting you on speaker. I have Zaida here with me. Go ahead." He closed the door to Zaida's office suite.

"Did some more digging into exactly what that worm was doing," Max said. "It's basically collecting certain information and passing it along to a database on a private server. That server wasn't hard to get into, but it also wasn't widely accessible to general users. You had to know what you were doing to get into it."

"So, what kind of data was it collecting?" Levi asked.

"The worm seems to be doing some analysis on whether the user of a computer is a potential Muslim terrorist," Max said. "It gathers info from emails, social media accounts, bank and credit card accounts, mortgage accounts. Basically, it evaluates all the info it can find and determines a terrorist quotient from one to ten. Anyone with a quotient of five or more gets their data sent to this server. Your girl's data is on that server. The worm gave her a terrorist quotient of seven."

Zaida gasped.

"Obviously, I need to do more analysis of what it's doing in order to really understand how those quotients are determined. Be advised that I'm likely not the only one who's been able to get in to this server. The worm began a month ago and has already traveled from the U.S., across Europe, gone through the Middle East, Far East, Russia, and has come back to the U.S. It also appears to have some ransom code that locks up a person's computer for a while, alerting them to the fact that they've been identified as a potential terrorist and ordering them to pay a fee to keep their info hidden. If anyone attempts to pay that fee, however, the link they're provided doesn't work. The database does keep track of those who click it. If people think your girl started this, well, she's made a world of enemies."

"Shit," Levi said. "What would make them think she started it?"

"Hers is the first record in the database. She's ground zero. Fun stuff. I'll get back to you soon." Max ended the call.

Levi stared at his phone for a long moment, then said, "I need to check in with my people." He made another call. This time, he didn't put it on speaker. "Commander, Jones here. We found the starting point of the Freedom Code worm. Zaida didn't start it—the computer wasn't in her control when it was set loose... Right... Jamal has tried twice now to take Zaida. He said he's got a brother and sister, friends of Zaida's, and is keeping them for their safety. No idea what he means by that. One of his students, Abdul Baqri, is the brother of the woman who had control of the computer when the worm was released."

Zaida listened while Levi and the commander, whoever that was, talked about what Max had discovered on the server connected to the worm code. "Zaida's stuff was in the database of content that had been scrapped from high-quotient computers. Hers was the first record stored. Max said it wasn't hard to get into the server and he likely wasn't the only one who had reverse-engineered the worm code to find that database. That explains why Zaida's early manuscript was found in the Syrian camp. And it explains why Mike Folsom had come back here to talk to her… It might explain why he was attacked, since the Syrians have friends here in the States following the same trail Mike was following… The FBI, huh? So Jamal's legit? Copy that…" Levi gave her a dark look. "Yes, sir. I'm out."

Levi's expression was frightening. He stood. Zaida watched him warily. "Jamal's working with the FBI. Commander Lambert's handing your parents over to him and his team."

"Will they be safe?"

"Yes. Lambert wants me to leave you with Jamal."

"No."

"I know where Jamal is. Let's go talk to him. You'll be able to see your parents and friends. Then we'll decide."

She caught Levi's arm. "He's already tried three times to take me."

"Only been twice. The men who broke into your place are confirmed terrorists."

Zaida wrapped her arms around her waist. That news was terrifying. She looked at Levi, realizing he was the only one she truly felt safe with. "Don't leave me with him. Please?"

"I need to see him to get a read on the situation. If I feel you're safe there, leaving you with him—and with your parents and friends—frees me up to go do some hunting. We'll decide it together. My contact said Jamal's working with the FBI on this. Makes me feel a lot better about him. And if he really does have your friends, then at least they're safe."

Zaida dumped the coffee and hot water she'd made for the group meeting. "If he has them, then who tossed their apartment? Did the FBI do that?"

"Good question."

Zaida faced Levi. "Just because Jamal's working with the FBI, doesn't mean he's all in with them. I don't trust him."

"Why not?"

"I know how single-minded he can be. With him, the means justify the end." She shut off the office lights as they went into the hall, then locked the door.

"But that doesn't include harming you, does it?"

She met his hard gaze. "It never has before. But then, there never was a time when people were dying all around me. I'm just saying something is not right with all of this."

13

Levi and Zaida drove across town and pulled into the parking lot of the Mountain Suites Hotel. They walked straight through the lobby, past a man in a suit who was reading a newspaper. Everything about him screamed Fed. He'd no doubt already reported their arrival up to his teammates in Jamal's rooms, but he didn't try to stop them.

They took the elevator to the fourth floor where another man greeted them. He didn't search either of them, but perhaps that would come in Jamal's rooms. Either that, or Lambert had cleared the way for him.

Their escort used his room key to open the door. The suite Jamal was in consisted of two rooms off a central living room and kitchen combination. The space was packed with people. The Hussans were there. As were Abdul and his sister. Plus Jamal and three agents.

Zaida hugged her parents, then went over to hug

her friends. Levi noted she only nodded at Jamal. Everyone was talking fast in Arabic; it was hard for Levi to keep up. Zaida's father came to greet him. His dark eyes were sharp. The distaste he felt for Levi was clearly broadcast by his expression and the rigid way he moved. Levi shook hands with him.

"So you're the farmer," Zaida's dad, Darim, said.

"Yes, sir."

"I expect you're treating my daughter well."

"He's been the complete gentleman, Father," Zaida said, coming to Levi's rescue.

"Mr. Jones." Rayna, Zaida's mom, followed her daughter over. "It's very nice to put a face to a voice." She held out her hand as she gave him the piercing look of a protective mother.

Jamal joined them. Levi and he exchanged hard looks. Levi tried to get a read from Jamal on what he was up to, but the professor carefully schooled his expression.

"Where are Zaida's things?" Jamal asked. "In the car?"

"She may not be staying," Levi said.

"You were ordered to leave her with us," Jamal said.

"It was a *suggestion*…and I haven't decided to take it or leave it. What I care most about is her safety."

"And I don't?" Jamal's eyes narrowed at the perceived slight.

"After I hear more of what's going on, I'll let you know her status."

Levi excused himself so he could go meet Abdul and Hidaya. They were young, earnest, and scared as hell. Hidaya wore a soft peach hijab and a long black dress. "Glad to see you're both safe. When we went by your apartment, it had been tossed."

Their frightened faces turned to Jamal then one of their FBI handlers. "We didn't toss it," one of the suits said. "You were there while we searched your place."

"I'd already given my computer to my friend to give back to Zaida," Hidaya said. "I'm sure that's what they were looking for."

The agent who'd spoken came over. "I'm Special Agent Jack Graham. Thanks for joining us," he said to Levi. "I'm glad for your help."

"Glad to be of help," Levi said, then walked over to the counter in the little kitchenette and leaned against it as he faced the room. "Jamal, bring me up to speed."

"What do you already know?" Jamal asked.

"I know that a spyware worm called Freedom Code was released into one of Zaida's old computers about a month ago," Levi said. "I know that worm makes threat assessments of the computer owner's potential for being a terrorist, terrorist supporter, or potential victim of one. I know that worm has circumnavigated the globe and has returned here to Colorado."

Levi looked at Abdul. "I suspect it's your pet project." He then looked at each of the FBI agents.

"And I suspect that your agency is highly interested in the worm's findings. I also know that the worm locks down computers it considers pose a significant threat, blocking that computer from being used for a period. This worm has made enemies around the world."

Abdul sighed. "I wrote it, yes, but I never intended to set it loose."

"It was my fault that happened," Hidaya said. "The worm was on a flash drive that I used on Zaida's old computer. I didn't know it was there at the time or I would never have done that. When I came to you, Zaida, I didn't know about any of this." She looked at her brother. "I didn't know you'd created such a thing."

Abdul nodded, looking upset with himself. "And I didn't realize Hidaya had taken my flash drive. We have several—they all look the same," he said. "One day, data started showing up on the server I'd set aside for the project."

"I thought you didn't intend to use the worm," Levi said. If he hadn't meant to release it into the world, why did he need a repository for its data?

"I didn't. It was my end-of-year project. I couldn't turn it in with only a theoretical construct. It was a practicum—I had to have a fully functioning prototype. I worked for months on the design with Dr. Abd al-Mukhtar. All of us in the course were working on interesting technical solutions to real-world problems. My project led a discussion about the ethics of such a project, why it couldn't be released without proper search warrants. We discussed as a class the data analysis I'd written the worm to perform. It was supposed to collect and analyze the social behavior and financial health of each person whose computer it visited in an attempt to identify people who had the psych profile of terrorists or who were at risk of being exploited by terrorists. For each computer it accessed, it gave a value of one to ten, ten being someone with a high probability of being an active terrorist, one being a non-threat. It didn't store information on anyone whose score was five or below. If someone was scored six or above, then the information the worm used to make its assessment was stored in the database I'd built. As it migrated from machine to machine, its understanding of threats versus non-threats improved. The worm was teaching itself."

"It was brilliant…and illegal as hell," Jamal said. "I read his code and his written analysis and was blown away. Nonetheless, I believed we were still in the realm of hypothetical—until the day Abdul came to me to tell me it had been released inadvertently. Already, a month had passed."

"I should have reported it sooner," Abdul agreed, "but I was scared. It ran through our community first, collecting info on Zaida and me and many others. I didn't want anyone to know that I had done this. I didn't even talk about it with Hidaya. But then I began to see some new data coming in, data that came from men in the Middle East and Africa, locations that I knew were terrorist hotbeds. They'd begun hacking the database. I had protections in there so that none of the data could be modified except by me. Above that, my system recorded any attempts at penetration from anyone who wasn't me." He looked around the room. "I didn't want any of my classmates to mess up my project. But when I began to see that it was getting attention—and returning results—from real terrorist groups, well, then I knew I had a serious problem on my hands. I went to Dr. Abd al-Mukhtar and told him everything."

Jamal nodded. "We immediately brought it up to the university, who reached out to the FBI."

"I had no fail-safes in the code, no way of stopping the worm once it was loose," Abdul said.

Hidaya leaned forward and covered her face as she started crying. "This is all my fault."

Zaida went over to comfort her.

"It isn't your fault, sister," Abdul said. "It's mine. I created the monster."

After working his share of cybercrime, Levi had come to believe coding was like modern wizardry. Everything now was dependent on it, from coffeemakers to fridges to cars. There were low levels of entry to the world of programming—anyone could do it; some failed, some succeeded, and some excelled. It was an open-access kind of thing, like giving magic wands out willy-nilly to people without regard for the danger they could do with their new tool.

Levi bent his head and rubbed his forehead. He

didn't know what the answer was to controlling the genie that was modern coding. Code itself was agnostic. It had no emotions, no loyalty, no inherent ethics. It could be used for good or evil. But when it was taught how to learn, how to improve itself, how to become more than it was when it was created, well, that was a whole realm of holy hell that humans were not ready for. And if terrorists were reverse-engineering code, learning its secrets, then they were also learning how to reproduce what it did.

"I believe one of the reasons the worm was so successful at what it does," Abdul said, "is because I didn't take a purely technical approach to it."

"Meaning?" Levi asked, almost afraid of the answer.

"I'd spent so much time on my computer science class that I'd gotten poor marks in my sociology class. I also had a year-end project in that class. I decided to make the code I'd written do double duty. You see, so many of us in the Muslim community are under extreme scrutiny. We are always considered guilty of being complicit with any violent behavior of radical factions around the world. I wanted my worm's analysis to show how that wasn't at all the case. I wanted it to give us our freedom. Hidaya told me about Zaida's Freedom Code. This was mine."

"So that's why you called it the same thing," Zaida said.

Abdul nodded. "I worked with my sociology professor to frame out the behavioral profiling that might intrigue intelligence communities even as it exonerated those of us who are innocent." He sighed. "Both professors gave me top marks for my project. And now look what I've done. I've broken the world. I've put my friends and family in jeopardy. I've done the very thing my community was afraid I would do—bring it harm. I can't...I can't make this right."

"The truth is," Jack said, "the information you inadvertently captured has put us ahead of several bad actors in the war on terrorism. I would expect there might be some type of amnesty the government can offer you, your professors, and the university in exchange for the cooperation you're providing and the help you've given our intelligence communities."

The room fell into momentary silence as everyone absorbed Abdul's story.

"Mr. Jones, you're...a farmer, right?" Jamal said, breaking the silence. He sent the agents in the room a glance. "I think you're out of your league here. Leave this to the experts. They don't need you underfoot."

Levi never let that hit show in his expression. "I am a farmer. And I'm also a concerned citizen. While all of you huddle here in this room talking about safety, I'll be out there ensuring our safety."

None of the agents backed Jamal up, which flustered the professor. Levi supposed Lambert had carved a space for him on the team. Whatever the cause, Levi took the latitude offered him. "Tell me about the Facebook posts you've been making recently," he said to Abdul.

"They're not from me. I've been hacked. Even now, I'm locked out of my account."

"Uh-huh. So who's been making them?" Levi asked, not convinced.

Abdul gave Jamal a pained look. "There are some kids in my class I don't get along with. They hate Muslims, people of color, Jews, anyone who's different from them. I know for a fact they belong to an off-campus group of white nationalists."

Jamal frowned. "You didn't tell me this."

"I didn't want more drama than I'd already created," Abdul said. "The worm hit their computers and identified them as Muslim terrorists. Their info was in the worm's database and I recognized their names."

"So there's an error in your profiling code," Levi said.

"No. Maybe not," Abdul said. "Not if they were doing a lot of research on Islam or were writing social media posts about hating Muslims or Jews. Or researching and preparing the texts they posted on my Facebook account—all of that would have looked the same to the worm."

"These kids are terrible," Hidaya said. "They've attacked him, physically, several times. Abdul went to the hospital after two of these encounters. They were getting worse, too, before he went to Dr. Abd al-Mukhtar."

"They wanted me to give them access to the database, but I wouldn't," Abdul said. "I said no. I said it over and over. And then they hacked my Facebook and Instagram accounts."

"These neo-Nazis and the Tahrir al-Sham groups have put out calls summoning their people to get to Fort Collins this week," Jack said.

Levi frowned. "Why this week?"

"The county fair kicks off Friday," Jack said.

"Aw, hell. That's two days from now."

Zaida gasped. "I've rented a booth there. I'll be selling my books and promoting the women's literacy foundations I'm associated with." She sent a worried glance toward her parents. "I'm also giving a talk there."

Shitballs. That was not news Levi wanted to hear. "All right. Let's lay this out again so we're all on the same page. Abdul created a worm that Hidaya inadvertently let loose. It crawled through…thousands of computers?" He looked to Jamal for confirmation.

"Millions," Jamal said.

"Millions of computers," Levi continued. "It's identified some local and some international groups of interest. We have confirmation that Tahrir al-Sham has activated some of its cells here in the U.S. And Jamal has twice tried to take Zaida."

"For her own well-being," Jamal interjected. "I wanted her here with us, safe."

Levi gave him a hard look. "Let's give you the benefit of the doubt. Tahrir al-Sham has tried for her once. Abdul has made enemies of some seriously bad actors. As has Zaida, since she's record number one in the worm's database. Now we have the impending threat of some unknown activity, perhaps in retaliation for the worm, that's due to happen during the county fair." He looked at the special agent. "That sound like a fair summary?"

"Yup," Jack said. "If we're going to stop this, we have to figure out what they have planned for the fair, and who's doing what."

Rayna grasped her daughter's hand. "This is unacceptable. You are in so much danger. You need to cancel your appearances at the fair."

Zaida sent Levi an intense look. "Should I?"

"Possibly." Levi nodded. "The whole fair may have to be canceled. But we still have time to take this op down. Going into hiding is not gonna stop this ball from rolling right into the fair. For one, terrorists are looking for any gathering of U.S. citizens where their impact can be the greatest. To that end, they've already been triggered."

"That's not all that's happening at the fair," Jamal said. "Some of my students are running a fundraiser booth for the robotics lab."

"It's a drone rental booth," Abdul said. "There was a sign-up sheet the last month of classes. When those skinheads saw that my friends and I had volunteered to run the booth, they said they didn't want to have anything to do with us, that we tainted everything."

Levi frowned. "You think the skinheads know the Tahrir al-Sham cells have been called up? Could they be working together? Or plotting independently of each other?"

"Great question," Jack said. "Did these white nationalists in your class ever actually get in to your database?" Levi asked Abdul. "You'd said they were roughing you up for access…"

"They did, last week," Jamal said.

"But I have code that they haven't cracked prohibiting edits to the database," Abdul said. "All they did was read it. Maybe copy it."

"In fact," Jamal said, "the code that tracks who hacks his worm was put in place to help focus attention on which of the terrorist groups the worm identified who were the most technologically savvy. These are especially dangerous bad actors. They're the groups who have the skill to hack things like our power grids, banks, medical systems, and other high-profile targets."

"So, if these two groups aren't working together, are we looking at a battle at the fair?" Levi asked. "A rumble between the Tahrir al-Sham and these neo-Nazis? Or are the white nationalists setting themselves up to protect the fair to curry favorable public sentiment?"

Jack scoffed at that. "Since when have white supremacists protected anything but their own twisted beliefs? No, I'm sure they want to spread their terror as badly as Tahrir al-Sham does. And if they can take out Zaida and Abdul in the same op, even better."

"We know that Tahrir al-Sham operatives are in

town. Have we seen an influx of the white nationalists?" Levi asked.

Jack nodded. "We've been getting reports from the sheriff's office that a larger number than usual are coming in. They're keeping a low profile, however."

"Have there been permits pulled for a protest or anything during the fair?" Levi asked.

"No," Jack said.

Levi lifted his hands. "Right. We got two days to figure this out. We need to work together. I'll share any info I discover. I expect the same courtesy from you."

"Agreed," Jack said.

"And I want Zaida's info removed from the worm's database," Levi said to Abdul. "You left the door open to the server. Every time one of our enemies decides to investigate who's looking at them, they're going to see her info as ground zero, keeping her a target for a whole bunch of bad guys." Levi looked at the agents. "In fact, by now I'm sure you've investigated everyone the worm reported. Take out all the innocent civilians. I don't care if you make shit up to replace it, or just leave the bad guys in there and let them fight it out, but get the civilians out of there fast."

"I will, Mr. Jones," Abdul said.

Levi straightened. "Great. We're outta here."

"No," Jamal said. "Go get Zaida's things from your car."

Zaida stood, as did her parents. She gave them

both a hug and a kiss. "I'm not staying, Jamal," she announced.

"Of course you're staying with us, daughter," her father said, a stern expression on his face. "You will be safer here."

"It was my computer that started all of this. I need to help resolve it."

"That is a foolish excuse to throw yourself into danger," her mother said. "Leave this to the experts."

"Zaida," Jamal said, gripping her arm, "you are not leaving this suite."

Levi read the panic on her face. Until he saw that, he'd been inclined to make her stay. "Actually, she has to come with me. If the bad guys watching her don't see her do at least some of her normal routine, they'll know something's up. We can't risk throwing them off. Not yet, anyway."

Zaida pulled free of Jamal and her parents and moved to stand beside Levi.

"Thanks, everyone. This helped a lot." Levi looked at Abdul and his sister. "I'm glad you're safe." His gaze took in Zaida's parents as well. "All of you. Shouldn't be but a few more days. Stay calm and stay focused. If you think of anything else, let me know. And like I said I'll be keeping you informed," he told Jack.

Jamal's dark eyes were blazing. "Where are you going to be?"

"Around town," Levi answered. "Your agents have my address, if it's needed. So do the Hussans."

Because Levi knew it rankled Jamal, he took Zaida's hand and drew her toward the door. An agent opened it for them.

She looked up at him when they were in the hall heading toward the elevators. "Thank you for not leaving me there."

Levi faced her while they waited for the elevator car. "Look, I don't want to come between you and Jamal. Or you and the plans your family has for you."

"There's nothing between Jamal and me. I've made that clear to him, but he isn't getting the message. And my parents don't get to decide my future, though they would like to."

"Okay." The cab arrived. Levi held the door open for her. Inside, she reached for his hand. They hadn't exactly communicated very well since this afternoon. Something had upset her, but Levi was damned if he knew what it was. Maybe things had just gotten hot too fast. He was going to have to be patient and follow her lead. The female psyche was complex; he didn't have a fucking chance in hell of making sense of it, but if she took comfort in holding his hand, then he'd count that as a mark in his favor.

They got to his Jeep without incident and went about a mile down the street before pulling over in an office complex's empty parking lot.

"I need to make a call," Levi said. He took the keys and left the car, moving away about ten feet. Zaida got out and stood at the end of the Jeep, watching him.

He called Max. "Go, Levi."

"You might want to make a copy of the Freedom Code database. It's about to get corrupted."

"Already did it."

"Great. The cult you guys are after is a white supremacist one, right?"

"It is. I'm a little busy with my woman right now. Can we pick this up in the morning?"

"Aw, shit. Sorry. Yeah, I'm out." Levi hung up. Next he dialed Lambert.

"You know what fucking time it is?" Lambert said.

Lambert was on the East Coast, two hours ahead of Colorado. "What, you only work daylight hours, commander? Go you."

Lambert sighed. "What do you have?"

Levi updated him with the info he'd gotten at the meeting tonight. "I know your people have had a look at that database. Better grab a copy soon; it's about to get corrupted. I told them to get Zaida's info, as well as that belonging to any other regular Joe, out of there, since everyone seems to be helping themselves to that shit. We don't need civilians becoming targets. If they don't clean it up, Max will."

"You're racking up a big bill with Owen Tremaine."

"You shoulda hired a hacker for this op, not straight muscle. You know we never went on an op without a full complement of resources. I called in what I needed."

"Need I remind you you're a lone operator now?"

"If you're gonna fucking micromanage me, commander, you can have the job back. But I'm keeping Zaida."

"That how it is? You got your head and dick tangled up?"

"No. I learned tonight that we're looking at trouble not only from the Tahrir al-Sham faction, but also from a local white supremacist group that got spotted by the worm. We suspect something's going down at the county fair this weekend. Zaida has a booth at the fair and is giving a talk. Abdul, the worm's creator, is manning a robotics rental booth for the university. They'll both be targets. I don't know if the skinheads are buddying up with Tahrir al-Sham, or if they're both planning independent attacks. I'll let you know when I figure that out. I couldn't have gotten this far without Max's help, so pay Owen's bill when it comes."

"Copy that. Keep me in the loop."

"Roger. I'm out." He walked back to the Jeep.

Zaida was still standing there, frowning at him. "You're keeping me?"

"I'm keeping you outta trouble." Levi pocketed his phone. "Look. We're dealing with hackers, some pretty serious ones. My phone's secure, but my Jeep's computer and comm systems aren't. Until we get this issue resolved, let's not talk about it in the car. Before tonight's meeting, I didn't realize what calibre of coders we were dealing with."

"You think they would hack your car?" Her eyes were wide.

"Sure." His teams had done it in the past. "Anything connected to a network and run by code can be hacked. Easy as shit. Your fridge, your computer, your home security, your TV's cameras, your remote controllers." He hooked a thumb over his shoulder. "The cameras on this office building. Even your ereader. Anything. At any time. There's very little security a good hacker can't crack."

They got inside his car and continued down the road, heading toward Levi's place.

"I hate knowing that," Zaida said, rubbing her upper arms. "There's nothing I can do about it, but now I feel like everything is watching me. Like spiders all around me."

"Good. Because you *are* being watched. Add to that everything you do online, your social media footprint, your Google searches, your convos with your home assistant devices, the DNA results you bought just for shits and giggles, anything about you that exists digitally—all of it makes for a very rich profile that can be used for or against you, as Abdul's worm demonstrates."

"I don't like that."

"There are no secrets anymore, that's for sure."

14

Though it was late when they got back to his house, Levi busied himself with some maintenance tasks he needed to do for the plants in his greenhouse. He could have put it off, but the work helped him think. And, truthfully, he was a bit of a coward.

Zaida had shut him out after their encounter this afternoon. He didn't know why, but he certainly wanted to give her a little room. He wondered if she regretted being with him. She hadn't seemed to at the time, but add in everything else that had happened—meeting up with Jamal, seeing her terrified friends, learning the FBI was involved in all of this, then Jamal ordering her to stay with him instead of leaving with Levi—well, none had been easy on her; a little time alone to process everything couldn't hurt.

It had been a relief to learn that Jamal had been truly acting for her benefit. Perhaps she regretted being intimate with Levi now that Jamal had been cleared. Hard to tell. Zaida was a sensitive, amazing woman. Levi just needed to give her room to deal with the maelstrom that had taken over her ordered life.

When he came back into the house, he got ready for bed, then checked on Zaida. Her room was dark, but the door was open. In fact, lights had been dimmed in the kitchen and living room, too. He walked past her room, peeking in to see if she was sleeping.

She wasn't. She was sitting up in the middle of her bed, leaning against the wall, her knees bent to her chest. He leaned against her doorjamb. "Can't sleep?"

"I'm a night person."

"And I've been rushing you along each morning. Tomorrow's not going to be any different. You know, it's usually easier to sleep when you're stretched out and relaxed."

She reached next to her and dug her fingers into Beau's soft fur. "Your dog's trying to help me relax."

"What's keeping you up, Zaida?"

"What isn't?"

Levi chuckled. He walked into her room, then climbed on her bed, sitting next to her. "Talk to me." He leaned back against the wall. Their shoulders touched, but he kept his hands folded in his lap. "Do you want me to take you back to Jamal?"

"Jamal?" Zaida rumpled her face as she looked up at Levi.

"He wanted you to stay with him."

"I slept with him, you know…before."

"Oh?"

"Yeah. That's why I don't like him in that way."

"Oh." He couldn't help his grin. "That good, huh?"

"Sex is like a metaphor for what married life would be like. His marriage would be all about him. It's one of the reasons I'm a big advocate of premarital sex."

"How'd I do?"

She looked up at him and blinked. "You gutted me."

"What?" Levi was shocked. "How?"

"You were wonderful. Everything I ever wanted. Everything. And I'm scared to death I'm falling in love with you. I have this awful feeling about us."

"What kind of feeling?"

"Like I want to vomit."

"So I make you sick." Levi knew he was arching a brow at her.

"No. I do."

He took her hand in his. "Baby, I'm having a real hard time following you."

"What if…what if I fall in love with you—and I mean real love, not just lust—and then we just separate when this is done?"

Levi sighed, rocked by the fact that she'd been feeling the same terror he'd been fighting. He wrapped his arm around her and pulled her up against his chest. "What if we fall in love during this horrible event and stay together afterward? It could go either way."

"Are you feeling what I'm feeling?"

"I'm scared of losing you…now that I've found you," he said.

"Yes. That's it. Just exactly."

Levi kissed her forehead. "What if we don't label this—whatever it is—just yet? What if we just let it be what it will be while we discover each other?"

"Because I'm clingy and needy and extremely possessive."

"That's hot as fuck, you know. I would love to matter to someone."

"You matter to me, Levi."

He grinned. "You matter to me, Zaida."

"I think Jamal thought, up until now, that I would change my mind and go back to him."

"So did you date for a while?"

"No. Not really. There was just always that assumption that we'd be together. And then I saw him with adult eyes and knew he wasn't for me."

"And he's a sucky fucker."

Zaida chuckled at that, then broke into big laughs that made him laugh. He hadn't meant to say it like that, but he was tired and his words had tangled.

"Yes. He's a sucky fucker. I love that. Next time I see him, I'll think of that and laugh."

"It's a relief knowing why he was trying to grab you."

"You believe him?" she asked.

Levi shrugged. "I do."

"So, we're just going to matter to each other for a while?" she asked.

"Why not? At least until one of us is ready to call it."

"Call it what?"

"Call it what it is. Love."

She gasped and turned so she was lying across his chest. "You said it first."

He grinned. "That's 'cause I'm braver than you."

She got serious and touched his cheek with her fingertips. "I'm really scared about this."

"Don't be. Love is easy. You should know. You're an expert in it."

"In *fiction*. Not real life. I'm such a poser. I've never been in love before. Have you?"

He put his knees up so she could lean against them. "Yes. Twice. Both times I thought something was real, but it was just a passing thing."

"What happened to the latest one?"

"She was in the intelligence business. Got in too deep on a case. She was murdered when she tried to get out."

"Was she the real deal?"

"I think so. She could have been."

"I'm sorry, Levi. That's a hard loss to take."

He nodded. "She's why I got out of the service, why I switched to farming."

"And yet here you are, back in the thick of things."

"Kinda hard not to roll toward it, when so much is at stake."

"Are you going to keep doing these cases?"

"I don't know. The money's good. I'm still something of an adrenaline junky. I want the world to be a better place. It's nice to be needed by my country. And I don't like innocents like you, your family, and your community getting dragged into danger."

Zaida sighed. For a long moment, they just sat there in the dark and silence.

"We better get some sleep. Will you stay with me?" she asked.

"You know it. Let me just go shut things off." They both got out of bed. He held up the covers for her then called Beau out of the room and ordered him to sleep on the sofa. He locked the front and back doors and shut off the lights, then joined her under the covers.

The twin bed, though extra long, was way too narrow for them to sleep in any position other than their sides. Or her on top of him, which worked too. She settled her head on his chest. She was quiet a long moment, but then he heard her whisper, "I love your flowers, Levi."

"I love them too." Only it wasn't his flowers he was responding to. He'd fallen off the deep end for

Zaida. If she wasn't who he thought she was, it was going to fucking kill him.

∼

It was early the next morning, not yet eight a.m., when the rumble of a Harley cut into the quiet summer morning. Levi had already made a partial tour of his lot, checking the irrigation flowing to his sunflowers. They were drought- and heat-tolerant, but they needed a good supply of water for another month or so before he let them start to cure.

He'd made a quick breakfast of scrambled eggs, bacon, and fruit. Zaida was already up and moving around, which was good because he had a lot of ground to cover that day.

The Harley triggered Levi's motion sensors. He went outside with Beau to see who'd arrived. His dog barked and ran down the stairs as Max shut off his engine. He wore a loose beige T-shirt and a leather vest that was inside out. He reached down and rubbed Beau's head, then grinned at Levi. Geez, the guy looked crazier every time Levi saw him.

"Thought they kept you chained to your desk," Levi said.

"Usually, but we need to talk."

Levi went down the front stairs and shook hands with the hacker. "Want something to eat? Just made breakfast."

"Sure."

The screen door slammed. Levi turned to see Zaida standing there, wearing a silky floral robe that was only partially on one shoulder. Her hair was a sexy mess. She looked like she'd just come from a tumble in bed.

Levi wished that had been the case.

"Hi, Max," she said, frowning into the morning sun.

Max arched a brow at Levi, then gave her a quick nod. "Zaida."

Beau ran up the stairs to greet her. She bent over and scratched his ears, entirely unaware of the luscious view she gave the two of them. "I'm just going to take a quick shower, Levi. Don't wait breakfast for me."

"Yes, ma'am," Levi said, wishing like hell that Max had picked another time to show up. "C'mon in," he said to Max. They got their food and coffee, then brought it back outside to the picnic table.

"This is quite the place you have here," Max said. "You got a thing for flowers, huh?"

"Yeah. And I grow herbs for local restaurants. It's a fairly steady living."

"Moonlighting helps."

"Sure does. Speaking of which, what brings you here?" Levi asked.

"Zaida's out of that database."

"Good."

"I went back through it, I found a group of students at the university who are skinheads."

"That's what I wanted to talk to you about last night. Abdul said he was being harassed by some of those kids," Levi said. "They knew about his worm because he had a few of them in his class. When they weren't able to hack its repository, they roughed him up a few times—bad enough he went to the hospital. When he didn't cave, they hacked his Facebook feed to plant some jihadist shit. What if that damned worm stirred things up among the skinheads? We know it froze the computers of everyone who met its profiling requirements and alerted them that they'd been identified as potential terrorists. Maybe that triggered them, kicked these kids into gear to fight back."

"That's my theory. I was going to check them out. Wanna come?"

"You bet...but first I want to have a look at the fairgrounds and Abdul's robotics lab. I hear something may be going down at the county fair. Abdul—the kid who wrote the worm—is manning a robotics booth at the fair. And Zaida's got a booth, too. I have a feeling we're headed toward something bad." He frowned as he looked at Max. "You know, when I asked for some of your time, I didn't mean for you to be hands-on."

"Well, too late. We've been investigating a cult. They're not like a regular cult. These guys are organized and they're big. They've infiltrated international governments, compromised CEOs, own half the world's glitterati. And they're a white supremacist group. They're sophisticated, rich, and dangerous.

Long before I joined the Army's Red Team, this cult tricked me into hacking some high-profile Wall Street accounts. I was caught, went to jail. I was just a kid, barely eighteen. For my own self-preservation, I hooked up with a prison gang the cult owns called the White Kingdom Brotherhood. The connections I made in jail were what drove the Red Team to recruit me. The WKB population not incarcerated runs drugs and weapons and acts as the enforcers for the cult. I'm a member of their club." Max hooked his thumbs in the arms of his cuts. "I've maintained my membership for my team's investigation. I came down to check out this group and see if they are affiliated with the cult we're tracking."

"What's your cult called?"

"The Omni World Order. Nasty SOBs."

Levi leaned back and gave Max a long look. "I never knew that about you, that you went to jail. We met when you were on the Red Team. Never gave a thought about your background or what brought you to the service. I made all the choices that led me to this spot; I chose to join the Navy, chose to try out for the SEAL teams, chose to stay in as long as I did, chose to get out when I did, chose this as my second career. You…were created. You didn't freely choose anything."

Max glared into Levi's eyes before slowly lowering the mug he was holding.

Jesus. Levi knew better than to reach into a man's soul and pull out his guts. "Forget it."

"It's true." Max shrugged. "At least up until I joined the Red Team. From there out, my choices have been my own. I'm cool with where I ended up. I'm loving what I'm doing now. I guess it worked out. I lost every fucking thing I loved, but I'm alive. I got my woman, a team I care about, work that's challenging."

"Good." Levi sighed. "It's not like we get out of this alive, anyway."

Max's faced eased. "Yeah. We should just march through it like fucking flamethrowers."

Levi grinned. "That's what I'm thinking."

Max pulled something from his pocket. "Brought this for your girl. All of us at our team headquarters wear one. The panic button alerts us to any problems. If Zaida gets taken, we'll be able to track her. Owen's loaning you two of his team—Selena and Ace. They're badass. They'll keep Zaida safe."

Levi took the necklace and stared at it. "When I put out a call for help, I didn't mean to make my problems yours."

"No big deal. We're all in the same fight, no? If we get in a bind, I'm sure you'll help us. Speaking of which, you should talk to Owen when this is done. He's always looking for guys like you. Wouldn't be bad to have a few frogmen on the team."

Levi chuckled. "I got all I can handle here. I'm not looking for a permanent gig, but thanks. These one-off jobs I get are enough for me." He paused. "I'm trying to make them enough, anyway." He held up the security necklace. "Thanks for this. I'm gonna round up Zaida so we can head out."

"Leave your phone with me," Max said.

"Why?"

"So I can install the app that goes with that necklace."

Levi handed over his phone. "If you want more coffee, help yourself. We'll just be a minute."

Max grinned. "I got all day."

Levi returned his grin, knowing Max probably meant the opposite. Inside the house, the scent of Zaida's body soap teased the senses. Levi set the dishes on the counter, then went and knocked on Zaida's door.

"You about ready?" he asked.

She opened the door. She wore a pair of tight jeans with a loose, rose-colored V-neck cotton sweater over a beige tank top. Her hair and makeup were done. Her feet were bare, which made her seem super short. He'd gotten used to her in heels.

"Almost."

Levi handed her the security necklace. "I know it's not pretty to look at, but it will let us find you fast if you go missing. Just hit this button if you have an emergency when I'm not around. Max said he and his team all wear one."

She draped it over her head, then adjusted her hair and slipped the flat plastic under her tank top. "Thank you."

"I'm going to drop you at your apartment while Max and I go check some things out."

Zaida's eyes widened. "Maybe it would be better if I joined my parents for the day?"

"You'll be safe. Owen Tremaine's loaning us a couple of his operatives through the weekend. They'll be with you today at your apartment. You can get some work done. Get ready for your presentation this weekend. Rest. Whatever."

"Do you think I'll be able to go forward with my presentation?"

"I hope so."

She held his gaze a long moment, then nodded. "Okay."

"Pack your stuff up. You may be staying at your place for a few days."

"What about you?"

"I'll be with you at night."

Her eyes locked on his. He knew she was waiting for a promise that everything would be fine. He couldn't say that—not yet, anyway.

"Okay," she finally said, with a nod.

"Okay." Levi stared down at her, wishing they didn't have to rush today, wondering if—when this was over—they'd get a chance to explore this thing between them. He left her doorway and went to the kitchen to quickly clean it up. He refreshed Beau's big upside-down water jug and made sure the timed feeder was full.

Levi's go bag was already packed. He took it out

to his Jeep. Beau followed him from the house to the car. "Sorry, boy. You're staying here to guard things for me. Mrs. Nolan will be over to check on you a few extra times over the next few days."

Max heard that and shook his head. "What is it about people and dogs? They always seem to think their dogs speak human."

"Don't they?"

"They speak dog," Max said.

Levi shrugged. "Whatever. You're clearly a nonbeliever, so I got nothing to say to you."

Max laughed and put his helmet on. "I'm going ahead. I want to check a few things out."

The roar of Max's bike drowned out Levi's answer, so he waved instead. He took Beau inside. Zaida was ready with her bags. She wore high-heel sandals that had wide brown leather straps across the top of her feet. Why that gave Levi a hard-on, he didn't know. And really, it didn't matter, because everything about her had that effect on him.

"Ready?" he asked.

"I am," she said. "Will we be coming back here?"

"Maybe not for a while, but when this is done, I sure as fuck hope so."

She smiled at him, her lips shiny and pink. Levi let out a quiet sigh. Maybe Lambert had been right: he had gotten his head and his dick tangled up. He grabbed her satchels and led her to the front door. She paused briefly to say goodbye to Beau.

Fuck Max. Beau did understand. His pup actually looked sad.

"Later, boy. Be good for Mrs. Nolan," Levi said as they left.

~

MAX WAS in the atrium of the apartment building when Levi and Zaida entered. Several men took note of Levi walking with Zaida. He would have smiled, but he was too focused on making sure there were no threats in the area.

When they got to Zaida's apartment, there was a tall woman already in there. Selena. Levi recognized her from his visit to their headquarters in Wyoming. She had long, dark brown hair, and green eyes. She was wearing a pair of slim jeans, hiking boots, an army-green safari type jacket, and a white T-shirt. She was the lone female who'd made it into the Red Team. No small feat.

He offered her his hand. "Levi Jones," he said.

"Selena." She looked at Zaida. "You must be Ms. Hussan."

"Zaida's fine." The two shook hands.

"Great. Ace and I will be your shadows until this thing is resolved," Selena said.

"Thank you," Zaida said. "Really. I can't thank you enough. But I hate that you're in danger because of me."

Selena lifted a slim brow. "Are you planning on harming us?"

"No."

"Then we aren't in danger because of you. We're in danger because of the bad guys hunting you, bad guys who are going down—hard—very soon." Selena followed that with a happy smile, one that gave Levi a chill. Female fighters always set him on edge, especially beautiful ones like this one. Yeah, he was old school, believing women should be the soft side of humanity, wonderful beings that needed protection and care…even as he knew how effective they were as fighters—decisive, accurate, and deadly.

"Is Ace here?" Levi asked. Just as he spoke, Zaida's front door opened and closed, admitting a purple-haired woman who was short, skinny, pierced, and feral looking. Her lipstick and eyeshadow matched her hair. Damn. Owen employed a fucking fairy. But if he'd sent her over, she had to be as lethal as Selena.

"You must be Ace," Levi said. He introduced himself and Zaida. "I think it's best, Zaida, if you keep to your routine. Make sure you take Ace or Selena with you anytime you leave the apartment—just stay in this building."

"I agree," Ace said. "Our guy back in ops, Greer, has a handle on the building's security. He'll know if anyone else is in and watching us."

"Good," Levi said. That made him feel much better.

"And we got the keys to Kelan's place if we need to bug out," Selena said.

Ace smiled at Selena. "We need to go check his place out. For security reasons. Besides, he's had it for how long and he's never asked us over?"

Selena laughed. "We can take a field trip…when it works for Zaida."

Zaida sent Levi a perplexed look. He held his hand out and had her walk him to the door. Working a isolated career as an author, she knew nothing about team dynamics. The girls were probably going to TP Kelan's place.

"When will you be back?" she asked.

"That's unclear. I'll stay here tonight, though," Levi said.

She nodded, then caught his forearm and leaned up to kiss his cheek. "Be safe."

"Don't you know the good guys always win?"

Zaida nodded. "They do in my world. Can I connect to the internet?"

"Sure."

"What about my parents?"

"I'm going to see them in a few minutes. Max and I are headed over to grab Abdul. I'll let them know the plan. You can call them. If you like, tomorrow I can take you to see them. Maybe you could spend the day with them."

Her expression twinkled. "I feel like I'm in Zaida daycare."

He pulled her into his arms. "It's the care of

someone who is important, someone the world needs to have alive. Put this out of your mind. You must have looming deadlines to meet."

"I do."

"So forget about the chaos and focus on your work."

She nodded. "Thank you. I don't know where I'd be if it weren't for you."

"You'd be bunking with your mother, thinking of all the ways your life was fucked."

She laughed. "My mother's really not that bad. We're very close."

"Good." He kissed her forehead. "I'll call when I'm headed back here."

∼

"If you got things here," Ace said to Selena, "I think I'll go watch things downstairs."

Selena winced. "Maybe I should go. You kinda stand out." She waved a hand over her face and hair.

Ace shook her head. "No, I don't. I'm so camouflaged. No one looks at punks. We scare them. Those fucking terrorists especially will not lower themselves to observing me since I'm such an aberration to them."

"Okay. Bring back lunch," Selena said.

Zaida hurried to her purse and took out a couple of twenties. "Here. Get whatever."

Ace pushed her hand away. "Forget it. It's in our per diem. Owen'll bill for it."

"Bill who?" Zaida asked.

Ace shrugged. "Whoever's running Levi's op."

Zaida looked from Ace to Selena and back. "I think it may be the CIA."

"Could be," Ace said.

"But they aren't supposed to operate on U.S. soil," Zaida said.

"Yeah, and bad guys aren't supposed to invade a woman's home or blow up a county fair or be fucking terrorists in the first place." Ace shrugged. "It is what it is, and we do what we do to stop it. Sometimes, the lines get blurred."

Zaida had never had she seen such fierce women. Their bravery was what she wanted for all the women she worked with. They were tough, resilient, and perfectly capable of never being a victim of a man's cruelty… Or had she read them wrong? Maybe it was a man's cruelty that had hardened them into the women they were now.

Ace left. Selena went over to look out the windows, gently pushing aside an edge of the curtains she'd drawn.

"I guess I'll get to work." Zaida started for the hallway but stopped. "Selena, will you and Ace be at the fair this weekend?"

"You bet."

"Good. I want several of my friends to meet you both."

15

Levi texted Max that he was headed out. He became aware of the Harley Panhead following him a few blocks away from Zaida's apartment. When they got to the hotel where Zaida's parents were staying, they parked next to each other.

"What's the plan?" Max asked as they crossed the parking lot.

"I want to walk the fair site. Then we go to the robotics lab so I can check out the drones Abdul will be renting in his booth."

Max stopped. "You know the fair site is going to be highly secured. They'll be checking purses and backpacks, taking dogs through the lines and the booths. They'll have blockades up to keep cars from plowing into the crowds. Just about the only way that place can be breached is via drone."

"That's what I was thinking," Levi said. "The

skinheads in Abdul's robotics class made a big deal about distancing themselves from the guys running the drone booth, which calls attention to their focus on the drones."

They continued into the hotel and up to the room where everyone was. The door opened before they knocked. Levi introduced Max.

Rayna hurried over to him. "Why didn't you bring my daughter?"

"She needed to get some work done. And she wanted to work on her speech," Levi said.

"But how could you leave her alone?"

"I didn't. She's with two armed guards."

Rayna wasn't happy about that. "Men she doesn't know? It was bad enough she was with you unchaperoned."

"They're female fighters. Trust me, she's safe with them."

Darim came over and put an arm around Rayna's shoulders, drawing her away. His dark eyes were no warmer than they'd been yesterday. Levi couldn't blame him. No father wanted his daughter to be the target of terrorists.

"You guys ready to go?" Levi asked Abdul and Jack.

"I'm going with you," Jamal announced.

"Suit yourself," Levi said as he turned and headed for the door. In the parking lot, Jamal told Abdul to ride with Jack.

The drive across town from the hotel to the site of

the county fair took only fifteen minutes…fifteen minutes filled with Jamal's barely suppressed rage.

"Got something on your mind, Jamal?" Levi asked.

"You know I do."

"Spit it out," Levi said.

"I want you to leave Zaida alone." Jamal said through clenched teeth.

"I don't think that's any of your business."

"In my culture, when a man touches an unmarried woman, he's claiming her."

"So?"

"You held her hand yesterday."

Levi sent Jamal a quick look. "It is a nice hand to hold."

Jamal banged his fist on the armrest of the passenger door. "She is not yours to touch."

"Says who?"

"She's been promised to me since we were kids."

"But you're not kids any longer. If she wanted to be married to you, she would have been…certainly by now, anyway."

"I am giving you only one warning."

"Jamal, look, don't do this. You won't win. You don't get to decide Zaida's future. Only she does. Let her make her choice."

"You're just a new toy. She'll tire of you fast."

Levi chuckled as he remembered his and Zaida's convo about Jamal being a sucky fucker. "Then she can have me until she's tired of me. But trust me, that won't be anytime too soon."

"You and I will never be friends," Jamal snarled. "I will see to it that her parents will never accept you."

"Do what you have to do."

Levi turned off the highway. He almost felt sorry for Jamal, losing the woman he loved to a man he considered unworthy. Levi parked and Jamal jumped out of the Jeep, slamming the door behind him.

That much frustrated desire wasn't good. What if that worm hadn't been released by Hidaya as everyone thought? What if Jamal had done it? What if Jamal had intended the worm to endanger Zaida so that she'd have no one to turn to but him?

Max rode into the parking lot and stopped next to Levi. Jamal had already gone on to walk with Jack and Abdul. Max took off his helmet and looked from Jamal back to Levi. "S'up?"

Levi told him the crazy new thought he'd had.

Max let out a grunt as he thought it through. "It's possible. You got your digital footprint locked down? 'Cause I can lock it down for you. Jamal has the skills needed to make your life miserable."

"I'm good. This ain't my first cyber-rodeo. I've learned a thing or two along the way. You know Mike Folsom? The CIA agent who got beheaded in Boulder? We were friends. Cybercrimes were his specialty."

"I wondered about that," Max said. "Sorry to hear you lost a friend."

Levi remembered the day he lost Julia, too. You didn't take on this line of work without expecting those types of losses. He just wished the hurt dulled over time.

They walked over to join the other three just as two other men came up to the group; Walter Harris, the manager of the event grounds, and Steve Wheeler from the county fair organization met them to give them a tour of the area.

There was a large outer perimeter of booths already set up, then several inner rows. At the very center was a big tent set up with tables and chairs—a place for people to bring their food and get a break from the sun and heat. Fort Collins in early August could have record-breaking temperatures. And the dry heat made it hard to realize how dehydrated a person was getting.

Next to the meal tent was another big tent set up as a lecture and demonstration area. That was where Zaida was going to be giving her speech. The event site rep gave them a full rundown of their security plan. It was as thorough as Levi thought it would be.

"Gentlemen," Wheeler said to the group, "I'll be honest—having the FBI take an interest in our security makes me a little nervous. You guys know something I don't?"

Jack sighed. "There's always more chatter around events like this. These days, the chance to take out ten or more civilians is tempting to a lot of different groups—domestic and international. We've intercepted noise from two such groups, one a disorganized group of white nationalists. The other a sleeper cell of Syrian terrorists."

Wheeler looked at his peer, then around at the guys. "Then maybe we should cancel or postpone the fair."

"Maybe," Jack said. "That's got to be your call—or that of the city council, the mayor, and the governor. They've all been alerted and are having that convo now. But know that whenever you decide to reschedule, the threat will be back on. It's better to continue as if nothing is amiss. It's our job to shut the threat down."

Levi could see anger building in Wheeler's mind. "This is unacceptable. People work hard to put this together. Kids show their farm animals. We have a big livestock auction. Dozens of food and craft demonstrations. A *New York Times* writer is giving a talk. We have tons of booths featuring the work of area artists. We have a rodeo and some big-name bands coming in. The cost of canceling and logistics of postponing are untenable."

"We aren't advocating either of those things," Levi said. "We are going to take care of the threat. Can you show me where the university's drone rental booth will be? And I'd also like to walk through Zaida Hussan's booth and lecture area."

The man stared at him a long moment. "Yes. Follow me."

They got to Zaida's booth first. "Here's a copy of the schematics she submitted for her booth."

Harris handed Levi a paper with a proposed layout showing where tables and various bits and pieces would be. Levi didn't like it. The fair had so many moving parts. It would be too easy to make Zaida disappear. Her booth had only the one opening—in the front—but with all the other booths around hers, it would be easy to slice through the canvas and drag her out.

Max came up beside him. "Selena and Ace will be here, too."

"Good." But was it good enough?

They went to see the drone booth that Abdul was going to be manning with some of the other students. The men giving them the tour showed them how the flow would work into and out of the drone booth, as well as the field where renters would be operating the drones. Abdul's booth wasn't far from Zaida's.

Levi looked at Jack. "We need to add to the list of prohibited items anything that looks like a drone or might be drone parts. I don't want anyone assembling their own drone inside the fair."

Harris frowned. "Is there some specific information you have on that threat?"

"No. Just a hunch," Levi said. "It's another way to limit potential problems."

"We can do that," Harris said, making a note. "I'm happy to add it to the list. However, you should know that there's no way we can properly monitor the airspace over the fair. Someone could fly their own drone in, and it wouldn't be easy to spot."

Levi and Max exchanged glances. "You've got ground security locked down, but you also need air security.," Levi said. "We need a full complement of SWAT teams deployed in oversight positions around the entire compound. We'll also need a helicopter doing rotations and satellite oversight in place."

"We don't have a budget for that," Wheeler said.

"No?" Levi said. "Then I hope you've got sufficient liability coverage for your event. What do a few thousand lives value out at these days?"

Wheeler stepped into Levi's space. "You said it was your job to neutralize the threat. Do your job."

"It is, and we will," Levi said. "Doesn't mean something else won't slip through the cracks. Better safe than sorry."

Jack set a hand on the rep's shoulder and drew him away from Levi. "Chatter is never specific, Mr. Wheeler, and it's all we have to act on right now. Sometimes it's enough for the bad actors if they just scare us into chasing our tails. Sometimes, they have concrete plans. We've heard chatter about small airborne drones, and that's what we're acting on. You need to find the budget to secure the air around your event. That's all we're saying. I'd be happy to talk to your people to make a plan."

When Jack took over the conversation, Max and Levi left the group to walk the far edge of the grounds, looking out at the surrounding area. There were fields on the north, east, and south sides of the event compound, and a highway and service road on the west. Way out in the northeast and east directions were sprawling neighborhoods.

The whole place was an open target for any air strike.

"Fuck. Me," Max growled.

"Yeah. That's pretty much what I was thinking," Levi said. "Let's wrap this up and go see Abdul's robotics lab."

∼

THE ROBOTICS LAB was on campus. Jamal used his ID to open it for them. The place was a large steel warehouse. Worktables lined the outer walls. Mismatched desks and file cabinets took a quarter of the space at one end. More worktables were in the middle. Open metal bracket bookshelves took up wall space here and there. Tools were neatly stored in rolling tool chests. There was a big open area where different small robotics could be tested.

On the worktables on the center of the room, were three rows of handmade drones. They were small—the biggest was two feet wide, a foot high. They were all made from various parts that could have been sourced from a hardware store or different mechanical toy kits. No two were alike.

"What type of payloads do these drones have?" Levi asked.

"None," Jamal said. "They have built-in cameras. They have different speeds they can go as well as some unique features that were encoded by their developers, like detecting colors or patterns or certain items. All rudimentary stuff. You saw the field today where these drones will be operated. There will be an obstacle course they'll be put through. Whoever completes the course without error will receive a ticket for a prize." He gave Levi a hard glare. "None of these can be weaponized."

Max picked up one of the drones and activated its control panel then moved through several of its configurable options.

Levi asked Abdul to put one of the drones through its paces. Jamal was right. The drones were just simple machines, running over, around, and through obstacles.

"These will be flying no more than six or ten feet from the ground to navigate the obstacle course," Jamal said. "They have a max battery life of fifteen minutes. It usually takes ten for an unskilled operator to go through the course. Our volunteers will be with each operator the whole time. Only three will be active at a time. Three will be in charging stations. And the last three will be queued up for play. I don't see how this can be hijacked for any evil intent."

"Unless somehow a different drone is added to the mix," Levi said.

Levi met up with Max across the street of the house rented by the skinheads who'd showed up on Abdul's database. The lot was in an unincorporated area of town, a few square miles that showed it couldn't decide what it wanted to be—industrial, residential, or ranch. It was scrappy and best seen from a moving vehicle.

The half-acre the little farmhouse was on had a steel frame warehouse in a back corner. Cars were parked haphazardly on the lot, which was crowded with piles of discarded metal parts and weeds. No one stood guard, not even a dog. Clearly, they weren't expecting the company that was about to rain down on them.

Max pulled a flamethrower rig out of one of his saddlebags and handed it to Levi. "This is yours."

"So when you mentioned flamethrowers this morning, it was a literal kinda thing, huh?"

Max laughed. "Maybe." He pulled an HK G36 out of the other bag and slipped it over his shoulder. "And this is mine. I'll take the lead on this."

"Go for it, G.I. Joe."

"Hey, at least I get to be a man. You're just a frog." Max tilted his head as he looked at Levi. "You know, you missed out. You should have joined the Red Team."

Levi chuckled. "Really? Guess if you thought you could have made it as a SEAL, you woulda gone that direction. Should,a coulda, woulda, huh, Max?"

Max shook his head. "Fuck. Me." He flipped his cuts to patch side out then started toward the house.

Levi could see movement in the house. Max didn't knock on the door; he just kicked it open and walked right in. He caught the first kid who came in an arm's reach and lifted him off the ground by his neck. The kid was shorter and skinnier than Max, no match at all for the Red Teamer's bulk and meanness.

"Which one of you's the boss?" Max snarled. The kid getting his neck stretched pointed to another kid sitting on someone's old porch sofa. Max dropped him and took two steps toward their leader before a couple of very brave or very stoned kids moved into his path.

The kid he'd just discarded got a look at Max's cuts. "Jesus, Carl. He's WKB," he announced to the others.

Levi saw the tension blow across their faces. He took up a position near the hall where he could see all threats. Max glared at the two kids who thought to block him. Faster than Levi expected, Max caught the sides of their heads and smashed them together, then shoved them out of the way. The leader still kept his seat on the cruddy sofa.

Max kicked his knee. "Stand in the presence of your betters, Carl."

The boy slowly stood. His face was twisted in an expression that was halfway between hate and fear. Levi wondered if he'd pissed himself. Maybe that was just the stink of the couch.

"My boss got word you're neck-deep in a planned hit," Max said.

The kid sneered. "I don't work for your boss."

"You call yourself skinheads, boy. So, yeah, you do work for him. He's got the corner on this market." Max kicked the coffee table over, pouring the short streaks of white powder on the filthy carpet. "And what the fuck's with this snow? We move heroin."

"It ain't nothin'," the kid Max had first accosted said. "The hit, I mean. Just taking care of some stinking Muslims. World's a better place without them."

"Shut up, Alex," one of the other guys admonished the chatty guy.

"Be that as it may," Max said, lowering his voice to a menacing growl, "our kind don't need the extra scrutiny right now. We've got bigger things in play. Your small-time shenanigans are a distraction."

"Small time," the leader, Carl, scoffed. "We're gonna make a big impression." He fisted his hands near his head, then popped them open and made an explosive sound. "Believe me, because of us, the stinking ragheads are going to be run out of the country."

Max laughed, then wrapped an arm around the leader's neck and turned him to face Levi. He rubbed a knuckle over the guy's head. "Cute, isn't he? I love baby skinheads. They think they can fart in public and make a difference in our cause."

"We aren't farting." The kid struggled against

Max's hold, but his arm only tightened around his neck. "We gotta plan to take out a few thousand Muslims and their sympathizers. You know they got a fucking bitch at the fair talking about saving women? That's bullshit. She's going down, too."

Max shoved him away. "You know what I got? I got clearance to burn this shack down." He looked at Levi, who fired up the flamethrower. "With all of you in it." Max nodded toward Levi, who started to torch the wood slats that framed the narrow entryway.

"Stop! Stop!" the leader shouted. "Jesus! We're on the same side." A couple of the guys rushed to put the fire out.

"If we were on the same side, I wouldn't have been sent down here to level this place." Max leaned close to Carl. "You wanna run with the big dogs, you better know your place in the pack. You don't make your own plays. Tell me what you got planned. I'll relay it to the boss. Maybe you'll live to ruin another of my days."

"We're gonna blow them up," Carl said.

"Who?"

"Everyone at the county fair. A couple hundred thousand go through the fair over the weekend. We can take out at least ten thousand of them."

Max frowned. "Who put this bee in your boxers?"

"We got hit by a worm," Carl said. "Went through all our computers. Locked them up for a week. It said we were Muslim terrorists." His eyes narrowed. "I know who did it, too—a kid at school. One of our own's in the same computer class. Abdul Baqri was bragging about his code, laughing at how it would identify all of us as terrorists. Well, that turd's going down."

"So you're fucking over all of your brothers because a kid tripped you at school?" Max asked.

"It wasn't just him. We hacked his worm. That man-hating bitch, Zaida Hussan, started it to call us all out. We got a plan to take out both of them, all while turning the entire community—the whole goddamned country—against the fucking ragheads."

"Big words for a baby skinhead," Max said. "How're you gonna do it?"

"Abdul's running a booth for drones to rent out. While all those drones are flying around, we'll bring in a dozen of our own, loaded with claymores ready to blow…right when the bitch is lecturing us all about love and acceptance and women's rights. People will remember Abdul and his friends were in charge of the drones. They'll check him out and see all the jihadist crap on his Facebook. They'll know who did this. It's beautiful."

"It's stupid," Max said. "Guess you're itching to visit Guantanamo."

"I gotta right to be heard," Carl said.

"You gotta right to die, too," Max snapped. "I'll let you know what the boss says."

"You can kill me," the kid scoffed. "You can kill all of us. Don't matter to me—we're soldiers for the cause. Won't stop the ball we've started rolling."

Max turned to Levi and started for the door. "Let's go. We're done here."

"No, we're not," Levi said. "These wet-nosed boys think they can A) build their own drones capable of delivering a payload, and B) build their own bombs. You bought their bullshit. The boss ain't gonna like that."

"I didn't say we *can* do it," Carl interjected. "I said we *had* done it."

Levi ignored him. "If we leave without seeing their little science experiment, the boss is gonna get riled up for nothing. You know how he is when he's fired up."

Max sighed. "We'd just be wasting our time. They got nothing to show for all their big talk."

"That's right," Carl said, approaching them. "We don't have anything to show you. Words don't make us big players. Actions do. We have an opportunity, and we're taking it. After we've made a name for ourselves, we can talk again."

Max shook his head. "All ops go through the biggest player in the area. Our White Kingdom Brotherhood president."

"He's not my president," Carl said.

Max caught his shirt and twisted it as he lifted Carl close to his face. "There's a lot of big fish in this pond. You ain't one of them. You're not even pond scum. If your little stunt brings fire down on the club, you can kiss your skinny ass goodbye."

Carl held his hands up and backed away when

Max released him. "Shock and awe...that's all I'm sayin'."

Max looked around the group of bullyboys whose masks of belligerence were a poor cover for their fear. He pointed a finger at each of them and said, "If you're wasting my time, one of you will be sacrificed and taken up to the White Kingdom Brotherhood with me. Decide now who that will be."

"Show them, Carl," Alex said. "Show them it ain't just talk."

Max looked at the kids' leader impatiently.

Carl's eyes narrowed. "Fine. We'll show you."

He led the group outside. Levi thought they'd go for their vehicles, but they just walked around behind their little shack and went into that steel farm building. Carl went in first and flipped the lights. The place was much more squared away than their house. Four folding tables had been pushed together. On them were twelve drones.

"We built these from schema we found online for delivery drones," Carl said. "They're capable of carrying a ten-pound payload. All you do is put in the coordinates where you want the package delivered. The drones drop their payload and return to their point of origin. Right now, the drones' power systems can only fuel them for fifteen minutes, so we have to be within a seven-minute radius of our hit zone." He shrugged. "We have a lot of options in that range where we can set up without attracting much attention."

"So walk us through your pyrotechnics," Levi said. "We both have military experience. We'll let you know how viable they are. You don't want to screw something like this up. And while your professors might have classes on robotics, I doubt they cover bomb making."

The boys shared looks among themselves, then Carl gave a nod toward one of them. In a separate corner of the building, an assembly line was set up that included gunpowder, prepared shrapnel, wire, large funnel cups, blast caps, cheap cell phones, and the other bits and pieces needed to make remote-controlled claymores.

Briefly, it stole Levi's breath. All he saw laid out on that table was human blood—Muslim, Christian, male, female…it all ran red.

Levi hit Max's chest. "Boss ain't gonna like this. These baby skinheads don't have the money to buy a pot to piss in. Where'd they get the money for an op like this? Not to mention the technical expertise."

"Good points." Max pivoted to glare at Carl.

"They're partnering up with someone," Levi said.

Max's eyes narrowed. "Here we go again. You're out there making associations without permission. What do you know about the people you're hooking up with? Maybe they're cops."

Carl laughed. "They're not cops. They got an ax to grind, like we do. Enemy of my enemy is my friend, you know."

"Who are they?" Max asked.

"Don't matter. The deal's done. We got the bombs. We get the glory."

"I want a demo," Levi said. "Show me one of your drones delivering a box. No need to explode it. Just deliver it."

"You still don't believe me," Carl said.

Levi slowly smiled. "I'm prepared to be wowed."

The group spilled out of the workshop. Levi and Max walked a good distance away from it. One of the boys loaded the drone with an empty box, then sent it flying around the property once, twice.

Levi heard Max say something, and wondered if he was wearing a comm unit. The kid running the drone brought it down low enough to release the box at Levi's shoulders. If those claymores exploded at chest height in a crowd, they'd spread death and destruction more than twenty feet around. With twelve of these drones flying in low, hundreds of people would be taken out.

All hell broke loose around the field before that box even hit the ground. SWAT vehicles, cop cars, and a bomb disposal unit swarmed over the property. A few of the boys tried to take off, but the K-9 units took them down swiftly. When the cops didn't take Max or Levi down, Carl said, "You said you were WKB."

Max grinned. "I did. I lied. Got this vest from evidence lockup."

In almost no time, the whole site was locked down. The bomb squad shut down a wide perimeter, keeping curious onlookers from getting too close. Max and Levi watched from across the street.

Max looked over at Levi and huffed an exasperated sigh. "We got 'em. Why don't you look happier?"

"Because we didn't get them. You saw the drones that kids with comparable skills built in the university labs. They were constructed out of scrap parts and had no payload capabilities. These drones were professionally manufactured. Who paid for them? Not these kids—you saw the flophouse conditions they were living in. Never mind all that gunpowder and the claymore components. Someone's funding them. These kids aren't the ones who cut off Mike Folsom's head. And they weren't the ones who tried to take Zaida from her apartment. These are just stupid kids who got tripped up by their hatred. They aren't the end of this. You heard what they said about 'an enemy of my enemy.' They're working with Tahrir al-Sham. I'll bet my left testicle."

Max grunted.

"Maybe they tried to leverage these kids—either as a distraction so we'd think we found our bad actors and quit looking," Levi said. "Or maybe they hoped these kids could pull off the hit and they wouldn't have to get their hands dirty. But now that these guys are out of operation, they still have a hit to make."

"All right. So we start over," Max said. "It's going to take time for the Tahrir al-Sham crew to get their shit together after this. They may not be able to recover as quickly as you might think."

"Well, we already know they can source small, payload-carrying drones," Levi said. "And they know how to build the bombs the drones will carry." He shook his head. "We still have a rogue cell to identify, find, and take down. And only hours to do it."

He called Lambert. "Go, Levi," the commander said.

Levi gave him an update on the situation. "I need someone to dig into these kids' finances and contacts, pronto. Someone was funding them. I'll get with Jack to see if his crew can find out if any large gunpowder sales have been made within a hundred-mile radius of the fair. Or maybe back in Michigan, where you think this cell came from."

"I'll call Owen and buy some of Greer's time for that background search," Lambert said. "You've cut this threat in half. That's progress."

"Not enough," Levi growled. "The fair starts tomorrow afternoon."

"Keep me posted," the commander said before he hung up.

Jack came over. "You guys don't look as pleased as I'd expect you to be."

"We've only taken half the threat down," Levi said. "We've got to find the Tahrir al-Sham players, and we're running out of time."

"An APB has been issued for all the men we think are in the cell," Jack said. "Their photos have gone out to all hotels, motels, B&Bs, RV parks, campgrounds, and short-term rental houses. We're going to find them."

"I hope they don't run to ground," Levi said. "They have to know these kids are going to give them up pretty easily."

"We'll find them," Jack said. "And we'll get this locked down." He left to talk to a couple of his agents.

"Hey, I'm going to take off," Max said. "I'm staying at Kelan's. I want to dig into a few things. I'll head out with you in the morning."

They hooked arms and shared a fast hug. "Thanks. I really appreciate everything," Levi said.

16

Zaida was with Ace and Selena in her living room when Levi got to her apartment. All three women stood. All three looked as exhausted as he felt. Zaida didn't approach him. She just stood there as if glued to the spot, her hands clenched.

Levi nodded at Ace and Selena. "Thanks for keeping her safe today."

"It's what we do," Selena said. "We good for the night?"

"Yeah," Levi said. "We head out in the morning by eight a.m."

"We're bunking at Kelan's," Ace said. "We'll be here in the morning."

Selena gave Zaida a nod. "Holler if you need us. Otherwise, see you tomorrow."

The women let themselves out. He and Zaida exchanged wary glances. "You okay?" he asked.

Her hands were clasped in front of her. "I'm scared for tomorrow. I can't not be there."

Levi went over to her and gripped her shoulders. "We'll have to make that call tomorrow. It starts late in the afternoon."

"And what if this isn't resolved in time? What if Abdul and I abandon our booths, then something really does happen? Everyone will think we had advanced knowledge that we didn't share with them. We will still be blamed for what happens."

"I'm not willing to sacrifice you for the sake of appearances. The FBI has kept the fair organizers up to date with everything. They have the info they need to make the call. What they choose to do with it is up to them. I don't know if you heard, but we did get Abdul's attackers. They were planning to hit the fair."

Relief washed across her face. "Well, that's it, then. It's done. We're in the clear."

Levi stepped away from her. He went to her fridge and looked for a beer, but remembered as soon as he saw her empty shelves that beer—or sustenance of any type—wasn't her thing.

"No, we're not." He faced her with the counter between them. "They had help implementing their plan. We still think that help came from the Tahrir al-Sham cell. The same guys that hit your place. We're trying to track them down. It's gonna be a long night. Did you eat?"

"No." She came around the counter and pulled a small notebook from a cupboard. "Here's the list of places that will deliver up here. Whatever you want works for me." She opened the notebook and pointed to a Mediterranean restaurant. "This place has great Greek salads."

Levi looked at the opened page. Anything he picked was good for her as long as it was Greek salad. At least her signals were clear. "That sounds good." He called in their order.

When he hung up the phone, the silence between them was oppressive. So much was at risk, and all of it was out of his control. Finally, he'd found a woman who filled all the hollow, empty parts of him that he hid even from himself...but he had no idea how solid what they had was.

Julia.

He closed his eyes against the echo of that name. He'd failed Julia. He couldn't fail Zaida.

Their food came a little later. Neither of them was in much of a talking mood. After supper, Zaida went to take a shower. Levi sat on her sofa with his laptop. He researched the brand of drones the kids had primed for use, reconfirming their payload capabilities, their flight-time capacities given different payload amounts. He came up with three different scenarios that gave the terrorists different ranges for setting up their attack.

Zaida came into the living room, wearing that silky robe she'd had at his house. Her hair was toweled dry. She wore no makeup. Her dark eyes were intense. "Will you come to bed with me, Levi?"

Her voice was soft. His dick responded as if she'd whispered those words just to it. "Can't. I have to finish this."

She nodded, then pivoted and returned to her room. He focused on the analysis he was doing, forcing himself to put her hurt look out of his mind.

He pulled up a satellite image of the area around the fairgrounds, overlaying his three rings of danger. It showed a lot of open ground—some undeveloped, some ranch land. A few neighborhoods. A chunk of interstate. Some businesses, standalone restaurants, and isolated residences. A new, unopened gas station. He'd seen that area today with Max. He used Google Street View to look at the developed properties in the search zone. The gas station was still under construction, but that image was old.

Anything going on in the open fields would quickly be identified. Jack had succeeded in getting a no-fly zone put in place during the fair, providing a dome of safety. Police helicopters would be able to quickly respond to a large drone penetrating the airspace, but not so much a fleet of smaller drones. And their helicopter would be grounded during the fireworks both tomorrow night and Saturday. Perfect time to deploy a dozen claymore-carrying drones to unleash hell on unsuspecting fair-goers.

The more he thought about it, the more it made sense that the cell had to be planning their attack between sunset and when the crowd left the fairgrounds.

Tomorrow, they were going to have to clear the entire circumference he'd plotted around the fairgrounds. And once they had, they were going to need continued police presence in the target area.

He called Jack and told him his findings.

"We already came to the same conclusion," Jack said. "We've alerted the proper teams. We'll sweep the area in the morning. By the way, we contacted the manufacturer of the drones the boys had. They confirmed they only fulfilled one large order placed directly with them. It was for the twelve drones we recovered. They gave us the names of their distributors in the area. We've got calls in to them as well. So far, we're only coming up with one or two on each sale, and none to the names we're tracking."

"Okay," Levi said.

"We've got this as locked down as we can, Levi. The fair isn't going to be called off."

Shit. Shitshitshit. "Roger that." He hung up.

Levi tossed his cell on the cushion beside him and leaned back, forking his fingers through his hair, fisting it as he stared at his computer. What the fuck more could he do? One shoe had dropped. He knew the other would follow…it was just a matter of where and when.

∽

ACE AND SELENA came down at seven thirty the next morning. Levi let them in. Zaida hadn't come out of her room yet. He was already up and showered. He'd managed to crash for a few hours last night.

He brought the fighters up to speed on his analysis and what Jack had put in motion for security sweeps and the establishment of a wide perimeter security.

"I don't want Zaida to go today," Levi said.

"We'll be there with her," Selena said. "Everything that can possibly be done is being done."

Levi shook his head.

"Look," Ace said, "this means the world to her. You said you think the biggest threat comes after nightfall. We'll get her out of there by seven. She'll be back here and safe long before the fireworks start."

Levi shook his head again. "I don't like it. I gotta go with my gut."

"You don't like what?" Zaida asked as she came out of the hallway. Damn, how did she always look like a runway model? She wore a tight pair of white jeans, a loose red tank top made of some crinkled silk material, a faded blue jean jacket, a cascading necklace of dozens of strands of turquoise beads and matching earrings, and a pair of pointed-toe pumps that had just the toe and heels covered, leaving the sides of her feet exposed.

She always stole his breath.

"What don't you like?" she asked.

Nothing. There was not a fucking thing about her he didn't like and didn't want to devour right then. Selena elbowed him. "Um. Right. The fair. I don't like you going to the fair."

"But we've worked it out," Ace said, shaking her head at him. "Unless the threat becomes clearer by this afternoon, we'll get you to your booth and keep you protected."

Joy spilled over Zaida's face. Levi growled to himself. She ran over to him and clasped his face, bringing him down for a kiss with those blood-red lips of hers. He almost forgot they weren't alone.

"Thank you, Levi," Zaida said.

"Don't thank me." He nodded toward Ace and Selena. "They made the case for you."

She smiled at them. "Thank you, ladies. Do you think we can get these boxes in your Jeep?" she asked Levi.

"Not all of them."

Selena held up her keys. "We've got one of the team's big SUVs. They'll fit in there."

There was a knock on the door. Max announced himself. Levi let him in.

"Ready to go?" Max asked.

"Sure. After we load some boxes," Levi said, taking Selena's keys.

Max narrowed his eyes at Levi. "You letting her do the fair?"

Ace hissed a sigh. "Got it covered, Max."

AFTER THE GUYS had left with the boxes, Zaida looked at Selena and Ace. "Are the rest of your team all knuckle draggers too?"

Ace rolled her eyes. "Yes."

"How do you deal with them?"

"Logic. Lots and lots of it," Selena said. "They get wrapped up in the emotion of being alpha protectors. We have to keep them grounded."

All three of them laughed at that.

∽

ZAIDA'S MORNING didn't go quite how she wanted. Levi gave her a couple of hundred-dollar bills, then asked Selena and Ace to run some errands with her. He wanted them to stop at a game store and pick up some things for everyone trapped in the hotel room. If there wasn't a break in the case soon, they'd all be in protective custody for a few more days and would be badly in need of something to do besides watch TV. And then he wanted Zaida to pick up lunch from a local deli.

It was thoughtful of him. Zaida wondered if his intent had been to keep her from worrying about the fair. If so, it had worked. She wasn't sure what she would find when she entered the suite where her parents, Jamal, and the Baqris were. Her parents were both Type A personalities. So was Jamal. The Baqris weren't, but perhaps only because they were the youngest of the group. Add to that mix the FBI agents, and the energy in the confined space had to be near explosive after so many days together.

Selena opened the door. The TV was on in the

living room. Her mother saw her first. She looked stressed, but who wouldn't in the same circumstances? Zaida smiled at her. She set her shopping bag on the coffee table. After greeting everyone and introducing Ace and Selena, she showed her mother what she'd brought. Mahjong, dominoes, some board games, some crossword puzzles and sudoku magazines. She even brought coloring books and colored pencils.

"It was nice of you to join us today," Rayna said.

"Of course, Mother." Zaida hid her smile, knowing her mom was truly glad she'd come today, but equally upset she hadn't been there yesterday. "I'm sorry I didn't come yesterday. I found some quiet hours to do some work. This is putting me behind schedule."

"It is affecting all of our jobs," Rayna quipped.

Zaida nodded and led her mother to the kitchen. Levi had sent them to his favorite deli to pick up buffalo meat Reubens and several salads. He'd figured the group were getting tired of pizzas and other delivery options.

"Is everything okay at your office? Who's taking your patients?" Zaida asked her mom as she unpacked the meal.

"It is fine. Fortunately, we'd already planned to cover for each other for our vacations. I just had to move my vacation up in the schedule." She gave an angry glance around the room and sighed. "This was not the vacation your father and I had planned."

"I know. It isn't what I had planned either. I'm

worried this won't get resolved before this afternoon. I might be forced to cancel. It was important to me to present what the different literacy foundations are doing."

"We didn't even know you were working with them," Rayna said.

"They aren't the cause of this trouble, Mother."

"But if not for them, if not for your dangerous stance, none of this would have happened."

"No. This is happening because some very small-minded people decided to express their hatred in a violent and awful manner. This has nothing to do with the foundations that I work with. It has nothing to do with the women I work with. It has nothing to do with you or me or Daddy or anything, anyone, that we love."

Her mother pursed her lips, the typical way she had of showing her displeasure. "And yet here we are."

Zaida nodded. "Yes. Here we are. Safe. Together. Thanks to these agents. And Levi."

"And Jamal," her mother added, shooting Zaida an admonishing look. She leaned close. "We have much to discuss after lunch."

Why, at twenty-nine years old, did that still strike terror in Zaida's heart? She smiled as she thought of Levi saying yesterday that after spending time with her mother, she'd think of all the ways her life was fucked.

"What has you grinning so, Zaida?" Rayna asked.

"Nothing in particular. I'm just feeling very grateful right now. I'm very lucky to have been raised by you and Daddy."

"Yes, you are."

Zaida reached over and took Hidaya's hand. "And I'm very lucky to have friends like Hidaya and Abdul."

Hidaya sniffled and gave Zaida a hug. "How can you say that after what we did to you?"

"You didn't do anything to me. You didn't do this on purpose. How could you know any of this was going to happen? This will all be successfully resolved very soon. We have to have faith in our helpers."

~

IT WAS AFTERNOON, almost the middle of a very long day. Zaida's anxiety over what was happening and her worry about Levi's safety were eating at her.

The women had retreated to one of the guest bedrooms, the men to the other for an afternoon rest. Selena went with Zaida, her mom, and Hidaya, while Ace stayed in the main room. Rayna drew her daughter over to the sofa. Her face was all business, her grip on Zaida's wrist relentless. Zaida knew exactly what talk was coming.

"Zaida, I'm your mother," Rayna began.

Zaida kept from smiling. All of their serious discussions began this way, as if being her mom entitled Rayna to special rights that allowed her to cross Zaida's boundaries.

Perhaps it did. Zaida wondered if she'd do the same when she had a daughter who needed a blunt conversation. At least her mom's words were whispered, though Zaida had the feeling she was making something of a presentation for Hidaya's benefit, since her friend had no mother to guide her.

Zaida smiled. "Are you sure?"

"Sure what?" Rayna asked.

"That you're my mother."

She was not amused. "This is a serious conversation, daughter."

"Very well. I'm listening."

"You are almost thirty years old. You aren't a child any longer. You aren't a student. You're settled in a career…such as it is."

"It's a very good career, Mother."

Rayna waved that away. "It is what it is. Your father and I have always thought the arts important, however they present themselves. That is not what I wanted to talk to you about."

"Oh."

"As I said, you are of an age where it's time to accept your adult responsibilities."

"I pay my bills. I haven't missed a mortgage payment to you and Dad yet."

"Yes, you are very good at managing your money. Your social life…not so much. A woman only has so much time before her physiology begins to age. It is time you married and had children."

"Says who? Is it written somewhere?" Zaida asked.

"What does it matter? Your father and I say it's time. We've chosen a wonderful man for you, yet you refuse to even consider him. Jamal is perfect for you. He is strong, successful. He'll be a good provider for you. He wants many children, too."

"You've worked this all out with him?"

"We have."

"I see."

"Good. It's clear you have an infatuation with Levi, but he is not one of us. And you're not a child. It's time to face life as an adult woman."

Zaida sighed. Up to now, her mother was covering Zaida's hands with hers. Zaida pulled free and took hold of her mother's hands, shifting dominance in their conversation to her favor.

"You know I love and respect you and Dad. You gave up everything in your world to come here so that I could have this world. I can understand the points you make about Jamal. He is a fine man, but he is not to my taste."

"This is not a decision that should be made based on hormones. It is one your intellect must make."

"I don't know what part of me is making this decision. Maybe my heart. Jamal doesn't make my heart jump. Levi does."

"Has Levi asked you to marry him?"

"Of course not. We've only known each other a few days."

Rayna grunted and pulled her hands free. "This is your last chance with Jamal. If you dally with this Levi, Jamal will not linger to pick up the pieces when your life crashes around you."

"I set Jamal free a long time ago. It is not my fault that he persists in his fantasy that we'll be together. I've been very clear that would not be the case, even before Levi came on the scene."

Rayna's shoulders slumped. She looked as if the world would never again be right.

"Mother, how many times have you told me the story of how you and Dad met? Of how you knew, only seconds into your acquaintance, that your lives would be forever entwined? Your story is why I fell in love with love. I've wanted what you and Daddy have all my life. I never felt that with Jamal. Never. But the first moment Levi and I looked at each other, I swear the ground shook. It was like a herd of elephants surrounded us, stamping on the ground, forcing me to pay attention. He's everything I've wanted all my life."

Rayna sighed. "So. That is the way of it, then. Does this Levi feel the same for you?"

"He's been a little busy since we first met. I think so. I see it in his eyes." Zaida shook her head. "We haven't talked about it yet."

"Well, if you love him and he loves you, and he will honor our family, then your father and I will consider him."

"What would you have done if your family didn't accept Dad?"

Rayna's eyes narrowed. "Do not give me an ultimatum. I have said we will consider him."

Zaida laughed and leaned forward to hug her mom. Life hadn't been easy for Rayna. War, oppression, religious practices that should have made enemies of her parents, a new start in a new country, language barriers, gender barriers...she had survived all of it to build a successful career and make for herself a thriving life, against all the odds a human could face.

Zaida was deeply proud of her parents, but they still could not decide her future for her. "All I need you to do, Mother, is accept that this decision is mine. You've raised me to be like you. Now it's time to let me be me."

17

Zaida was in the shared living room later that afternoon, when Levi texted that he was coming to pick her up. Jamal, Jack, and one of the other FBI agents had already left with Abdul.

There was a heavy silence in the room. Her parents did not want her to go. Her dad looked close to a full-blown temper tantrum. That he didn't cut loose made her proud. He wasn't treating her like a child, giving her ultimatums. He accepted her decision, even though he didn't agree with it.

When Levi came in, he looked like a cable wound too tight. "Ready to go?" he asked.

She nodded.

"I have all of your things in your booth already. Max is keeping an eye on it."

"Thank you." She hoped he wouldn't try again to dissuade her from going. If he did that here, her parents would pile on. To her relief, he took her hand, nodded at her parents, and led her out of the room, leaving Selena and Ace to follow.

They parked in the lot set aside for vendors. Selena stayed with them as Ace wandered off to do her thing. K-9 units were checking out the booths and each vendor.

While they waited to get through security, Levi turned to Zaida and said, "I reconfigured your booth."

"You did what?"

"I had to fortify it." He stepped close and lowered his voice. "If there's an active shooter or fucking claymore unleashing its payload near you, you need to have some cover."

Zaida was grateful he'd done that. They got through the security checkpoint and went straight to her booth. Levi had set up two wide pillars of black shelves at both front corners of her booth. Originally, she'd had two tables set up so people could walk around them. People could still walk around the bookshelves. And all of her paraphernalia regarding the foundations she wanted to feature was nicely arranged on the shelves.

"Why change from the open tables to bookshelves?" Zaida asked.

"Because in the center, behind the clustered bookshelves, are a couple rows of sandbags. It'll give you and anyone in your booth some cover to duck behind."

Instead of the two folding tables set up side by

side at the back of the booth, he'd put up two smaller tables separated by another tall column of bookshelves. She walked over to those tables, knowing she was going to have to rearrange her books and signs and little giveaways. But her foot collided with something under the table. She lifted the table skirt and found a dense stack of sandbags there.

She looked at Levi. He lifted both brows. The look he returned made it clear that if she didn't like it, he'd physically remove her from the fair.

She said nothing, just continued her exploration. In the far back, there was another setup of small tables, sandbags, and a sandbag-filled column of bookshelves.

"You don't know what direction an attack might come from," he said. "There's space under the tables for several of you to take cover. If shit breaks loose, you get down."

"You've reduced the size of my booth by about a third. Fewer people will fit in here."

"Fewer people crowding around you is a happy thing for me today."

Zaida couldn't help the tears that filled her eyes. He'd made her a mini fortress—he hadn't been kidding about that. She went over to him and set her hands on his waist. "Thank you. I feel much safer now."

His nostrils flared as he released a long breath. "I added sandbags to Abdul's booth too."

Zaida caught his face in her hands. "You're a good man, Levi Jones."

"If I were a good man, you wouldn't be here." He took a little sting out of those words by pulling her into a hug. He kissed the top of her head. "Let's get your booth set up how you want it before the hordes descend on the fair."

~

THE FIRST AFTERNOON of the county fair was well attended and went off without a hitch. Zaida's translators were there, greeting visitors. She'd told them about the security features Levi had given them.

Ace and Selena actually had fun talking romance novels with booth visitors. They filled in for her and her translators when any of them needed a break. Zaida was grateful she was never left on her own. She'd sold some books and had several opportunities to talk about the literacy foundations she was featuring—it had been a great start to the weekend.

But now, it was nearing the time she'd promised to shut her booth down.

People milled about in chaotic patterns that Zaida could tell stressed Levi. None of the fair-goers showed any signs of stress. Some debated the need for SWAT on fairground highpoints. Some said they felt they were in a prison, but most were thankful the proper security measures had been taken to ensure their safety.

Freedom Code

None seemed to know the truth of the threat hanging over their heads.

She went to the opening of her booth where Levi was. There was something strange in his eyes when he looked at her...something like dread.

"Thank you for today," she said as she set her hands on his folded forearms. "I sent the translators home. I'm going to start shutting the booth down."

"Are you pleased with the event so far?" Levi asked.

"I am. It's been great seeing my friends become so animated when they talk about their work with our foundations. You'd be surprised how empowering that is."

Levi's lips moved into a smile as he stroked her cheek with his thumb. "Can I get you something cold to drink? Something to eat?" he asked.

"I'm fine. Selena just made a run for us."

He caught her hand, just the tips of his fingers against hers, but before he could speak, he jerked back. His eyes focused away from her. He frowned, then tapped his ear and said, "Copy that." He took her arm and led her deeper into her booth. "Sorry, I have to go," Levi said, more to her guards than her. As soon as Ace and Selena surrounded her, he took off.

"No worries," Selena called after him. "We'll be here having fun. Catch up when you can." Selena smiled at Zaida, and Ace gave him a wave.

Sheer panic paralyzed Zaida. She sent Selena a

questioning glance, but the woman shook her head. There were civilians milling around near her booth. None of them could talk.

She couldn't get the look Levi had had off her mind. This was bad. Very bad. She made short work of locking things up. She took her money box and a few papers. When the booth flaps were lowered and tied up, she let Ace and Selena rush her off.

"Wait!" Zaida stopped, but the girls strong-armed her along.

"No waiting," Ace said.

"But we need to get Abdul."

"The agents with him and Jamal are already getting him out of here," Selena said.

∾

Max met Levi with his bike. Took little time to cross the fairgrounds. The event center's op room was almost military grade, and it was full of top emergency response brass from the county and state—and with Jack and his crew, federal level, too.

Jack must have cleared Levi and Max as part of the team; no one balked at their joining the group.

A man wearing a stained pair of jeans, a T-shirt, and a faded blue cotton shirt was pacing wildly around the room. "Finally, are you gonna listen to me? I'm telling you something's not right."

"Mr. Powell," Jack said, "please start at the beginning."

Powell looked at Levi and Max. "I own a few gas stations up in Wyoming. Small deals. They do okay. A couple of friends and I went in on the new one just up the street. It was supposed to open today. I called a few times to see how things were going. My partner said everything was great, but he was too busy to talk. I called at noon to get the morning's tally. The numbers he read off didn't make sense for the day he should have had, especially with the county fair right here. I came down from Wyoming today to see if he needed help, and I find the station never opened at all. In fact, there are barricades up with handwritten signs saying it wasn't open.

"When I went into the store to question him, he looked terrified. I only saw one other guy there. Someone from the city inspection crew. They'd found a safety violation and had shut the station down."

"And that's bad because…?" Levi asked.

"Because all of those inspections had already been completed. We were ready to go. Everything was a go," Powell said.

"I showed him the photos of the group we've been tracking." Jack spread them out on the table. Both he and Powell pointed at one guy. Suhair Rashid.

Levi shut his eyes, relieved they'd finally caught a break. He looked around the room. "Wasn't this gas station checked in this morning's sweep?"

"It was," Jack said. "The police cleared it. No one was there. And there were no vehicles he could see."

"They must have come in afterwards," Levi said.

"They've been lying low an entire day. They could have taken action at any point, but they didn't."

"They're waiting for dark," Max said.

It was nearing dusk now.

"Right," Levi said.

Powell shoved his hands into his hair and squeezed his head. "I've been telling this story all day. See something, say something. Well, I fucking did, and no one's doing anything. And now you tell me my gas station is being held by a known terrorist. He's going to kill my friend."

Levi looked at Max. "I want Greer on those cameras now." When Max stepped aside to talk to Greer, Levi set a hand on their informant's shoulder. "Sir, I know you've told others all of this before, but tell me again everything you saw."

"He and my partner were both sweating bullets. That man had a heavy accent. He was wearing a jumpsuit." Powell closed his eyes. "He had a headset on, like, um, a phone headset."

A schema of the gas station was up on a big screen. It was a sprawling setup with a main office and store combination that was flanked on both sides by separate gas bays for cars and larger ones for RVs. It also had two separate wash stations, one on the RV side, one on the car side.

"Show me where they were when you saw them," Levi said.

Powell walked over and pointed to the cashier station in the store. "Here."

"Do we have a live satellite image of the site?" Levi asked. One of the ops room technicians brought up an image. The place looked vacant. No vehicles were anywhere in sight.

"All right. We're going in there," Levi said. "This is what we've been waiting for. We have until nightfall."

Powell looked around the room. "Until night for what?"

Levi led him out of the office. "Sir, your persistence has potentially saved a lot of lives. I need you to stay here in case we have more questions." Levi pointed to some seats in a waiting area, then shook his hand. "Thank you."

Back in the office, the group had convened around the station's schematics.

Levi had Max call Greer and put him on speaker. "Do we have confirmation that the drones are on the gas station premises?"

"Negative," Greer said. "Only the external cameras are still functioning, but I was able to crack their security footage for the day. The station's manager arrived at five a.m. He was followed shortly after by what must have been our tango. They both went inside. A few minutes later, a pickup truck towing a flatbed arrived and backed into the first wash bay on the RV side. After that, men came out of the bay and set out the blockades at the station's entrances. There's been some movement between the bay and the office—the men go into the office building and return. No one's left the premises yet."

Levi looked at the schematics as Greer talked. That first wash bay was constructed for big but noncommercial trucks, things like RVs and livestock trailers. It wasn't an automated wash bay; it just had a hose mounted on one of the side walls for manual washing. It did have garage doors that covered both entrances.

"Their hostage is still with them," Greer said. "We identified his vehicle as that belonging to the station's manager. They parked it inside one of the other RV bays. The inside cameras have all been shot out. I saw the flatbed in the wash bay, but there was a tarp over the back, so I couldn't get a clear view before they trashed the camera. I've counted six men in the wash bay."

Levi watched the live exterior video feed. All the overhead doors in the three wash stations were down. He looked at the county fair rep, Harris. "They're going to unleash hell once the fireworks start. Delay the pyrotechnics until my word."

Harris stepped aside and dialed a number on his phone.

"Commander," Levi said to the man leading the SWAT team, "get your guys into position here and here. With spotters. Our tangos are going to release those drones under the cover of the fireworks display. Watch for them to come out of either side of that wash bay. If any make it out, they have to be taken down in this field, well before they reach the crowd."

"We can storm the wash bay and take them out before they unleash their hell," the commander suggested, obviously itching for action.

"Negative," Levi nixed that. "We're still reviewing the security feed. They could have booby-trapped the hell out of that place. And even if not, they have some number of claymore bombs—at least six but possibly double that. If you send your guys in, these bastards will happily go to heaven and send you all to hell. Won't be the big impact they were hoping for as far as civilian lives, but each of your guys has to be worth a hundred non-combatants to them."

Levi shook his head. He and Max exchanged hard glares. "Get your guys in place, commander. Max and I are the only ones going in." To Wheeler, Levi said, "We need the bomb disposal unit nearby. Not too close; we don't want them to see it and take pre-emptive measures, activating their plan before we're ready. The firefighters are already on hand because of the fireworks, so we're good there. Have people in place to direct the crowds to the event buildings in case this goes south."

"So what's the plan for you two?" the SWAT commander asked.

"We're gonna ride Max's bike up to the main office and go in, neutralize the lone guy in there, draw the rest of his team to us, then jam all wireless transmissions so they can't get the drones off the ground.

We're not going to be able to communicate briefly. Your guys have to be ready to hit anything that comes out of that wash bay—drone or human."

The commander agreed and left to get his team in place.

Levi phoned Rocco. Max's whole team was on their comms, so Levi knew he didn't have to bring Rocco up to speed. "I need you to send me a recording in Arabic. Something from the lead guy in the main office calling his soldiers to him in a high state of rage. At least two minutes of ordering his men to come to him, that he needs their assistance, forget the drones, come to him."

"We don't know what he sounds like," Rocco said.

"Doesn't matter. His men know his regular voice, but probably haven't been with him when he's screaming in panic. They won't know your screaming voice from his. Send me that recording ASAP. I need it on my phone before we cut transmissions."

"Roger that," Rocco said before hanging up. Three minutes later, it came in. Levi smiled as he listened to it. He could understand a calm, slow convo in Arabic, but not this—words were flying fast and furiously. Something about infidels and Allah.

While they were waiting for the SWAT commander to bring Max a wireless jammer, Levi stepped aside to make a personal call. Zaida picked up before the first ring finished.

"Levi? What's happening? Are you all right?"

"I'm fine." He shouldn't have called. Jesus, what

was he going to say? That he loved her? And how would that sit if he was about to get himself blown up? "I just wanted to hear your voice. Where are you?"

"At my apartment. With Ace and Selena. Abdul got back to the hotel safely as well. When are you coming home?"

Home. Zaida was home to him. "Shouldn't be long. Will you wait up?"

"Yes. Levi...I love you."

All the breath left his lungs. He held the phone to his forehead, trying to figure out how she meant that. She was always telling someone she loved them—her parents, her friends, the women who worked for her. Love was something easy for her, something she handed out like baked goods.

"I love you too, babe," he said, telling himself he meant it however she meant it. He lowered the phone, staring at it a long moment before disconnecting their call.

Max punched his shoulder. "Ready?" The bastard actually grinned. "Time for a ride."

Levi looked at everyone in the room, gave them a nod, and followed Max from the room. Powell was still sitting in the waiting room. He jumped up when they came out of the office.

"We're gonna get your friend out of this," Levi said as Max went on without him.

Powell shook his head. "I don't give a fuck about the station. Do what you have to do. I can rebuild it.

Just get my friend out in one piece. And don't let anyone else get hurt."

Levi nodded. "Copy that."

It was nearly dark outside. He and Max exchanged glances as they jogged out to the bike. The ride to the gas station only took a couple of minutes. Max rode around one of the sawhorse blockades and went right up to the main office. They knew the door wasn't locked because the crew never paused to unlock it when they went in to use the bathroom.

"Hey, bro!" Max said to the room in general as he eyed the wall of cigarettes behind the front counter. "Need some smokes." He didn't spare more than a fast glance for the owner who was tied to a chair.

The Middle Eastern man rushed forward. "We're closed. You saw the signs—"

Max kept him talking for the seconds Levi needed to make sure there wasn't more going on at the station than the claymore-carrying drones they were about to send off. He'd been half afraid they'd rigged the gas storage tanks to blow too, but at a glance, Levi couldn't see any detonation devices.

Rashid pulled a gun and pointed it at Max, but fell back with a bullet in his head before he could say another word. Levi holstered his pistol and grabbed his phone, starting Rocco's recording playing at full volume. He tucked his phone up against the Bluetooth device the terrorist was wearing.

After that, shit broke loose. Two men slammed into the office. Max caught one and got him in a chokehold, incapacitating him fast. Levi fought with the other, throwing punches briefly before taking him down with a wrist hold that dropped him to his knees and broke his arm. Levi pushed him to the floor and kept a knee on his back.

Shooting sounded from outside. More shooting from farther away. And then the thing that filled Levi with dread: three huge explosions.

The fireworks display had started, which Levi hadn't signaled. Harris probably wanted to cover up the gunshots and explosions. Levi was breathing hard. With the screaming Arabic recording playing, it was hard to hear the sitrep coming over their comms.

"Shut that thing down," Max growled. Levi did. Quiet took over the room, with only the fireworks booming in the near distance.

Levi grinned at Max, who was giving the SWAT commander an update over their comms. They both heard the same thing. Three of the terrorists had run outside with their drones, trying to get away from the jammer. They were blown up with their drones. The other three had tried to make it into the main office. One was shot outside. Levi and Max secured the other two. At least two of the bad guys had survived; the FBI would have fun getting info from them.

Jack's agents came in and took them into custody. Levi and Max freed the station manager and led him outside. One of the Feds took him to an ambulance. It was a zoo outside with news vans and reporters everywhere, trying to get as close as they were allowed. Jack came over with Wheeler and Harris. They congratulated Levi and Max.

Levi saw Powell being led over to his station manager, who was sitting on the back of an ambulance. Levi went over to thank him.

"No, thank you for listening to me," Powell said, shaking Levi's hand.

"You bet. You did the right thing, bringing this forward and insisting someone take it seriously," Levi said.

The bomb squad came in to clear the site. Everyone was moved farther back. Levi and Max got on Max's bike.

"Where to, bro?" Max asked.

"My Jeep. Gonna head to Zaida's. You staying in town or heading back home?"

"Think I'll head back home," Max said. "Been away from my woman too long. We've got some celebrating to do." At Levi's Jeep, they exchanged a hug. "You know you're going to be hearing from Owen."

Levi shoved his hands in his jeans pockets. "About what? I told him where to send the bill."

"Yeah, no doubt he's already done that. I'm betting he's got an employment package for you. You may not have come from the Red Team, but you know your way around a bad situation."

"Tell him not to bother." Levi grinned. "I got flowers. Who needs terrorists?"

Max laughed. "Flowers. Right." They bumped

fists. "Later, bro. If you think you still need me, let me know."

"Nah, we're good. Thanks, man," Levi said, then watched his friend ride off.

Levi began to unwind as he made his way over to Zaida's. He knew Jack's team would go through the data to make sure the whole cell had been taken down. That wasn't going to be a fast process. And who knew how accurate his analysis would be? Terrorist cells were fluid organizations. They added and lost members all the time. Their parent organizations routinely dissolved and reformed as new entities. Getting an accurate head count on terrorists was an imprecise art.

Ten men in the cell were dead or out of commission—three of them had been vaporized. The neo-Nazis from the university might provide some info on who they worked with…but then again, maybe not.

There were still two more full weekend days at the fair. It continued into the week for another two days, but Zaida's participation finished Sunday evening.

Levi would really just like to hear they'd successfully terminated this threat.

18

Selena opened the door for Levi. She read his face, then gave him a relieved smile. Zaida and Ace stood.

"Is it really over?" Zaida asked, wringing her hands. Levi had texted the three of them that it was all clear and he was coming back. He knew Owen's crew had updated Zaida as they followed along on their comms.

Levi nodded. "I think so. No civilians were hurt." He gave the women a sitrep, moving through it fast because Zaida looked ready to drop.

"Righto," Selena said. "We're outta here. See you in the morning, Zaida."

"You're coming back?" Zaida asked.

"Coming back? We'll just be upstairs," Ace said. "Until we get a firm all-clear, we're your bodyguards for the weekend."

Zaida looked relieved. "Good. Thank you. I hope

this was the end of it, but I appreciate your being here."

"Later, Levi." Ace waved as she went past him.

The door shut behind the women, leaving him alone with Zaida.

So. This was it. This gig was almost up. It was time for them to face reality…time for him to accept Zaida's choice for their future.

"You okay?" he asked. Neither of them had moved toward the other.

She nodded, then followed that with a shake of her head. He went over and pulled her into his arms, holding her until her trembling eased.

"What happened?" she asked.

He told her the lite version of the story, telling her about the man who'd followed the see something, say something rule, that the guy's friend was saved and the business wasn't too badly damaged. "Everything worked out okay," he said.

"You make it sound like it was nothing."

He shrugged, giving her a little smile. "I guess I judge things by how badly the good guys get hurt. This time, no civilians were harmed. Yes, we lost Mike at the beginning of all this, but none of those claymores were set off in the crowds. Two groups of bad guys are off the streets; one's pretty much wiped out. I'd say it was a good day."

For a long moment, they just looked into each other's eyes. Levi wanted to ask what she'd meant when she said she loved him, but he didn't. If she put him in a friend zone, he wouldn't be able to walk that back.

He touched her cheek with his fingertips. "I'd kill for a shower. Want to take one with me?" He grinned, expecting her to shoot him down.

"I thought you'd never ask."

Zaida's shower was big, built for a man his size, not a little thing like her. There were two showerheads. They each stood under one, facing each other. Zaida's nude body was perfect. She was not in the least shy about her body or worried about his watching her as she bathed.

She'd had a long and stressful day, but she'd been brave as hell facing it. The last thing he wanted was to take more from her by asking for intimacy, but his dick was already long and hard, stretching down between his legs. When she looked at him with hungry eyes, he could no more fight his reaction to her than he could stop the sun from shining.

They washed themselves independently, each watching the other. When they both were rinsed, Zaida shut off her water. Levi was almost afraid to move, wanting what he knew he shouldn't.

"Levi, you should know... I mean, I want you to know...two things. I don't... I've been cleared, you know, of any STDs. I should have told you before."

Levi frowned at her, trying to make sense of what she was saying while the shower roared down on him. He shut it off. STDs. She didn't have any. Good. That was great.

"I'm clear too," he said. "I had that as part of my annual physical in the service. I haven't been with anyone since my last one. So..."

Zaida moved a step closer to him. "And I'm on birth control." She shrugged. "I started that with Jamal and just never stopped. It messes with everything, going on and off that stuff, so I just stayed on it. I was thinking of getting off it, but then you came along."

He moved toward her, catching her face in his hands. "I didn't want to press you. Not tonight, after the day you've had."

"The day *I've* had? What about you? You had to stop terrorists and bombs. You faced death head-on."

He shrugged. "That used to be a normal day."

"Make love to me, Levi. Please."

He nodded, then opened the shower door and got out. He handed her a towel. They both dried off. He watched as she put lotion all over herself. Such a girl thing, but that was Zaida: one hundred percent female.

He went into her room and turned her bedside lamp on. It had three brightness levels; he put it on the dimmest. He wanted to watch her as they made love.

Love.

Was this love? The real stuff? The kind of love you gave up everything for?

He looked over at her Kama Sutra couch. It would be wasted tonight. Tonight they needed slow and easy, sex and talk. When Zaida came out of the bathroom, he lifted the covers for her. The air conditioner was on super cold. Felt great after the blistering heat of the day. He got in after her and pulled her close, loving the feel of her soft body against his, their legs entwined. He knew she could feel the heat of his erection between them.

He leaned over and kissed her mouth, leisurely, taking his time, letting her body get used to his. He broke the kiss and looked into her eyes, losing himself there as he smoothed a bit of her damp hair from her face. He had so much to say to her, but he knew it needed to wait.

He kissed her cheek, wondering if his bristly beard bothered her. He hadn't shaved in a few days. He kissed her chin, her neck, her shoulder. She moaned. He caught her breast in his hand then inched down to mouth her nipple. There was the slightest taste of lotion on her. He rubbed her skin with the back of his hand, wiping it off before he sucked hard on her tightened peak.

Still holding her breast, he kissed her side, her ribs, her hip. Pushing her flat on her back, he opened his mouth and ran his teeth gently over her upper thigh, her inner thigh. She was open to him, relaxed and beautiful. His to take. He kissed her mound, then separated her folds and tongued her clit. She whimpered quietly, a frown wrinkling her brow. He smiled at her as he lay between her legs, then gave all his attention to her sex, letting her moans, quiet

Freedom Code

cries, and the movements of her hips direct his touch.

She tasted so sweet. One finger entered, teasing her. Two fingers. Her hips lurched up against his face. He draped an arm over them, holding her in place as her orgasm racked her body.

As it began to ease, he kissed his way back up her body. When he was almost lying fully on her, she pushed herself to sit up. Smiling at him, she ordered him to his knees. When he knelt, she took hold of his cock, stroking him, her fingers teasing him until he was huge and throbbing for her mouth. She leaned forward and brought him to her lips, letting her pink tongue swipe over his swollen head.

He hissed at the sensation, watching as her mouth opened and she took him inside her, deep. His breath came in short huffs as he felt her tongue stroke the sensitive underside of his cock. He moved his hips, gently thrusting into her mouth. She moaned, and the sound rumbled against his skin. She sucked him, drawing down against one of his thrusts, wresting a groan from him.

He eased himself from her mouth, feeling dazed. He bent down and kissed her, fucking her now with his tongue. When she sucked that, he almost came. "You're trying to kill me, woman."

She laughed, that sexy, feminine, laugh that reminded him she knew so much more about infinite things, things he'd never know or understand. She was a mystery, and she was his.

He scooped a hand behind her waist and tugged her lower on the bed, then kneed her thighs wider open and settled between them, rocking against her mound, grinding himself against her clit. When he guided himself to her opening, it was pure heaven. He tried to enter her slowly, so slowly, but she was wet and hot and ready for him, and slow was a demon right now. When she arched up, pushing herself against him, he slid all the way in, seating himself to his balls, stretching her.

He stared down into her eyes as he moved in her, realizing they weren't two people seeking their own independent pleasure; they were one being, one heart, each experiencing the other. He never wanted this feeling to end, though he knew he wasn't going to last long. Not with his balls so tight, banging against her.

She bent her knees and wrapped her arms around his chest, hugging him to her as she moved against him. He moved faster, tapping all the way against the back wall of her vagina. She was making delicious little sounds that drove him harder. He was so close. So close. He clenched his teeth, fighting his release, wanting her to go first. And when she did, her inner muscles gripped and pulsed against him until he could no longer resist.

He groaned as he released inside her in hot spurts. His orgasm set hers off anew. He kept thrusting, riding her passion, giving her what she needed.

It took a while for her body to calm from its excitement, but it finally eased away. She went limp under him. He smiled into her face, stroking her cheek with his thumb. Making love to her was like riding an earthquake. God, she was amazing.

She looked as moved as he felt. Her nostrils flared as her breath hitched. Levi frowned at the storm in her eyes. She caught his face and brought him close for a kiss. "I meant what I said, Levi Jones. I love you."

He gave her a sad smile. "I wasn't sure when you said it. You love everyone. You love easily. I was afraid you meant you loved me like a friend."

"I do. Like a friend. Like a lover. Like my man."

"Zaida, I can walk away now. I don't want to, but I can. But if you tell me I'm your man, then you gotta know it's a forever kind of thing. And I mean for fucking ever."

She circled her arms around his neck. "I want forever," she said, "with you. I want us. I want the world to know you're mine. Is that clear enough for you?"

He stroked her face. He wanted to smile, but it was hard with his heart in his throat. He nodded. "Yes." He kissed her forehead. "We need to talk, though. There are things you should know."

"Like what?"

Levi eased himself from her. For a moment, they lay side by side. Then he rolled over and faced her. "I took this job with extreme prejudice. I hate cyber-crime ops."

She touched him, her hand moving from his shoulder across his chest. "Why?"

"I told you I was in love twice…before now. The last time was when I was paired on a cybercrime op with an intelligence officer from the Navy."

"She was the one, right? The one you loved?"

"Yeah." He paused. "We were in Tbilisi, Georgia, trying to ferret out details about some Russian hackers. Those bastards were staying a step ahead of us, and we couldn't figure out their secret. My job was to provide Julia security so she could do her job. We posed as a married couple. It was an extended op. Things got a little heated. Fuck, they got a lot heated. I fell for her. Hard."

Levi sighed. He stared into Zaida's eyes, wishing things were different. Wishing he didn't have to tell her this story. She put her hand on his fist.

"Mike was there."

"My Mike? Mike Folsom?"

"Yeah. He was our CIA liaison. He was also working the case. He saw something I didn't. I was too blinded by Julia to see it. He did a psyops maneuver, releasing a bit of false info to see where it spilled out."

"What happened?"

"Well, it spilled out of Julia. We discovered she was a double agent. She was working for the fucking Russians."

"Oh my God."

"Took a while to convince me. I tried to prove him

wrong. But once he was onto her, the things she did became clearer. He got confirmation from a couple of his sources."

"What did you do?"

"I did what I was sent in to do. Neutralize the threat." Levi opened his fist and looked at his fingers. He could still feel Julia's hot, wet blood on his hands. "I killed her."

"Levi."

"Yeah. I killed the woman I loved. I never gave her a chance to get away. I took her life."

Zaida leaned up on her elbow and looked at him in horror. He closed his eyes and rolled to his back, knowing her next words would be for him to leave. Her hand was cold on his face. He sat up, dropping his legs over the side of the bed as he held his face in his hands.

Zaida crawled over to lean against him. She wrapped one arm over his back and the other under his arm. Joining her hands, she kissed his shoulder. "When was this?"

"Two years ago. Nothing was the same after her. That's when I knew I had to get out. I already had the farm. It was time to go. My tour was up in January, so I left." Left everything. His brothers. The teams. The Navy. The only life he'd known as an adult. "I've had a hard time trusting women since Julia. There's really been no one. I never expected you."

She smiled and kissed his shoulder again. Wait...

why wasn't she kicking him out? Couldn't she see what a monster he was?

"That's what I meant when I said I took this job with extreme prejudice. At first glance, you looked a like another Julia."

"I'm not Julia redux."

He looked at her and nodded. "I'm sorry for being a bastard when we first met."

"I didn't understand what was happening." She rested her chin on his shoulder. "You were overwhelming."

"This—you and I—we've happened fast. So fucking fast. I don't want to take any of this for granted, especially not you."

"Do you believe in love at first sight?"

"I haven't believed in love for a long time. I really haven't given it a thought. I'm not exactly batting a thousand in that department."

"I believe in it."

"Well, you would, given it's your career."

"Or is it my career because I believe in it?"

Levi sighed. He scooted back on the bed and drew her over his chest. He was afraid to move forward with her. What if he failed her? If he opened himself and let her in, and then at some point in the future they didn't work out, he would fucking die.

"I know what we should do," she said.

"What?"

"We should swap hearts. You give me yours so

that I can heal it. I'll give you mine so that you can protect it."

Zaida's hair was drying in long, fuzzy curls. He gripped a fistful and lifted them over her shoulder. "If we do that, we won't be able to live without each other."

She smiled. "That's kinda the point."

He pulled her all the way up his chest, loving the soft feel of her nude body. "You are so much braver than I am."

"I know." She nodded sagely. "In this, anyway."

He stared into her eyes until the humor left them. "Zaida Hussan, I give you my heart, to hold near your soul, to heal and keep forever."

A big tear slipped from her eye and splashed down on his cheek. "Levi Jones, I accept your heart and give you mine, to guard and protect and keep forever."

Levi choked on a strangled breath. His eyes watered as he brought her close for a kiss to seal their promises.

Never in his life had he felt so much joy.

19

Levi's motion sensors alerted him to an uninvited arrival. A week had passed since the end of the county fair. Jack had given the all-clear regarding the Tahrir al-Sham terrorist cells. Of course, that assessment wasn't worth the time it took to say it, since they really never were out of the woods when it came to hate groups.

Zaida had spent most of the last week with him, working on her book while he worked the farm. They'd made love on his roof once, when they'd gone up to watch his sunflowers one night. Levi had had the locks updated on her apartment, since it seemed everyone and their brother had a key. Life had settled back to a new normal.

Levi had been waiting for a group of sunflower seed buyers from Spain. They'd promised to come look at his hybrid crop of black seed and consider it for a gourmet line of sunflower seed oil they'd developed. He hoped they could make a deal. These buyers were offering a premium price.

He walked out of his greenhouse and headed toward his house. A man in a Lexus SUV pulled into the parking area. Jamal. Levi pulled his work gloves off and dropped them on the picnic table. He wasn't entirely surprised that Zaida's one-time-almost-fiancé had come out for a face to face.

Zaida was worth fighting for, and well he knew it. Levi was just glad that she'd stayed in town last night. Jamal didn't need witnesses when he left with his tail between his legs.

Jamal walked over to greet him. They shook hands. He sent a glance around them at the walls of sunflowers, which were even taller than when this nightmare began.

"Zaida told me your place was beautiful," Jamal said. "She was right."

Not bad, as opening pleasantries went. Levi nodded, accepting the compliment, even though he knew where this friendly meeting was headed. It was the same, really, in any culture. *Leave my woman alone. Get the fuck outta Dodge.* Levi wasn't going to comply.

"You're a long way out of town, Jamal. What brings you out this way?" Levi asked.

Jamal took his sunglasses off and looked straight at Levi. Nice move. His gesture indicated this would be an honest and frank discussion—just the kind Levi liked.

"I wanted to thank you for helping Zaida. I wasn't

sure of your motives that night we met on the street."

Levi kept himself from grinning. Fuck honesty; Jamal knew exactly what Levi wanted from Zaida that night.

Jamal looked down at his own neatly manicured hands, then at the greenhouses behind Levi, then at Levi, who became aware of the farm dirt under his own nails.

"And now that the crisis is over," Jamal said, "it's time for you to let Zaida move on with her life."

Levi held up a hand. "Save your breath. That ship has sailed. Zaida's mine."

Jamal's dark eyes hardened. Geez, he was so easy to read. "She isn't part of your world," Jamal growled.

"She's part of whatever world she wishes to be part of," Levi said.

"You confuse her. You take her from her parents, her people, her destiny."

"No, I don't, actually. Free will does none of that. Everything in her life is her choice. Not mine. Not yours. It's her Freedom Code, you know."

"I've known her all her life. I know what's best for her."

Levi grinned at that. "Says you. Can I offer you something to drink? Coffee? Tea? Water?"

Jamal glared at Levi. This wasn't going to be a short discussion. "Coffee. Espresso if you have it."

"I do. Come inside. It's cooler there." Levi held the door for Jamal. This meeting was a pivotal one if

Levi wanted Zaida to have any harmony in her life. It was no secret her parents far preferred Jamal to Levi. Making peace with Jamal was a long shot, especially when so much was at risk. Levi knew Zaida had already made the choice between him and Jamal, but Jamal didn't.

The professor had proved himself to be a man of honor, helping his student, helping his country, trying to keep the woman he loved and her parents safe from danger. Levi was glad Abdul had been exonerated. Jack's team had confirmed the worm had come from the flash drive Hidaya had used on Zaida's old machine; Levi was glad it hadn't been Jamal who'd released it. And it turned out that the worm Abdul had crafted had become a boon to his chosen country and its spy networks. The FBI had even rewarded him with a scholarship and an offer of employment upon graduation. The secrets Zaida had been keeping from her parents were all out in the open.

All in all, things had worked out well. But much depended on whether Levi and Jamal could make peace with each other. He wanted Zaida's parents' acceptance of him to be as frictionless as possible.

Beau came into the house from his dog run and silently approached Jamal. He got a good sniffing in before Jamal even became aware of him. When he looked down at the dog and Beau looked up at him, there was a tense moment, but then Beau wagged his tail and let Jamal scratch his head. That went a long way toward alleviating Levi's concerns about the guy.

Levi washed the garden dirt off his hands then ground the espresso beans. The rich scent of coffee filled the air. He and Jamal talked about the beans and Levi's espresso setup as Levi made the coffee. It seemed they were both connoisseurs of good coffee.

Jamal sat on one of the counter stools. Levi pushed his small espresso cup over to him, offering him cream and sugar. Taking his own cup, Levi leaned against the opposite counter and waited for Jamal to state his case.

Jamal sipped his cup. "That's good."

Levi nodded.

"The thing is, Levi, one cannot know a culture by making war with it."

"I'm not at war with your culture. Or your people. Or your religion. I'm out of the war business."

"No, you're not. If you were, your government would not call upon you like it just did."

"*Our* government, no?"

"Yes. Our government."

"We are one people, Jamal."

Jamal scoffed. "My people are a significant minority."

Levi looked down at the counter. How easily an us versus them mentality was to set up. And how difficult it was to resist that very thing. "You can consider yourself separate, unique, special. I consider myself human. I try every day to improve how I represent my humanity, but the truth is I am nothing more or less than a man, however well I do it. And this man is in love with Zaida. And because of that love, I gave her the freedom to choose me, you, or neither of us. I don't presume to know what's best for her, but I suspect she does. And she chose me."

"And this is where your not being one of us causes everyone problems. This isn't a choice she can rationally make. It's a choice her parents, as her elders, and her suitor, as her superior, should make for her."

"Why can't she rationally make that choice for herself?" Levi asked.

"Because it is too emotionally charged, as she herself is right now. This will affect the rest of her life. She needs guidance."

"Wow. That's a whole bunch of bullshit. This is the twenty-first century. Get with the times. Zaida is the only one who can make this choice for herself... and she's already made it."

"Again, that is a sign that you do not respect our culture."

"I walk a gray line, Jamal, which is the perfect balance between all extremes. It's where peace is. Where hope is. Where joy thrives. I've fought my whole life to find that line. And now that I'm on it, I'm not going to lose sight of it."

"What does that mean? What do you stand for, then, if you are in the middle of everything?"

"I stand for you. For Zaida. For her parents. Her friends. Peace. I'm not in the ultimatum business. I don't know what's better for her, for you. Only for me."

"Then you care nothing at all for her, only for yourself."

"You can twist my words all you like. We both know what I'm saying."

"So you won't withdraw your pursuit of her?"

"She has my heart." Levi held his free hand up. "I can't take it back. What she decides to do with it, I will have to live with. And so will you."

"I gave her my heart first."

Levi slowly smiled. "And now we talk like twelve-year-olds."

Jamal glared at Levi with narrowed eyes. He straightened and set his cup on the counter. "Thank you for the coffee. I will leave now."

∼

LATER THAT NIGHT, Zaida came over. Since the fair, she'd been splitting her time between her place and Levi's. He was glad she was here; he wasn't himself when she was away from him. They were finishing their dinner, sitting at the picnic table. He was trying to think of a way to tell her Jamal had come out for a visit. He didn't want to make drama, but felt she should know that her old boyfriend was still carrying a torch for her.

"You seem distant, Levi," Zaida said. "Is something the matter?"

"Not really. Jamal came out this morning."

Her mouth made a big O. "What did he say?"

"That you were his and I should go to hell." Okay, so he'd made a little drama.

"I'm sorry. He is tenacious. I will have another talk with him."

"I'd rather you didn't. He needs time. He's thought of you as his for a long while. He has to ease himself into a new paradigm." Levi had an idea. "Maybe he just needs to meet a new love interest. There anyone you know?"

She winced. "I can't. He's a sucky fucker, remember? I wouldn't wish that on any of my friends."

Levi laughed at that. "Right. I forgot." He pushed his plate away. "So how did I do the other night at dinner with your parents? We seemed to get along. I'm trying very hard to get them to like me."

Zaida put her hands on his. "I know. And I appreciate that. They'll come around, sooner or later. Mom actually laughed at some of your jokes. I think I even saw Dad smiling a time or two."

"I figured laughter was a good way in. I had to distract them from this." He held up his scraped knuckles and waved a circle around his face with his finger. "It's a big reminder of what we just went through."

His phone rang. Levi took the call, recognizing the Nolans' number.

ZAIDA LISTENED to Levi talk to someone she assumed was a neighbor. She liked that he had a support network out here. It was such a remote place—the fact that he had friends near gave her a little peace of mind.

"Hey, babe," Levi said as he got up from the picnic table. "Mr. Nolan's working on the harvest schedule. We cost-share some equipment that we need to book. I know it's late, but I've got to run over there." He kissed her cheek. "I shouldn't be too long. Wait up for me?"

"Of course."

Zaida sat outside a little longer, but as dusk fell, the mosquitos got aggressive. She took their dishes to the house and cleaned the kitchen for Levi. Smiling, she thought she wasn't utterly helpless; she could load and unload a dishwasher.

There was a knock at the door. Zaida looked at the clock. It was almost eight p.m. Levi had been gone an hour. She wondered who was knocking, then remembered he was expecting a Spanish delegation from a sunflower growers' organization. It was a little late for them to come by, but she didn't want to harm his business by not opening the door.

Beau growled. She shushed him and opened the front door. Four men were there. The porch light showed their Mediterranean features—fair skin, dark hair and brows. She smiled at them, wishing she spoke Spanish. They had to be the guys Levi was waiting for.

"May I help you?" she asked. Beau crept closer to her, still growling. She frowned at him.

As soon as her attention was off the men, they shoved their way inside. Beau went crazy. He leapt at one of the men, who had pulled a gun. She screamed and spun around, trying to run for the back door, but two men grabbed her. The last man also had a gun, and he was trying to get a bead on Beau, but the man and the dog kept twisting about, blocking his shot. His friend screamed frantically in Arabic, shouting at him to shoot the damned dog.

Zaida kicked at the man's arm before he could, causing him to shoot his friend. The men were shouting at her, at Beau, at each other. She fought against them and managed to break loose in the mayhem, charging toward the front door. Beau disengaged from the man's arm and chased after her…as did the men. She ran straight into Levi's sunflower field, seeking the only shelter immediately available to her.

Too late, she realized the thick flower stalks would provide no real cover as the men fired into the field. Leaves popped all around her as bullets hit them. Someone was running after her. He was shouting directions back to his men. Beau was keeping up with her, thank God. She turned to the right and ran in a different direction. She changed directions often, but always keeping to right angles, hoping that would make it harder for anyone to watch from the house and see where she was headed.

The flowers were so densely grown that it was hard to run in any direction other than an east-west axis. The spiky stalks slashed at her skin. The sun had set, so the darkness inside the field was complete. She slowed down, trying to judge how close the men were behind her. She seemed to have a lead. Maybe they'd stopped to get a fix on her location. She paused. She was breathing loudly. They'd find her fast if she didn't calm herself.

And then the gunfire started. She could hear stalks cracking after each round. Beau caught her hand and dragged her down. She hugged him close, burying her face in his soft fur. Someone was coming close. Beau didn't growl, but he turned toward the threat.

Zaida was more terrified than ever before in her life. She knew she was staring at her own death. These were going to be her last seconds on earth. The man was coming nearer. Had he located her? Or was he going to just pass right by? She forced her breathing to slow so that she could hear him. But it was another sound she heard that absolutely paralyzed her.

Rattles.

Two of them, flanking her. Too late, she remembered Levi warning her about the snakes in the fields. Oh. God. Hers was going to be a terrible death, riddled with bullets and snakebitten.

The man turned on his flashlight. The rows were too narrow for him to move through other than sideways. He kept ducking down to see what the light revealed. He stopped two rows from her, probably hearing the rattles.

With the benefit of his light, Zaida moved her

head slightly so that she could see the snake to her right. The triangle head had to be the size of her fist. Bigger, maybe. It was sitting atop its coiled body, its big rattle shaking behind it. She looked to her left to see the same thing, but from a slightly smaller snake.

It was then she remembered she still wore her security necklace. Levi had asked her to keep wearing it until the chatter on the dark web truly settled down. She freed a hand from Beau and reached for the slim plastic pendant, squeezing it over and over. A sob broke from her as she thought how Levi would take her death.

The man who'd been chasing her bent forward and shined his light toward her. He crouched down. "At last, I've found the bitch who caused so many of my brothers to die." He started to crawl toward her.

Zaida whimpered. Her fingers dug into Beau's chest. She could feel his growl more than she could hear it—her blood was thundering in her ears, fueling a fight-or-flight reaction she couldn't yield to because of the snakes on either side of her.

She blinked. The man screamed and twisted back. She saw a snake attached to his neck and another at his wrist. He fumbled for his gun and shot willy-nilly into the dirt and air around him, but by then, the snakes were gone.

He screamed, "Help me! Help me!" in English and Arabic.

But no one came, for him or her.

20

Levi was already on his way back from the Nolans' when the app associated with Zaida's security necklace started to go off. His phone rang. A glance at the screen showed Max's number. He tossed the phone aside. Zaida was his only focus. He floored the gas pedal, flying the last mile down the long dirt road, slowing only enough to turn onto his property.

A man was standing beside the picnic table as Levi pulled in. He pointed his flashlight at Levi, then started firing at the Jeep. Levi ducked as he floored it again, driving straight for him…and over him. He slammed on the brakes and spun the Jeep to a stop. Of course, he'd left the house unarmed except for the knife in his ankle holster.

He walked behind his car to make sure the guy he'd hit was dead. He wasn't moving, but he still had a finger on the trigger of his pistol. Levi took the guy's gun and put a bullet in his head, just to be safe.

"Zaida! Beau!" he shouted. He heard a single bark out in the middle of the field directly in front of his house. Before he could start her way, two guys came out of his house and began shooting at him. Levi shoved his picnic table over, then dove behind it, only to be body-slammed as soon as he was down by one of the guys.

Levi struggled to get some leverage against his attacker. They were tangled up under the picnic table bench, which was freestanding. The other guy from the house was only steps away, but Levi had to keep his attention on the gun his opponent had in his hand. Keeping a grip on the man's wrist, Levi waited until the guy from the house reached them before kicking the bench, flipping it up at the third man.

Levi rolled over, getting on top of the man he was wrestling. He planted a fist in his face. Twice. Levi was able to grab his knife from its holster in the brief pause that followed, and stabbed it into his opponent's neck, then rolled over again, keeping the guy's body as cover. Levi took the gun the man was holding and shot the third guy as he was getting back up to his feet, hitting him in the chest.

Levi pulled free and shoved one of the pistols into his waistband. He'd dealt with three bad guys. They only had one vehicle. The odds were good that there would be at least one more, unless they'd parked another vehicle where he didn't see it.

"Zaida! Call out!" he shouted. She didn't, but Beau did, another single bark. "Beau! Good boy." Levi could see a glow ahead. It killed him that Zaida wasn't responding. Was she hurt? Dead? Gone? He tried to hurry, but the going wasn't easy. The light was getting brighter.

"Zaida! Answer me!" Still nothing from her, but Beau gave another bark. Whatever that light was, it was where Beau was. Maybe Zaida had turned on the light on her phone. "C'mon, babe. Answer me."

A few feet farther in, and he saw Beau lying on the ground, facing a man who seemed unresponsive. Levi released Beau and stepped in front of him, his gun pointed at the man. He was breathing hard and sweating like crazy. The whites of his eyes were red. Levi grabbed his gun, and as he did, he saw the red, swollen patch with a V-shaped bite mark.

He had a matching spot on his neck. Yeah, that guy probably wasn't long for this earth. "Where's Zaida?" Levi asked. The guy's lips moved, but nothing intelligible came from him.

Levi looked back at Beau, but only saw his tail as he slipped into the rows of sunflowers. And then he heard her, just faint gasps for air. Motherfucker. Had she been bitten, too? Obviously, there'd been two snakes in the area. Maybe there'd been more. Levi followed his dog, terrified of what condition he'd find Zaida in.

"Baby, it's me. You're safe." He stepped through another row, and there she was, huddled on the ground, shaking. He knelt in front of her, looking at her through a dense row of sunflowers. "Hey." He swiped his hands over her face. She still didn't look up at him or move in any way other than the shivers racking her body.

"There are more men," she whispered. "There were a lot of them. Four, I think. And snakes. Snakes everywhere."

"The men are all dead." God, it was a relief that she could talk. "C'mon. Let's get back to the house."

"No! I told you—there are snakes everywhere. Don't move."

"Nope. I don't see any. They're long gone. They don't hang around after a confrontation, especially if what they bit isn't prey. It's okay. I got you. I'll carry you. If I have to walk through a pile of them, they'll get me, not you. You weren't bitten, were you?"

"I don't think so."

"Honey, for sure you'd know if you had been. C'mon, stand up now so I can lift you."

She stood very slowly, holding his forearms in a death grip as he pulled her into his row between sunflowers. When he lifted her, she wrapped her arms around his neck and squeezed tightly. He pushed through the tight crop of flowers, leaving the snakebit guy behind with his flashlight so it would be easier to find him. He wasn't super interested in attempting to save the man's life. He'd come onto Levi's property with the intent of harming Zaida. Levi figured he'd gotten what he deserved.

Zaida relaxed just a little when they were out of the forest of sunflowers, but that relief didn't last long once she caught sight of Levi's torn-up front yard and three more dead guys.

Off in the distance, coming from a northerly direction, was a helicopter. Not something that ordinarily would catch Levi's attention now that he was a civilian…but this one was flying low.

Fuck. Maybe it was unconnected to everything, but maybe not. He ran up the stairs to his house with Zaida and Beau. He needed to get his weapons. He locked the front door, then crossed the room to his big wall unit. After flipping up a light switch panel, he pressed his right thumb on the panel it hid. A section of the wall unit separated from the rest of the built-in, moving forward, then to the side.

He heard Zaida gasp at the armory he exposed, but he didn't have time to calm her fears. That chopper had landed nearby, probably in the empty field across the street. His driveway's motion sensors triggered an alarm. He took out an M16 and its magazine. He heard heavy footsteps on his front steps.

Levi grabbed Zaida and called for Beau to follow him. He rushed them into his bedroom and then into the bathroom. "Lock this door. I'll lock the bedroom door. Don't come out until I tell you it's clear, understand?"

There was a loud banging on his front door. He looked at Zaida one last time, then ordered Beau to guard her. He set the lock on the bedroom door as another loud banging came against his front door.

"Levi! Open up!" Max's familiar voice thundered through the solid steel door.

Levi laughed as he heaved a relieved breath. He opened his front door, admitting Max, his friend Val, and their team lead Kit. They plowed inside his house, visually sweeping the room for hostiles.

"What the hell are you doing here?" Levi asked.

"There a fucking reason you can't answer your phone?" Max snarled.

Levi patted his pocket, then remembered he'd dumped his phone on the floor of his Jeep in his rush to get to Zaida. "Oh."

Max spread his hands wide and looked like he was about to strangle Levi.

"Ohhh. Zaida's necklace," Levi said.

"Yeah," Kit said. "We're still tethered to her. When her alert came through and we couldn't get you, we had to come down."

"It's good we did, judging from your lawn decor," Val said. "There more enemies out there?"

"I don't think so. As far as I know, there was just the one vehicle with four bad guys. I haven't had a chance to search."

"We checked for heat signatures on our way in," Kit said. "Only caught one faint one in the field. That someone you care about?"

"No. He's one of the bad guys," Levi said. "He chased Zaida into the field, then got some special attention from a couple of rattlers. A little natural justice, if you ask me." Levi went over and knocked on his bedroom door. "Zaida, it's safe. Come on out now."

He heard her unlock the bathroom door, then she fumbled with the bedroom lock. As soon as she opened the door, she threw herself into his arms. He held her in a tight, one-handed grip, his other hand still on his M16. He led her over to his sofa so she could sit down. He still hadn't gotten a chance to give her a once-over.

Zaida looked at his friends nervously. All three were watching her with intense expressions. She was fighting tears. Levi thought she looked like she wanted to jump up and flap her arms to shake off the adrenaline she'd built up over the last hour. When he moved away to put his rifle back in its case, she did just that. Her breathing was irregular. The flapping didn't help. She went over and gave Max a big hug.

"Thank you," she said, looking at the other two who'd come with him. "Thank you for coming down. You barely know me, and yet here you are, once again hurrying into danger to help me." She shook her head. "I know I won't ever be able to repay you."

"Don't worry about it," Max said. "Levi's paying for us." He got an elbow in his ribs for that flip remark from the big blond. Val, wasn't he? Zaida tried to remember.

"We woulda come anyway," Val said. "Not like we'd leave a little girl to fend for herself."

Kit shook his head. "You've collected some wicked enemies, Zaida." He looked at Levi. "You're not going to be in the clear until Tahrir al-Sham forgets the impact she's had on their operatives."

"I know," Levi said. "I thought we were out of the woods, but more of them crawled out of their shitholes." He pulled Zaida out of Max's hold and led her back to the sofa. "I need to call this in," he said, looking at Kit. "Can you guys hang here for a minute?"

"You bet," Kit said.

Levi went outside to his Jeep and grabbed his phone. He leaned against it as he called the commander. "Hey, sorry for the after-dark call…"

Lambert huffed a laugh. "Forget it. What's up?"

Levi told him. "The suits thought we'd pretty much wiped out the cell. So who are these guys?"

"Send me their info. Any of them alive?"

"Not sure. I killed three, and one's dying in my sunflower field from two rattler bites. Hope he'll be dead by the time your cleanup crew gets here. If not, guess they'll have to take him for medical treatment."

"How's your woman?" Lambert asked.

"Shook up."

"Sorry about that. I'll find out what I can about any persistent threat against her. I'll update you when I know something. I'm going to call this in to Jack as well. Let me know if you need something else."

Briefly, Levi thought about the guys' helicopter flight down here, but decided not to say anything.

Lambert would know about it soon enough, when that bill came in.

"That's it from me. Later, commander." Levi gathered the licenses of the three guys in his front yard and snagged a picture. Then he sent those and pics of the men to both Lambert and Jack.

When he went back inside, he found Zaida was sitting on the sofa, a damp cloth on her forehead. One foot was in Val's lap, her other soaking in a big roasting pan full of soapy water. Val was bent over her foot with a pair of tweezers, pulling out slivers.

Levi heard his water kettle scream and looked over to see Kit manning the stove for a cup of tea. Max stood near the sofa, his arms folded, glaring at what Val was doing.

Geez, Levi hadn't even seen to Zaida's welfare before calling the attack in. Her feet were cut all to hell from running barefoot into his field. It was going to take several days for all the spiny hairs from the sunflower stalks to come out of her skin. She really needed a bath and a change of clothes.

Levi sat next to her and took hold of her hand. "You guys can take off. There's a team coming out to do the cleanup."

"We'll stay until they get here," Kit said, handing the mug of tea to Zaida. "Just on the off chance there's another team waiting to strike if the first one failed. Max, go outside and secure the site until Levi's guys get here. I'll be out in a minute."

Max nodded and left.

Kit looked down at Zaida with worry in his eyes. "Zaida, I hope the next time we meet, it's just for fun."

"Thanks, Kit." Zaida smiled up at him, then winced as Val tugged a splinter free. "Me too."

"Levi." Kit nodded, indicating they should talk in the kitchen. He handed Levi a card with Owen's info. "The boss wanted me to tell you that you've got a job, no questions asked, whenever you want one."

Levi smiled as he looked down at the card. "Good to know. If this farming gig doesn't work out, I may just take him up on that." He shook hands with Kit, then the team lead left the house.

LATER THAT NIGHT, after Max and the guys had left, after Jack and his team had recovered the bodies and evidence, Levi put his home back in order. He parked his Jeep, righted his picnic table, tidied the kitchen and living room, and repacked his first-aid kit. It was almost midnight. Zaida had long ago showered and gotten in bed after letting Levi bandage her feet.

Everyone was gone now. His home was once again ordered and quiet. Zaida hadn't come out of the bedroom; he hoped that meant she was sleeping, because he needed time to think.

He sat on the sofa. Leaning forward, he put his head in his hands. There was a fifty-fifty chance that Zaida was finally out of danger. Those weren't odds he liked. Even if Jack once again reported the Tahrir al-Sham cells were finished here in the States, Levi wouldn't have a sense of peace. Any other cell in the allied ISIS network could take up the *fatwa* against her. Even if Levi somehow got the *fatwa* lifted, there was no guarantee the sick bastards wouldn't continue to target her. He could go hunting, but hatred and crazy ran deep. No matter how many he took out, ten more depraved men would take their place.

At some point, an eye for an eye wasn't the answer. Maybe only love was. Zaida's Freedom Code had to apply to men as well as women.

Levi didn't hear Zaida's door open, and didn't know she was there until her bandaged feet came into his field of view. He looked up at her. Her eyes were serious. Sad. She reached for his hand. He pulled her into his lap and leaned back on the sofa.

"I'm sorry about tonight," he said, breaking the heavy silence.

"It's over. Don't dwell on it."

"I don't know what the answer is, Zaida. I don't know how to stop this."

She leaned against his chest. He felt her shake her head. "Greater people than us have fought for peace. It's always seen as a weakness."

"You know you're a warrior, right?" Levi said. "Your Freedom Code is the change we need."

She pushed up to look at him. "Do you think so?"

"I do. It ain't gonna be easy. I told Jamal I was out of the war business." He sighed and brushed a lock of her hair behind her ear. "But I will fight to my death for you."

"For peace."

"For love." He smiled at her and pulled her into a tight hug.

EPILOGUE

Levi's phone rang. Zaida was calling…at seven a.m. Since when was she up this early? "Zaida. Everything okay?"

"No. It's awful," she said.

"What is? Are you in danger? Where are you?"

"My parents have just left. They spent the night here. They're on their way to see you."

Levi slumped against the counter, relieved. "Why aren't you coming with them?"

"I was forbidden."

"Forbidden. Really? Can they do that?"

"I'm so sorry, Levi. I knew this was coming…I just didn't think it would happen so soon."

"And…what exactly is happening?"

"They're coming out to negotiate. For me."

"What? I have to buy you?" Levi laughed. He was not at all surprised her parents wanted to grill him about his intentions, but it was fun torturing Zaida about it.

"No. Yes. Maybe. They want to be sure you can afford me."

"Ah. Well, if I show them my bank account, they might turn around and drive away."

"Oh, God. Are you poor? I should put some money in your account. We never talked about this."

Levi could hear heavy breathing from her end of the phone, her panic ratcheting up, so he took pity on her. "We should have talked about it. I'll tell you what I'll tell them. I was in the service for twenty-two years. I partied my way through the first decade. By year eleven, I guess I grew up, figured out my body couldn't take doing what I was forever. I started to save every penny I could. I went to school nights, weekends. The university worked around my schedule. SEALs are damnably unpredictable, but the university helped me make it work."

"What did you study?"

"Ag sciences. I saved up to buy this property, which I did about ten years ago. It's almost paid off since I took a fifteen-year mortgage. Between my Navy retirement and my farm's income, I think I got you covered, babe."

Zaida huffed a relieved sigh. "Don't tell them all that. Just the last part."

"Honey, don't you think I know how to negotiate for you?"

"Have you ever negotiated for a wife before?"

"Nope. First time around, we went to Vegas."

"Oh, God. Don't tell them that, either."

"They don't like Elvis?" Levi chuckled at her gasp.

"My parents are so old world in some ways. Many ways."

"Well, some things are tried and true. It's a respect issue. They want to know that I mean to do well by you. And, darlin', I sure do."

"I love you, Levi. We can run away. Be expats in Canada."

"No can do, sweet thing. Neither of us wants to be an expat and running away from your family won't fix your troubles. Besides, then they'll hate me for taking you away from them."

"It's true."

"They hate me?"

"No, they're afraid you'll take me from them."

"Never. I was kinda afraid they'd take you from me. See? We have common ground."

"When they're like this, they are so dreadful. I don't want you to hate me. Or them."

"Zaida Hussan, if your folks didn't confront me, I would worry about their commitment to you. It's all good."

"Just beware if my father starts speaking Spanish. That's bad. Very bad."

"Not if you speak Spanish and can back him down."

"Do you?"

"I do."

"God, there's still so much I don't know about you."

"That's what a lifetime is for, honey."

"I want to be there, with you."

"Then do it. Get your butt out here. I'll fix a brunch for us. Is there anything they're allergic to?"

"No."

"Anything they can't eat? Bacon?"

"I guess technically we shouldn't eat pork, but we're not devout. We're not even practicing our religion. And if we weren't supposed to eat bacon, why would it taste so good?"

"Good to know, but I won't push that boundary just yet. Go shower and get out here. I want to celebrate with you."

"I can't come out yet. These things can take all day."

"Honey, how long did it take you to fall in love with me?"

"As soon as you shoved Jamal from me that first night."

"Yeah. I'll have your parents on board as fast. I guarantee it. Pick up some champagne on your way out, okay?"

"Okay. I love you, Levi. Please remember that."

"Honey, nothing else matters. I love you. And I already love your parents."

"You barely even know them yet."

"Ah, babe. Just think about how much they're worrying over this, too. They probably were up most of the night strategizing for this convo. Hell, I bet they got up early hoping to sneak out of your place without you knowing and getting all stirred up. But you had to be a good hostess and got up early with them."

Zaida giggled. "I did hear them talking late last night. And they were a little disgruntled this morning."

"So, tell me…there anything you want out of this negotiation? Privacy rights? Freedom to choose when our kids will be born…?"

Zaida gasped. "They cannot dictate any of that to me."

"*Do* you want kids?"

"Yes. Do you?"

"Sure. I'm settled enough now. Wouldn't mind breeding a few laborers to help me on the farm."

"Levi. Jones. You will not speak of our children that way. And don't let my parents make demands in that corner. My mother's an ob/gyn. She could absolutely do it."

He laughed. "Fine. They stay out of our bedroom."

"Oh yes they do."

"What about religion? Want me to convert?"

"I don't care what you do. That's a personal decision, and it isn't required to marry me. Don't let them bully you on that front. I told you, we don't even practice our religion."

"When do you want to get married?"

"I feel awful. I just wanted this to progress in its own natural way."

Levi's nerves caught on edge. "You do want to get married, no?"

"Of course I do. I just don't want to rush you. I feel like your freedom's cornered now between my parents and me. That's not fair to you."

"Baby, you are my freedom. I'd marry you this afternoon."

"I have no intention of rushing our wedding, Levi Jones. I have certain standards, and I'm only going to do this once. I want the whole experience—picking a dress, sending invitations, the shower, sampling wedding cakes, poring over vacation spots for our honeymoon, picking your tux."

"Then I will defer that negotiating point to you."

"Okay. Are we really doing this?"

"Yes. But I haven't proposed yet. That you must leave to me. We aren't officially engaged yet until I do."

"Can I pick my ring?"

"Oh, fuck yes. It would give me hives trying to choose a ring for you. Hey, I gotta go. I need to get some cooking done before your folks get here. C'mon out when you can. We'll wait brunch for you, but you should know—I'm already starving."

"Right. I will. Love you!"

The warmth of her words went all the way through him. "Love you too." He dropped the call. His whole body tingled with joy—something he'd never felt before. He couldn't get the grin off his face as he started prepping for a big celebration brunch.

∽

Levi was alerted when a car pulled onto his property about an hour later. The dust trail showed its progress. He went outside and watched as the elder Hussans parked their Escalade in front of his house. He held his coffee in one hand and waved with his free hand.

It was a hot, still morning. He knew the day was going to be a scorcher—just the way his sunflowers liked it. The Hussans got out of their air-conditioned vehicle. He could tell the exact moment the heat hit them from their expressions. Though it was a midweek day, they were dressed for an elegant picnic. Zaida's dad wore a Cubavera shirt over khakis and loafers. Her mom wore a loose aqua-blue silk tunic over white capris with a pair of blinged-out flip-flops. Both also wore matching straw hats.

"Good morning," he called to them.

"Good morning," Darim said, nodding to Levi and giving a friendly smile, though he briefly looked apologetic. "Sorry to stop by so early and unannounced. I was taking Mother for a drive before the day got too hot. Before we knew it, we were right here, so we thought we'd stop. If it's not a convenient time, just tell us to be on our way."

"It's a perfect time. I have a quiche about to come

out of the oven and a fresh pot of coffee about to go on. Will you join me?" He shook hands with Darim, then took Rayna's hand and kissed her cheeks.

Zaida's mom frowned. "Hello, Levi. Who's here cooking for you?"

Ah, that was why she was put out. "I cook for myself, Dr. Hussan. I long ago figured out if I wanted to eat, I'd better learn my way around a kitchen."

"Yes, I would like to join you," Rayna said. She turned and faced her husband, who met her look with raised eyebrows.

Darim coughed, covering his momentary lapse. "Levi, I find I have an extreme urge to wander about your greenhouses. May I do that?"

Levi looked from one conniving parent to the other. Coward. Apparently, Rayna was in charge of this negotiation. Geez, they had this whole thing rehearsed.

"Of course." Levi held a hand out toward the greenhouses. "Help yourself. Later, we can walk through them together so I can explain what I grow. And perhaps your wife would like to see as well."

Levi led Rayna up the steps to his front door, which he held open for her. Levi knew he had one shot to win their approval. He didn't mind the game. Rayna was a formidable but fair matriarch who kept her husband and daughter in line; it would be nice to have her on his side.

The chilly air from his swamp cooler offered welcome relief from the heat building outside. The oven timer went off. Levi took the quiche out of the oven, then got the fresh pot of coffee brewing. Rayna came around to his side of the counter and inspected it.

"What type of quiche is it?" she asked.

"A simple cheese one."

"What did you put in it?"

"Chives, green onions, garlic, and parsley—all from my garden. The eggs come from a neighbor whose wife keeps chickens. The Gruyère is from a cheese shop in Fort Collins." He had puff pastry egg soufflés warming in the lower oven. In fact, he'd just finished whipping together their brunch, most of which he'd hidden in the fridge. He'd made a fresh garden salad, a bowl of cut fruit, and olive tapenade bruschetta bites. He hoped the quiche would throw Rayna off guard, as if he'd made breakfast just for himself.

"Hmm." She nodded. "It smells delicious."

Levi smiled at her. "Would you like coffee or shall I make some tea?"

"Coffee, thank you," Rayna said. "I expected not to like you."

"I can understand that. We've both seen the worst humanity has to offer. It's better to expect it than be blindsided by it."

Rayna nodded.

"Zaida's not like us," Levi said. "She's been sheltered—"

"Protected," Rayna said.

Levi nodded. "She's never had to develop that hardened skin we have. She loves everyone and they love her back. She reminds me of my sunflowers." He poured a mug of coffee and handed it to Rayna, then set out utensils, napkins, and cream and sugar.

She lifted a brow. "How so?"

"They are so full of joy that it pops out of them in a burst of yellow color, mimicking as best they can the thing they love the most—the sun. Love explodes from Zaida in her smiles and her eyes. It would be a special thing if she could be that way her whole life."

Rayna nodded, a little sadly. "You see it too."

"I do."

"You'll take her away from us," Rayna said.

Levi gave a slow shake of his head, feeling as if he'd made a giant leap forward in having his relationship with Zaida acknowledged. "Where would I go? My life is here. Her life is here. You two are here."

Zaida's mom frowned. "You don't have to go anywhere to close the door on us."

"That's something I feared from you," Levi said. "You are her world. She tries very hard to please you."

Rayna gave him a baleful glare. "I wouldn't have picked you for her."

That hurt, even though it was a fact he already knew. He started to speak, but Rayna held up her hand.

"I realize that what I thought I knew about my daughter…maybe I didn't."

That put Levi on alert. He'd never meant to drive a wedge between Zaida and her mom. He was on tenterhooks for her next words. God, if Rayna asked him to back off, he didn't know if he could. And the worst of it was, if that happened, he'd never be able to tell Zaida why, because he could never bring discord between her and her family.

Rayna jerked her head toward the rest of his house. "This place is too little to raise a family."

Levi's brows lifted. "Are you giving me your blessing?"

Rayna's chin trembled. "All this time wasted. She could have been married long ago and had a half-dozen children by now."

Levi shook his head. "She couldn't have because I wasn't here. I was out fighting the world. And she was becoming the woman she is now."

Rayna sipped her coffee. "Her father and I tried for years to have children. We'd given up when she came along. She is our everything."

"You have to let her decide for herself whether she wants children—and if so, how many." Levi cut into the quiche and dished out two slices.

"Would you give her that choice?"

Levi passed her a plate. "I would give her anything. I want what she wants."

"And see, that is what has always been missing from the men I tried to send her way," Rayna said. "Yes, Levi, I give my blessing to you and Zaida. Her choice was perfect. So much better than any of mine." She reached over to squeeze his hand.

Levi had to blink away a wash of moisture that hit his eyes. He came around the counter and hugged Rayna.

"But this house is too small for a family," she repeated.

"Dr. Hussan, I own a thousand acres. This can become a guesthouse. Zaida can design the home she wants."

Rayna's eyes took on a determined look. "Yes." She nodded. "And you should call me Mother. We have much to do before your wedding next year."

"Whoa…slow your roll, Mom. I haven't even proposed yet."

"She will accept."

Levi chuckled. "Let's at least give her the perception of freedom to make her own choice. And you and I will have to accept it—whatever it is."

She looked wounded. "But you are already calling me Mother. It can go no other way."

The front door opened. Darim peeked inside. Rayna waved him forward. His face was shining with joy.

"Levi has asked our permission to marry our daughter," Rayna said.

Darim nodded solemnly. "And did we grant it?"

"Yes. Yes, we have. Say hello to your soon-to-be son."

Darim laughed and shook hands with Levi. He

then pulled him into a hug and kissed both of his cheeks. Pounding him on the shoulder, he said, "Well done. You've conquered the dragon."

Levi grinned, checking to make sure that wasn't insulting to Rayna. "In this battle, anyway."

Darim leaned close. "I knew she would love you, because our beautiful daughter does. It was only a matter of formalities."

"It was never only a matter of formalities." Levi shook his head. "If I didn't have your blessing, then I would live forever alone, a man robbed of his heart."

Darim laughed. Keeping a hand on Levi's shoulder, he faced his wife. "You see, Mother, our daughter has made a wise choice. She has learned something from us after all. They will have a long and happy marriage, I believe."

Levi's phone buzzed as another car drove onto the property. He recognized Zaida's BMW SUV. Seconds later, she blew through the front door, carrying a bottle of champagne and a bag of treats from the bakery in her atrium.

Levi smiled at her, hoping to ease the panic in her face. She looked from him to her mom and dad.

"Zaida," her mother said, "we told you to wait at your apartment for us."

Zaida kissed her mom then her dad. "I know. But I couldn't."

"I asked her to come out and celebrate with us," Levi said. "You didn't think you could keep her out of something like this, did you…Mother?"

Zaida looked shocked, then joy poured from her smile. She set her things down on the counter, then ran around to hug him. She laughed as he kissed her.

"We've come to an agreement," Levi told her.

"Already?"

He nodded. "Yeah. Let's have brunch. I'll fill you in while we eat. There may be some finer points you want to tweak."

"I love you, Levi," Zaida said.

"I love you, Zaida. My sunshine."

OTHER SLEEPER SEALS BOOKS

All books in the Sleeper SEALs series are standalones and can be read in any order:

1) Protecting Dakota by Susan Stoker

2) Slow Ride by Becky McGraw

3) Michael's Mercy by Dale Mayer

4) Saving Zola by Becca Jameson

5) Bachelor SEAL by Sharon Hamilton

6) Montana Rescue by Elle James

7) Thin Ice by Maryann Jordan

8) Grinch Reaper by Donna Michaels

9) All In by Lori Ryan

10) Broken SEAL by Geri Foster

11) Freedom Code by Elaine Levine

12) Flat Line by J.M. Madden

OTHER BOOKS BY ELAINE LEVINE

RED TEAM SERIES

(This series must be read in order)

1 The Edge of Courage

2 Shattered Valor

3 Honor Unraveled

3.5 Kit & Ivy: A Red Team Wedding Novella

4 Twisted Mercy

4.5 Ty & Eden: A Red Team Wedding Novella

5 Assassin's Promise

6 War Bringer

6.5 Rocco & Mandy: A Red Team Wedding Novella

7 Razed Glory

8 Deadly Creed

SLEEPER SEALs

11 FREEDOM CODE

MEN OF DEFIANCE SERIES

(This series may be read in any order)

1 Rachel and the Hired Gun

2 Audrey and the Maverick
3 Leah and the Bounty Hunter
4 Logan's Outlaw
5 Agnes and the Renegade

ABOUT THE AUTHOR

Elaine Levine lives in the mountains of Colorado with her husband and a rescued pit bull/bull mastiff mix. In addition to writing the Red Team romantic suspense series, she's the author of several books in the historical western romance series Men of Defiance.

Be sure to sign up for her new release announcements at http://geni.us/GAlUjx.

If you enjoyed this book, please consider leaving a review at your favorite online retailer to help other readers find it.

Get social! Connect with Elaine online:
　　Reader Group: http://geni.us/2w5d
　　Website: https://www.ElaineLevine.com
　　email: elevine@elainelevine.com

Printed in Great Britain
by Amazon